NIGHTMARE POINT

Also by Carole Berry

Island Girl
Goodnight, Sweet Prince
The Year of the Monkey
The Letter of the Law

NIGHTMARE POINT

Carole Berry

ST. MARTIN'S PRESS
New York

NIGHTMARE POINT. Copyright © 1993 by Carole Berry. All rights reserved. Printed in the United States of America. No part of this book may be used or reproduced in any manner whatsoever without written permission except in the case of brief quotations embodied in critical articles or reviews. For information, address St. Martin's Press, 175 Fifth Avenue, New York, N.Y. 10010

Design by Judy Christensen

Library of Congress Cataloging-in-Publication Data

Berry, Carole.
    Nightmare point / Carole Berry.
        p.   cm.
    "A Thomas Dunne book."
    ISBN 0-312-08889-2
    I. Title.
    PS3552.E743N5   1993
    813'.54—dc20   92-43893
                                                              CIP

First Edition: March 1993

10 9 8 7 6 5 4 3 2 1

This is a work of fiction. All characters and incidents, and many of the locations, are products of the author's imagination and are not to be construed as real. The Provincetown police station has moved to modern quarters, but the author has chosen to leave it in its old town hall location. The dune shacks are very real, but Dromedary Point exists only in the author's imagination.

NIGHTMARE
POINT

1
Labor Day Week

Chapter 1

THE Shark hit the water an instant after the starter's gun sounded. There was scarcely a ripple. Even as the cold wet of the pool closed itself over his legs, his powerful arms were churning, pulling him ahead of the swimmers in the other lanes. It was mid-season; by now the rhythm came easily. His muscles were perfectly tuned. Arms, legs, lungs—all working together. His peripheral vision was sharp, and he saw that kid from Fremont High creeping up on his right. Not a chance. The kid was good, but he was no Shark.

At the far edge, the Shark turned fast and slipped deeper, until he disappeared beneath the pool's surface and nothing of him remained visible but a glistening fast shadow slicing through the water. He had reached the middle of the pool before he surfaced for air. That Fremont kid—he was still there, trying to close the gap. The Shark took a huge lungful of air and stretched for the finish.

From somewhere in the distance, a thin wailing sound began scratching at his senses. He let it drift past. He was a Shark. Not just a Shark. *The* Shark. He was the ultimate swimmer, 160 fearless pounds of speed and muscle. He had nothing to fear from anybody.

The wailing noise rose, climbing into insistent bursts. There was one voice, and then another, louder one. Sharp, jarring words that had scarcely penetrated his senses became clearer.

"Hey! You! Sleepin' beauty in the shit-brown Chevy. Wake up! This ain't the Hilton."

The noise tore into the Shark's world, blasting it apart in a torrent of horns. Still half-dazed, he pulled himself erect in the Chevy's front seat. He blinked, trying to clear his vision. The blue-green water that had cooled him seconds before disintegrated into a sun-beaten stretch of hot asphalt and overheated cars. From behind him, an angry driver shouted, "Come on, Bozo. Let's move it."

Bozo! Fully awake now, the insult registered. The guy had to be a fool. Asking for trouble! Well, the Shark knew how to handle him. Leaning out the Chevy's window, he called over his shoulder, "Blow it out your ear, asshole."

The two rednecks in the pickup didn't look like they were ready to back down. As the Shark turned away, one of them raised a finger in an obscene gesture. The Shark stomped the clutch angrily. The Chevy lurched and died. There was a jolt as the pickup nudged its bumper.

Mother's car, a voice at the back of his mind said. The voice began as a murmur, barely audible. It quickly gathered strength. *Don't you dare let anything happen to my car, Ronnie.*

He looked through the rearview mirror. The pickup's doors had opened. When the two sunburned men in shorts and open-necked shirts stepped onto the asphalt, his heart began racing. With his free hand, he reached down into the place beneath his seat where he kept the knife hidden. His fingers probed around the emergency brake and the edge of the passenger seat. A flicker of panic hit him, and his speeding heart beat faster. Then the knife's steel edge bit into his fingertips. Now the Shark could take them, grab the closer one, twist his arm behind his back, and hold the knife to his throat.

An image suddenly flickered through his head. Mother is standing in his bedroom door, her hands planted on her hips.

You learn to control that nasty temper, Ronnie, or you're going to feel my belt on your legs.

Mother is dead, he reminded himself. It was different now with Mother dead. It was better. The Shark could come out whenever he wanted.

The man from the pickup was next to his window, standing there, arms crossed over his chest. Here was the Shark's chance. Jump out of the car and take this sucker, quick, before the redneck knew what was happening.

No, no. It isn't better now that Mother is dead. Shame on you for thinking that. It's worse. Much worse.

Ronnie's breaths came faster. The great lungfuls from the swim competition had turned into short, panting gasps as he tried to calm himself, to force himself back to the safe place where the Shark took care of things. It was too late. The Shark had gone, and Ronnie's courage had gone with him. A paralyzing fear gripped Ronnie even before the man from the pickup spoke.

"Hey, turkey! Who you calling asshole?"

The man stooping by his door was big and flaccid. He had a mottled red nose. A visor cap with a charging bull across its brim perched on his head. As he spoke, the smell of beer washed over Ronnie. The other man was leaning through the window on the passenger side, smiling his ugly gap-toothed smile.

Ronnie slacked his grip on the knife. It slid from his hand and fell back to the floor.

"Sorry guys. I didn't mean anything. I just kind of drifted off. You know how it is."

There was a soft click on his left. The man in the hat was playing with his door lock, lifting the button, pushing it down. Up, down. The man's hands were huge. Ronnie suddenly had a terrible loose sensation in his bowels.

"You watch who you call asshole around here," the gap-toothed man said. The two men turned and walked back to the pickup.

"Dumb jerks," Ronnie said under his breath. After a few

seconds, he looked up into the mirror. The men were back in the pickup. "Dumb, ugly jerks," he said, louder. Restarting the Chevy, he rolled forward slowly, careful not to send loose gravel flying back onto the truck.

Some dozen cars ahead, at the moment when a baby finally cried himself to the edge of a light sleep, the four-year-old boy in the Bart Simpson T-shirt in the backseat of a station wagon locked his legs together and whimpered.

"Daddy, when are we going to stop? I've got to go pee."

The baby shuddered and his eyes half-opened. The girl cradling him, a slender thirteen-year-old, began rocking again, murmuring soft words into the infant's neck. Another child, a girl of nine, looked at her four-year-old brother in disgust.

"Daddy, didn't you hear what Frankie said? He said the word for number one. You said if he said that word again . . ."

The man, his hands damp and hot on the steering wheel, spoke softly, forcing his words between clenched teeth. "Both of you listen carefully. If you wake up the baby, you will not go to the beach all week. You will stay in your room without a television. Do you understand me?"

"But . . ."

"Quiet!"

Ahead, Frank Neuhauser could see the long line of Labor Day traffic disappearing around the curve toward the inlet and rising, finally, to cross the Bourne Bridge. The bridge was still far away; the cars visible along the top span were tiny as a line of ants.

Frank's face was slick with oil and sweat and fatigue. It had been too long since breakfast, and the needle over the gas gauge hovered near empty. The noon sun beat relentlessly through the aging wagon's windows, and the hot, still air smelled of soiled diapers. Not for the first time that day, nor for the last, Frank experienced a sour wave of nausea rising in his throat. A second later, tears filled his eyes, threatening to spill down his face.

"Damn this glare." He lowered the visor in front of him. "Joyce, I'm starting to think this was not a good idea."

The pale, obese woman in the passenger seat said nothing. For most of the year—from the middle of September until the first weeks of June—the tourists abandon Cape Cod. Only the intrepid year-round residents—the fishermen, the innkeepers who seal up their drafty upstairs rooms and warm themselves around fireplaces, a few hardy tourists who have come to love the winter sea wind on their faces and the special magic in out-of-season beach towns—those few have the Cape to themselves. They say there is a special aura then—a magnification—and good times, love, and friendship seem richer. Some even say that troubles, if they don't actually disappear, can take on such a romantic character that they are savored and burnished, much like the leaks in a proud old wood-hulled sailboat.

After Memorial Day, with the lengthening of the afternoons, the population swells. By summer, the tourists come in throbbing, bustling packs—carfulls, planeloads, busloads of them, drawn by the sun. The Cape's mood becomes the mood of the marketplace. Nothing escapes—from the toniest antique shops in Chatham to Provincetown's obscure alley doorways. The year-rounders hustle to bring in enough money in three months to last them through nine more; the summer people hustle to spend as much as they can in a "buy all you can, eat all you can" frenzied search for rejuvenation.

Frank Neuhauser wanted nothing to do with any of it. He had made that clear to his wife, Joyce. The heat, the crowds, sand, strange, uncomfortable mattresses and abysmal television reception. Not to mention the inflated prices. And definitely not to mention their . . . situation.

"Don't you think," he had asked, phrasing it as carefully as he possibly could, "that you would be more comfortable, at first, going straight home?"

"Actually, no," Joyce had replied. "I'm looking forward to the Cape," and she had held out for her vacation.

Frank couldn't imagine where her resolve had come from. After her six-week stay in a psychiatric hospital, during which time she underwent nine sessions of electroconvulsive therapy, he would have thought that just once she would have been glad to skip this yearly nightmare. No such luck. Thank God his boss had loaned him the condo. One less expense.

Out of the corner of his eye, Frank saw his little boy's hand, sticky with chocolate from a melting candy bar, slide over the back of the car seat. Frankie's fingers grazed his mother's neck.

"Mommy, I told Daddy I have to go pee. When are we going to stop?"

"Didn't I tell you not to bother your mother?"

"It's all right, Frank. We'll be stopping soon," she said to the child.

Frank sighed. Ahead, at some point still out of his sight, the traffic was merging into one lane. A blinking red light ahead signaled something—an accident or, more likely, road work. There was always road work along this stretch. They constructed and they ripped up and they rebuilt. Why shouldn't they? It was only the taxpayers' money. His money, and here he was sweating. . . .

His wife read his thoughts. "Traffic will move faster once we get onto Route Six."

"I'm sure it will fly right along," he said, unable to keep the sarcasm out of his voice.

"Daddy," his younger daughter singsonged, "Frankie wet his pants."

"What?" he said angrily, glaring over his shoulder at his son. "Oh, hell! Frankie, you are much too old for that!"

"Daddy, I told you. . . ." The little boy's words were choked with sobs.

His sister grabbed her nose. "Yech. Gross."

There was a small sound from the baby, just a cough, then another. Everyone in the station wagon froze. Within seconds, a full-throated howl filled the air.

"Damn! Couldn't keep him quiet, could you, Debbie? Too much to ask!"

The older girl scowled at the back of her father's head. "What was I supposed to do? Smother Andy?"

"You watch that attitude, young lady."

"Frank, why don't you pull over at the Texaco," Joyce said. "It will be cheaper than on the Cape, anyway, and I can get Frankie cleaned up."

The station was one of those big modern ones with eight pumps on two sides of an L—no lead, low lead, self-service. The wagon lumbered from one to the next. The shocks were gone and it swayed when Frank finally hit the brakes.

"Damn. A dollar thirty-four's the cheapest. This was not a good idea."

"We won't be long," Joyce said.

"Take your time. We're going to be sitting here forever."

Frank Neuhauser watched his family cross the pavement— Maryann skipping ahead, Debbie, the oldest, pulling Frankie junior behind her, and Joyce carrying Andy. Was it his imagination, or was Joyce even heavier than she had been when she went into the hospital? My God! Had she ever really been as pretty as he remembered her being?

"Fill it up?" a boy asked.

Frank nodded, eyes still on his wife. He was right—her body blocked most of the ladies' room door. She shifted, edging sideways through the entrance. "Warm in the winter, shady in the summer," he said under his breath. The moment the words were out of his mouth, Frank felt a twinge of guilt. He'd heard a coworker say that about an overweight secretary, and he'd laughed, but it wasn't something a man should say about his own wife.

"Pardon?" asked the boy at the pump.

"Nothing."

There had been a time, not many years before, when Frank had urged growth on his pretty, docile wife. "Take classes, join clubs," he had advised. "Expand yourself." In the most perverse way imaginable, Joyce had obliged him. The soft white hands that had once charmed him with their fluttering uncertainty grew until her wedding band had to be sawed from her finger. Her milk white breasts became gross and pendulous; the cushion

9

of her stomach rose like kneaded dough spilling from its bowl. After the birth of their fourth child, Joyce had outweighed her husband by almost forty pounds.

"That's fifteen twenty-eight, sir."

"What?" Frank thrust a credit card at the kid. "How much did it take?"

"Eleven point—"

"Forget it." He twisted in his seat and looked at the traffic. Still crawling. No, not even crawling. Inching. There was a young woman in a green sports car with its top down. Her long russet hair hung over her bare shoulders. Bare, *slender* shoulders, he noticed, and the thought that so often had run through his mind over the past few months repeated itself: Where have I gone wrong? Have I done something to deserve this?

The wagon swayed as Joyce and the younger children climbed back in. "All done."

Her voice sounded abnormally bright to Frank. Maybe she had taken one of her pills. A junkie's dream, that's what his wife's handbag amounted to.

"Where's Debbie?"

"She's getting us some soft drinks."

"Great! Probably a dollar each here." He tapped the horn. "Come on, Debbie!"

Joyce turned away from her husband and rested her chin on the hot window frame. Right from the start of the trip, she had found herself longing for her little room at the hospital, with its bare white walls and the tile floor that felt cool and good on her feet. She already missed the doctors and nurses, who never, no matter what, showed anger. Not that this was so bad. Oh, no. Her return to her family wasn't nearly as difficult as she had anticipated. During the long drive, she had smiled at their humor and sighed sympathetically over their problems. It hadn't been very difficult. The truth was, she felt so unattached to her four children and her husband that they might have been actors on a weekly television series.

Though her doctors had downplayed it, Joyce knew there

was a possibility of temporary memory loss with electroshock therapy. But was it memory loss that made Frank seem like an irritable stranger? Was memory loss the reason why she felt so tenuously attached to her children? Maybe. Maybe not. As she tried to make sense of her world, Joyce wondered whether her connection to her family had always been tenuous.

Her wedding album was tucked somewhere in her luggage. Frank, trying hard to do everything right, had brought it along at a therapist's suggestion. "Reattach yourself to the things that are important in your life," the therapist had told her. "Work your memory. Go through old pictures. See old friends. Eventually everything will come back."

Joyce glanced at the stacked luggage in the back of the station wagon. It will wait, she said to herself. A crowded car full of cranky people on a hot highway isn't the place to start thumbing through wedding pictures.

She watched waves of heat simmer off the hoods of passing cars. "When your mind wanders, try to think about absolutes," the therapist had said. Absolutes. A red car with Massachusetts plates passed them. Was it a reflection from the shiny paint that made the driver's face look so red, or was he as hot as she was? No flights of imagination, she reminded herself. She needed absolutes. A Toyota passed, absolutely. Then a little gray Honda. Japanese cars. Lots of them. Had there always been so many? An old yellow Volkswagen. "Look at the rust," she said quietly. A beautiful girl with Rita Hayworth red hair inched by in a sports car. There was a name for that car's color, wasn't there? English racing green. A bad-luck color? Where had she heard that? It probably wasn't true. The girl with the red hair didn't look as if she had bad luck.

Next came a Chevy, even older than the station wagon, dull brown. The driver's lips were moving. Joyce squinted, focusing on him. How odd. Not that the man was talking to himself. Lots of people talk to themselves. But how odd to spot a familiar face on the highway, a face that actually tugged at some fragmented memory.

11

The station wagon bounced off the curb and nosed into the lane next to the Chevy. Joyce's eyes hadn't left the driver.

Ronnie was trying to return to the dream, trying to bring the Shark back. For a moment, the Shark had spoken through him, but there were too many cars around. There was too much noise and confusion. The pickup truck stayed right on his tail. And that station wagon that had cut in alongside him! Why did that woman keep looking at him that way? For a second, her eyes locked onto his. Ronnie quickly looked away, then took a quick glance back at her. She was still staring at him.

Too bad the Shark wasn't there. The Shark would know what to do about her. The Shark would lean out the car window and say something to make her turn her fat face away. Ronnie lowered the sun visor into the open window, partially shielding himself from the woman.

"Joyce, what are you staring at? Joyce!"

"Nothing." For a moment, she and the stranger had looked right into each other's eyes. He had looked away abruptly, recoiled even, and that had touched something deep in her, something that made her uneasy. But that was ridiculous. Maybe the man hadn't recoiled. Maybe he simply hadn't wanted to be stared at.

"Frank, isn't that someone we know? Driving the brown car? I could swear I've met him."

"He's no one I know," Frank answered. "And please don't stare. He'll think . . . just don't stare."

"But . . ." She looked out the window again. The man had lowered his sun visor and his face was partially hidden. "Is he the man who bought the West's house when they moved?"

"No, he's not."

"Are you sure? Maybe I've seen him in the neighborhood. Could he be . . ."

For a second, Frank stared into the brown car. When he looked away, he began tapping his fingertips against the steering wheel. "No. That man is not anyone I've met. And he's obviously never met us, because he turned his head when I stared at him. He probably thinks we're a couple nuts. Please let's mind our own business."

Maryann piped up from the backseat. "Well I certainly don't know him. The man who bought the West's house is old and yucky."

Ronnie took another fast sideways glance at the station wagon. The woman was saying something to her husband. They seemed to have forgotten about him. Why had they been staring at all? Did they know something about the Shark? The thought frightened him. Nobody could know about the Shark. Where the two lanes merged into one, Ronnie tapped the brake pedal and let the wagon pull ahead. He let the girl in the green sports car edge in front of him, too. She didn't impress him. Too old. But the Shark would like her. The way her hair fell in red strands over her shoulders—the Shark would like that a lot. By the time the Chevy hit the metal grids of the Bourne Bridge, Ronnie had slipped back into the dream. The redheaded girl was standing at the edge of the pool, handing the Shark a white towel. She had a beautiful smile, the redheaded girl, and it was all for the winner. The woman in the station wagon was gone from Ronnie's mind.

The bedroom Joyce and Frank shared on the second floor of the condominium was warm and damp, and the sheets clammy. The air conditioner in the window leaked a widening ring of water onto the brown carpet. Their brief attempt at lovemaking had left Joyce wide-awake and apprehensive. The room was easily twice the size of the one at the hospital, but she felt cramped and claustrophobic. It wasn't really the room, she knew. It was Frank next to her, and her four children scattered around the condo. Life, pressing down on her.

"The kids are asleep," she whispered, "Why don't we sit out on the beach for a while. We could take a blanket."

13

"Huh? Come on, Joyce. I'm beat. Tomorrow's another day."
He brushed her cheek with his lips. "Will you try to keep the
kids quiet in the morning? I'd like to catch an extra hour. That
drive was brutal."

Joyce lay quietly for a few minutes, afraid to move but knowing sleep was impossible. If she took a pill, she'd sleep, but that
sleep wouldn't be a restful one. Over the last months, there had
been so many pills, so much time passed feeling half-awake.
Pushing away the sheet, she sat up.

"Frank, I'm going for a walk."

He came awake with a start. "What's wrong? I was almost
asleep."

"Nothing's wrong," Joyce said, trying to keep anything that
might alarm her husband out of her voice. "I'm not tired. I want
to get some fresh air."

Frank rose on his elbow and looked at her. "Are you sure
you're all right? Nothing's bothering you?"

"No, I'm restless. That's all. The air will help." She pulled her
beach coat over her nightgown.

"Put your shoes on," Frank said as he sank back onto his
pillow. "There's all kind of garbage in the sand."

Joyce fished her sandals off the floor. "Back in a few
minutes."

Frank lay awake, fighting his impulse to watch from the
window. She'll be okay, he told himself. Her doctor says she's
okay. A foot-high stack of medical bills says she's okay. A suitcase full of pills says that if she isn't okay, take one and she will
be. I can't watch her every minute.

The sleep of the exhausted soon overtook him.

The moon was a mere sliver that night. Joyce dropped her
sandals on the condo's porch and crossed the driveway to the
beach. The cold night sand on her bare feet gave her a rush of
energy. At the water's edge, she waded in to her ankles and
relished the cool, easy lap of the waves. Yellow dots shone from
the lighthouses out on the points of land to the west. Several

hundred feet from shore, a fishing boat trolled, barely touched by the crescent moon. To the east and south lay the miles-long stretch of efficiency cabins. Across the bay, the lights of Boston brightened the night sky.

Wading back onto the sand, she took a cautious look around. She was alone on the beach. Unsnapping the front of her robe, she pulled it from her shoulders and laid it on the sand. Then she lowered herself onto her back. The cool wind off the bay slid through her thin nightgown, caressing her body. She looked up through the black night into the Milky Way.

One day over with, and all in all it hadn't been bad. After dinner, she'd spent time playing with her younger children. They were thrilled to have her back, and Joyce had felt her own emotional connections being reawakened. Debbie was the only one who was keeping a distance. Debbie would take longer. And so would Frank. Oh, Frank would take a lot longer.

"It's not as if I ask a lot," Frank had often said to his wife, and Joyce knew that he didn't. Only that they might fit in, not stand out; that the right thing, word, house, job, children, would come to them as effortlessly as he imagined they came to other people. And hadn't he done his part? he would ask. Top-selling salesman and assistant manager at the number-one insurance brokerage in their area. A tract house, sure, but in a prime, safe, clean development. Four bedrooms, three baths, a basement recreation room. The price could only go up.

Joyce had tried. The eighteen-year-old bride of an "older man"—Frank had been twenty-two, and a new college graduate at that—Joyce had moved into the life her husband arranged for them with scarcely considered, never-spoken apprehensions. As years passed, she had begun to feel like a traveler moving through a foreign land, following illegible signs, hearing words she didn't really comprehend, and incorrectly interpreting jumbled signals.

Until the previous May night when Frank was out at a meeting, Joyce's anxieties had been her secret, her only secret. Frank had never suspected that the mountain of domestic tranquility

15

sharing his bed and board fell asleep with nameless fears and woke with a hopeless despair that never completely subsided.

Joyce Neuhauser's suicide was the one thing that was to have been all hers. There was no concern for what Frank or the neighbors thought. Not even for the children. It was all hers—the germination of the idea, the tranquilizers hoarded in the cup of an outgrown bra, the time, the place. That night the previous May, she had spread her red treasure on the kitchen table—thirty 10-milligram Seconal tablets prescribed by her doctor for sleeplessness. And a quart of vodka.

A fleeting realization of the enormity of what she was doing had made the first two Seconal hard to get down. She gagged on them, and on the rough taste of the vodka, and took two more pills. She drank and took two more, and then more. At some point—it could have been five minutes or twenty later—the month-old baby had cried from the back of the neat split-level house. Joyce started to rise but fell back into the kitchen chair. She took more tablets and looked around her kitchen. Once it had been crisp and pretty. Now the yellow print curtains were faded and limp. The black-and-white tile floor cried out for washing. As she stared, the squares paled into a dirty blur. Vodka splashed across the table when she raised the glass. She swallowed the remaining pills in slopping mouthfuls and laid her head on the wet table.

Joyce had wakened the next afternoon in a hospital bed. She couldn't move. Her arms and legs felt as if they were paralyzed. Her throat hurt terribly. Frank's face floated over her, hagridden, somehow more clearly defined than it should have been. "Why didn't you leave me alone?" were her first words. He hadn't answered.

A course of antidepressant drugs had followed. A few months, Dr. Weisman, the young therapist whom she first met in that hospital room, had said. Then they would see. Dr. Weisman had a wide, almost Oriental face, and had spoken to her with quiet, childlike words. He seemed wise beyond his years. Nothing she said had surprised him. After a time, when her system had proven unable to tolerate the drugs, he had suggested the electroshock treatment. Four months after her attempted suicide, Dr. Weisman and his colleagues had pronounced Joyce well enough to function normally.

The breeze coming off the water was quickening now. Joyce sat up and watched as feathers of sand drifted over her ankles. Strangely thin ankles, coming from such thick calves. What was that phrase? Well-turned. Can a fat lady have a well-turned ankle? Would anyone notice? Pulling up her gown, Joyce stared openly at her thighs. Under the dark sky, they had a fuzzy, amorphous quality. Shifting her hips, she pulled the gown farther, until her stomach and breasts lay exposed. She imagined her body as a mountain range seen, perhaps, from a distant airplane. There were towering peaks and rolling hills, tiny rills and valleys tucked away, enfolded by the vast landscape. Still fat, sure, but well enough to function. Well enough to function as what, though? Wife, mother, crazy lady? Pulling down the gown and gathering her robe around her, Joyce walked back to the apartment.

Frank woke as she slid into bed.

"I was worried. Are you all right?"

"I'm fine."

Joyce slept then, and sometime in the early hours when the light was just breaking over the eastern edge of the sea, she dreamed. Her feet were sliding, fighting for a grip on the painted slick blue-green bottom of a swimming pool. Her hands tore through the water in terror. Something was forcing her down—something strong pushing her under, suffocating her. She tried to scream but water filled her mouth. The hands gripped her harder. They were shaking her.

"Joyce! Joyce! What's going on? What's wrong with you? Wake up."

She woke with a start, gasping for breaths that wouldn't come. Frank knelt over her, his hands on her shoulders.

Tears began rolling down Joyce's cheeks. Frank shook his head and let out a sigh.

"You were dreaming, Joyce. That's all. A bad dream. Try to calm down. Take a deep breath."

For a moment, there was something, some important thing she had to tell him. It passed as quickly as the shutter of a camera opens and clicks shut.

"Joyce?"

She was afraid if she tried to speak, strange sounds, words she couldn't control, would come out and Frank would be upset by them. Then he was pushing one of her pills at her. A whole pill and a glass of water. She wanted to tell him she only took half a pill at a time, but the worry in his expression stopped her. After swallowing the pill, she sank back on the bed. The rest of the night, she slept.

When Ronnie had finished brushing and flossing his teeth, he washed his face with warm water, then rinsed it with cold. He patted his skin dry with a paper towel and ran a comb through his hair. The attendant at the public men's room behind the Provincetown Bakery never once looked up from his book.

Ronnie hated not showering, hated the feeling of the road on him, and the touch of the clothes he'd worn all day. His hair was much too long, too. It was the Shark who had told him he didn't have to go to the barber ever two weeks, but Ronnie could just imagine what Mother would say about that! Lately, he'd let the Shark talk him into doing a lot of things Mother wouldn't like.

He'd showered that morning, but he hadn't shaved. He'd lathered his face and pressed the razor against his skin. "Hell with this," the Shark had said. Now dark stubble showed on his cheeks. Tomorrow, he'd find a room and get cleaned up. A cheap room—he didn't have much money—but a clean one. In a private house, if he could. Mother said they were the best places to stay. "You can depend on an owner to take better care of a place than some motel maid," she had told him. Mother knew a lot.

That night, he slept in the Chevy in a slot at the back of the municipal parking lot near the pier. When the last traffic had quieted, Ronnie was able to slip into that quiet place and be the Shark again. His night was filled with competitions and cheering crowds. Girls handed him towels and rubbed his shoulders dry. Ronnie dozed that night, never really sleeping. That seemed right, though. Real sharks never slept. He'd learned that from a television show. Real sharks were always on alert, always ready.

Ronnie's eyes were open when the crack of light appeared on the eastern horizon.

Chapter 2

EMMA'S Grocery fronts on the bay side of Commercial Street. There isn't much of a sidewalk, and the grocery's small front porch, partially shaded by a second-floor dormer, almost touches the asphalt street. A sign on the screen door, under the rusty tin cutout of the blond girl in a red halter waving a Coca-Cola bottle, says NO DOGS. NO BARE FEET. No one pays much attention to either warning.

The store, a few blocks from the wharf on the West End of Provincetown, stretches like a shoe box all the way to the water, where a rear storage room rests on pilings that have seemed on the verge of collapse for twenty years. Wide oak floorboards, smooth and dull from generations of sandy feet, run front to back. Wooden shelves line the side walls floor to ceiling. Emma usually can be found at the checkout counter at the front, just inside the screen door. The counter is so cluttered with racks of suntan lotion and odd, out-of-style dark glasses that the customer could easily miss the small, bony woman behind the register.

That Saturday morning, the air was still and the temperature rising. Emma stretched her head up and fanned herself with the weekly guide to Provincetown's nightlife. People had often remarked that Emma, with her long neck and jutting chin, resembled the masthead on a nineteenth-century whaler, beaten and aged by the sea. The skin on her neck and hands was as dry and wrinkled as a crumpled paper bag.

At the side of the counter, Robin, the big old Labrador, slept, her graying muzzle resting on the dried mud that coated her paws. From time to time, she flicked an ear to send a persistent fly on its way.

Emma glanced toward the back of the store where Little Ned Mayo was stocking the soft-drink cooler. Taking his time, as usual, Emma saw.

"Looks like its going to be another scorcher. Better hurry with those," she said to him.

"Wouldn't be surprised," Ned answered laconically. "Shame when a man can't afford something to wet his whistle on a day like this."

Emma ignored him. Years earlier—no one really remembered how many years anymore—Emma and Little Ned Mayo had been an item in Provincetown. These days, if asked, Ned would deny ever offering to make an honest woman of her. Only the old-timers knew how, long ago, on a heart-melting spring night Ned had mustered his courage. Emma, however, showing either a streak of fierce independence for a woman of that time or, perhaps, as had been suggested, good Yankee sense, had chosen to go it alone.

As sole owner and proprietor of the store her parents founded, Emma had prospered. It became accepted that while Ned stocked the shelves and swept up and locked the front door at night, and some nights—though they had grown fewer over the years—followed Emma up the stairs at the side of the building that led to her dormered apartment, it was Emma who worked the register and took the receipts to the bank and paid Ned's salary.

"Squeezing those nickels till they scream for mercy," he had told his buddies at the Fo'c'sle Tavern when he was out of Emma's hearing.

It was a little before eleven that morning when the Neuhauser family filed through the door—Frank in the lead, Joyce behind him, carrying the baby, Maryann, and finally Debbie, leading Frankie. Emma sized them up fast: Sodas, sandwich fixings. Won't spend much, but won't steal anything, either. She grimaced as the little boy stretched into the packaged cupcakes, causing the wire rack that held baked goods to teeter on its wobbly legs.

The older girl crouched on her heels next to Robin and stuck out a hand tentatively toward the dog's massive head. "Does he bite?"

"He's a she," Emma said. "Can hardly even chew anymore, much less bite."

"I wish we had a dog," the girl said. "We had a cat."

"He died," said the younger girl.

"Cats are nice, too. They're clean. Keep down the mice." Emma looked toward the rear aisle. "Ned," she called, "if you're through with those sodas, there're some cartons in the storage room need unpacking."

Grumbling all the way, the old man disappeared through the door at the back of the building.

Joyce Neuhauser carried the baby to the side of the store. The pill she'd taken the night before had left her groggy, with a sickish feeling in her stomach. Sweat was collecting on her neck and in the fold of her bosom. Balancing the baby on her hip, she leaned her back against the frozen-food cooler and reached into her plastic bag for a cloth. The baby's head lolled to the side.

A dormant maternal streak rose in Emma. The poor little kid. Red as a tomato. Shameful, taking a child that young to the beach. She was about to offer to hold the baby when the screen door opened and slammed shut again.

Ronnie blinked and widened his eyes, adjusting them to the store's dim light. He looked around him, at the man squinting

22

at prices on bread wrappers, at the little boy, and back at Emma.

"Do you have cold sodas?"

"Other side of the frozen foods," she answered, hardly looking at him.

A moment later, there was a clattering sound from the back aisle. Stepping from behind the register, Emma peered over the rack of baked goods. The heavy woman holding the baby had stumbled away from the frozen cooler into a display of brooms and mops. The wooden handles rested on her arm, across the baby's back, and on the floor around her feet. Her hip was dangerously close to a pyramid of catsup and mayonnaise bottles. She clutched the baby like a shield as the man pushed past her to get to the sodas.

"Pardon me," Emma heard him say. She watched as he lifted the top of the red cooler, then called to him. "We just got through stocking that. Coolest ones are on the bottom."

He closed the cooler and walked back past the heavy woman, two cans of soda in his hand. As he pulled his wallet from his pocket, his glance fell on the costume-jewelry display in the old glass case. A shark's tooth on a gold chain rested among the jumble of seashell bracelets and sand-dollar medallions.

"How much is that shark's tooth?"

"Fourteen ninety-nine," Emma answered. "It's a nice one."

Ronnie shook his head. "Oh. That's a lot."

It sure was, Emma thought with great satisfaction. A lot more than the two dollars each they had cost when she'd bought them by the dozen.

"Chain's gold," she said, neglecting to add the word *plate*.

Debbie Neuhauser was still crouched on the floor by the Labrador, Robin. Giving the dog a final pat on the head, she rose and edged over to the counter. "Is it a real shark's tooth? Can I see it?"

Emma, sensing a sale, pulled the chain from the case and dangled it in front of the young girl, all the while looking at the man. "Give it to you for twelve dollars even."

Taking the chain in his hand, Ronnie examined the tooth.

23

Then he looked at Debbie for the first time. To Emma, it seemed as if he had to think about something before he spoke. "Sure," he said finally. He dangled the chain toward the girl. The tooth swung slowly back and forth.

"Mako shark?" Debbie asked.

"Great white," he answered.

"How can you be sure?"

He took a step nearer the girl and lowered the necklace until it hung directly in front of her eyes. "Look carefully." With his finger, he traced a ridge down the center of the tooth. "You can tell by the ridges," he said, so softly that Emma could hardly make out what he was saying.

Debbie's eyes followed the man's finger. She was oblivious to her mother's voice calling her name.

"Honey," Emma interrupted, "If you're Debbie, I think your mom wants you." And a good thing, too, the woman said to herself. This lecher's old enough to be your father.

Debbie rolled her eyes. Ronnie smiled at her. For a second, she smiled back, then blotches of red began to spread across her cheekbones.

"Better go," she said.

Ronnie paid for the soda and the necklace and left, closing the screen door quietly behind him. The Neuhausers, every available arm loaded with groceries, followed a few minutes later.

As the family made their way up Commercial Street, Emma pushed through the screen door, propping it open with her body. She watched the procession until it passed out of sight around the curve by the Coast Guard station: the overweight, nervous woman, the tired-looking husband, the sweet little boy, the two pretty girls. *And that poor little tyke.*

Ned shuffled up the aisle, groaning under the imaginary weight of a carton of cereal. "Some women aren't cut out to be mothers," Emma said to him.

"Didn't notice 'em. Busy hauling boxes. Awful lot of work for a man my age."

"If you'd worked harder when you were younger, you

24

wouldn't have to work so hard now," she said matter-of-factly.
"Emma," he responded, "you're letting in the flies. Next
thing, you'll have me running around like a fool, swatting
at 'em."

She moved back into the store. "An odd bunch there."
Ned laughed. " 'An odd bunch, a strange one.' Damned if
you don't get going about half the people who come through
that door. To listen to you, nothing but queens and perverts and
addicts around this town."

Emma took a swipe at a fat fly buzzing lazily over the counter.
"Ned, there's a rack of brooms needs picking up back by the
soda cooler."

Oh, man! The way she looked at him. Those blue eyes, and the
way her front teeth pushed at her lip. Not a lot. Just a little.
Innocent, and . . . so cute. That white shirt she was wearing was
unbuttoned at the top, so he could glimpse the top of her pink
bathing suit. Had she done that on purpose? She didn't look like
the kind of girl who would do things like that. She didn't look
like a tease.

From where he'd pulled the Chevy, into the shaded alley
across from the Coast Guard station, Ronnie had to twist in his
seat to see the front door of Emma's. A girl like that was worth
the trouble.

Had she noticed that it was kind of hard for him to start
talking to her? He'd been so nervous. The old lady had noticed.
Sometimes it seemed like old ladies noticed more than other
people. He'd seldom been able to hide his thoughts from
Mother, especially when he was thinking about girls. One time,
when he'd watched the girls down the street playing in their
yard, Mother had read his mind. He was a lot bigger than
Mother by then, but she'd slapped him hard, anyway—right
across the face.

Had the girl in the store known what he was thinking? Had
she seen how the sweat misted over his forehead? He didn't
think so.

25

So cute. Cute, cute, cute. The word echoed through Ronnie's mind, a quiet reminder of the bad time years before. He pushed the word away.

He liked the way the girl in the store had made that face when her mother called her. And the way she'd returned his smile. The minute she smiled up at him, he'd known she was a nice girl. More than nice. Her smile had made him feel warm. Analyzing that smile now, he realized that it meant something special. She had shared something with him—a little secret smile against her mother. Couples shared secrets like that.

He saw the family leave the store, watched them walk single file down the narrow sidewalk and around the curve. When they passed the Coast Guard station, they turned down one of the side streets leading to a small development of condominium apartments along the beach. Before they were out of sight, Ronnie started his engine. By the time Frank Neuhauser unlocked the door and the family disappeared into the two-story apartment, Ronnie had found a parking place at the end of their block.

Debbie tugged at the bottom of her pink bikini and squinted into the sun. Frankie, trotting a few feet behind her, stepped onto the sand, faltered, and jumped back into the shade of the building.

"Come on, Frankie," Debbie called.

"I don't want to. It's too hot. It's burning my feet."

"Okay then, baby, you stay there all day, or go back in the room and watch TV with Daddy and Maryann."

The little boy's high-pitched whine followed Debbie as she darted across the sand and splashed into the calm bay water.

"Debbie. Debbie!"

Her mother's voice rose in the tone Debbie knew well. Six weeks, her mother had been away. Her father had said there would be changes in her mother, but one thing hadn't changed: Her mother still treated her like a baby. So did her father. Okay, but if she was such a baby, why had she ended up spending most of her summer baby-sitting her sister and brothers? She was old enough to do that, wasn't she?

Debbie looked back up the beach. Her mother had set an oversized umbrella into the sand. She, Frankie, and the baby were huddled under it. Debbie shouted back, her voice shrill with annoyance. "What do you want?"

"Stay where I can see you. Don't go out too deep."

Ronnie had spread his blanket behind the rock jetties that separated the public beach from the one reserved for condominium owners and their guests. Through a space in the rocks, he could see the family. When the surf was quiet and no motorboats raced across the bay, he heard their voices, playing, arguing. He heard the mother's fearful calls, and he heard the girl's defiant answer.

God, he liked her. With every minute, he liked her more. Debbie, her mother called her. Ronnie would call her Deborah. It sounded nicer. Settling into the warm sand, his back against a rock and his eyes half-closed, he began thinking about the way she looked. There was nothing dirty or teasing about her, no squinty-eyed stares trying to get a guy excited. A nice clean girl.

Rousing himself, he reached into his khaki pack for the paper bag that held the shark's tooth necklace. He grasped the tooth at its flat end and ran the sharp ivory over the soft flesh of his inner arm. It left a white trail that faded quickly. Deborah would be soft and white where the pink suit covered her skin.

When Ronnie looked up, he saw Deborah's head above the water out at the end of the rock jetties. Her long light brown hair was clinging, smooth and glossy, and he saw that her face was shaped like a perfect heart.

Her father had been nicer to her when her mother was gone. That was one good thing. He'd always said, "Thank you," when Debbie took care of Andy and the other kids. Since yesterday, though, all he did was snap at her, the same way he snapped at the younger kids. Debbie was thinking about this when she saw the man from the store. She watched his hand go up tentatively.

27

For a moment, she planted her feet firmly on the sandy ocean bottom. There had been all those lectures in school about perverts doing things to girls. This man—it was hard to tell. He needed a shave, but he looked okay, and he talked to her as if she was a real person and not just a baby-sitter, or worse—a baby.

Debbie let the tide carry her into shore. When she was close enough, she waved back to him.

Ronnie could hardly allow himself to believe it. As she stood and walked out of the water, he swore to himself: No dirty ideas, no dirty thoughts.

"You think that's a real shark's tooth you bought?"

She crouched and rested one knee on the corner of his blanket. Her leg, still dotted with water, was inches from Ronnie's arm. He wouldn't look at her bare skin. He wouldn't. He would look only at her face.

"Sure it is. Why? Don't you think it is?"

"My dad says everything they sell here is plastic made-in-Taiwan junk for suckers."

A small wave of anxiety registered. Was she one of those girls who worshiped their fathers? He had to be careful here. He had to let her know that he was more important to her than her father was. But he had to do it in a cool way.

"So? Does your dad know everything?"

"Of course not."

The anxiety calmed. "How about your mother?"

The girl groaned. "Give me a break. She's worse than he is. She's . . . well, she's a hundred times worse."

"Do you think she'll come looking for you?"

"No. My mom's scared to put her head under the water. She'd have to go all the way around by the street," Debbie said, and she grinned happily.

"You want to see how I can tell this shark's tooth is real?" he asked, delighted by her smile.

She nodded.

28

"Give me your hand."

Debbie held out her hand, obedient. He placed the tooth on the flat of her palm, being careful not to touch her. With his finger, Ronnie traced the dark line down the tooth's side. "This is where the nerve was that connects the tooth to the blood supply."

She jerked back her hand, suddenly self-conscious. "Don't look at my fingernails. They're hideous. I'm trying to stop biting them."

God! She was sharing herself with him, already telling him her personal secrets. It was almost too much, to talk about something personal so soon. She wasn't fast, was she? Of course she wasn't, but he had to be careful. Talking about these personal things, he might say something wrong, maybe scare her. It was better to talk about safe things. The Shark. As long as she didn't know that the Shark lived in his head, he could tell her stories about the Shark.

"This tooth reminded me of one I took off a great white down in the Bahamas a couple years back," Ronnie finally said. "A fourteen-footer. One of the biggest ever taken out of those waters."

"You killed him?"

"Sure did."

"What with?"

He savored her innocence. How nice it was to talk to a girl like this. Not like those dirty girls at the laundry, with their dirty minds and their filthy jokes.

"First, I stunned him with my spear gun," he said, "then I finished him off with my knife."

Debbie's eyes narrowed. She tilted her head to the side. "Are you putting me on? I saw something like that on television, but you're not the same guy."

Could she tell he was lying? "No," he said hurriedly. "I'm not putting you on."

"Well, then, why didn't you keep the tooth from *that* shark?"

"I gave it to someone." As soon as he said that, he wished he

29

could take the words back. What if she thought he had given it to another girl? "I gave it to my boss. Sharks' teeth are good luck, you know. Magic."

"I never heard that."

"They are. Here." He held the necklace out to her. "Do you want this one?"

"Oh, I don't think my parents would let me keep it, but maybe. . . ." Stooping, the girl peered through the space in the rocks. Across the beach, her mother and the baby still huddled under the umbrella. Frankie had wandered to the edge of the water. He was digging in the wet sand. Sitting back down in front of Ronnie, Debbie lifted her hair from her neck. "Can I try it on?"

Ronnie put the chain around Debbie's neck and clasped its hook, still not daring to touch her. They were so close, he felt warmth rising from her skin. "Now close your eyes and breathe deep," he said. "You'll start to feel the magic. Do you feel anything yet?"

"No." She flopped down on her back, half in the sand so that her face caught the sun's full glare. "I hope at least I get a good tan. So far, this summer's been totally wasted. Hey," she said a second later—"I think I feel something."

Ronnie could hardly believe how cute and nice she was. Everything about her was perfect. Well, maybe not the bathing suit. Once they were together, he wouldn't let her wear one like that in public. In private, though . . .

"The magic doesn't work on everybody," he said, "but I thought it would work on you. How does it feel?"

Debbie giggled. "Hot. The chain's burning my neck. It's probably going to turn it green, too."

Ronnie leaned closer to her. The chain lay temptingly against the reddening skin of her chest. All he had to do was reach for it, pretend to be taking it back, and he could brush his fingers against her throat. The thought of it made him catch his breath. He breathed deeply. She even smelled clean.

"Do you want me to take it off you?"

30

"In a minute. What's your name, anyway."

"Ronnie," he said. "What's yours?"

"Debbie."

"What's your last name?"

"Neuhauser."

"Where are you from, anyway?"

"We live outside of Lincoln Township. That's near Boston."

"I know where it is. Do you go to Lincoln High School there?"

"No, but my mom did, about a hundred years ago. Did you go to Lincoln?"

The conversation was getting too scary. "No," he said quickly, and he was relieved when she didn't ask him any more about that.

"I go to Our Lady of Mercy," she said.

Still shaken, Ronnie said the first thing that came into his head.

"Do you have a lot of boyfriends there?"

She hesitated. "Come on," she said, and her face turned a deeper red. "It's a girls' school. Besides, I'm only thirteen. My birthday was last month. I mostly hang out with my girlfriends."

"Are they good girls?"

Debbie opened her eyes and stared up at him, and he knew he'd said something wrong. That was the kind of question a weirdo would ask. He couldn't let her think he was a weirdo. He looked offshore, his eyes following the billowing sails of one of the refurbished schooners that took tourists around the bay.

"I mean," he added, "good friends. Do you do a lot of neat things together?"

"Neat things?" She seemed to find the words funny. "Sure, sometimes," and she started grinning again. "We're good the other way, too. We go to Catholic school. My parents put me in there to *make* me be good. If I'm not, Sister Immaculata . . ." She drew a finger across her throat. "Colleen. She's in my class. She's my best friend. But Lisa—that's Colleen's sister—she's going to be sixteen. Tenth grade." A small pucker developed between Debbie's eyebrows. "Sometimes Lisa does these wild things. My dad says she's going to get us in trouble if we hang out with her."

Suddenly somewhere in the distance, a whistle began to blow. "What's that?" she asked.

"Lunch whistle for somebody, I guess."

Debbie sat up. "I better get back. My mom's going to think I drowned."

As if on cue, a woman called from the other side of the rocks. "Debbie? Debbie?"

Ronnie rose into a crouch to stare through the space in the rocks. Deborah's mother was on her feet. Her thighs were fat and ugly. And on top—gross! Out of the dark chasm at the back of his mind, a vision flared briefly into a shaft of light. The boys, hushed, smothering their giggles peering through the crack in the wall of the girls' locker room. The girls on the other side of the wall are peeling off their suits, unaware that they are watched. Ronnie doesn't want to watch. He doesn't like these girls. But he can't tell the other boys. . . .

A knot of fear had twisted Ronnie's stomach. He felt weak. By the time he looked back at Deborah, the girl was moving toward the water and fumbling with the clasp at the back of her neck. "I can't get this off." She hurried back to the blanket. "Here, quick undo it."

"Please keep it," Ronnie said. The bad memory was still there, and he was afraid to be near her. She might notice how his fingers shook.

"I can't. My mom would have a fit. This vacation's going to be boring enough. If I got grounded, I'd just die." Pulling the necklace free, Debbie dropped it onto the blanket. "You keep it for me," she added.

Oh, man! A shiver of anticipation ran up Ronnie's spine. She wanted to see him again. That had to be what she meant. The ugly memory disappeared. She was walking away. He couldn't let her walk out of his life. The thought of her rejection all but paralyzed him, but he had to ask.

"If you're really bored, you could meet me back here after dinner. We'll get some ice cream and talk some more."

At the edge of the water, Deborah turned and looked at him. He tried to read her expression. Was she repulsed by his offer? As she dragged her toes along the edge of the water, he held his breath.

"I can't," she said with finality. "They wouldn't let me, and if I tried to sneak I'd ruin my whole vacation. Bye."

She moved into the shoulder-deep water at the end of the jetty. A minute later, she had disappeared from his sight.

"I'm here, Mom," he heard her calling. "I was looking for shells."

Debbie stopped where her brother was building a winding road in the wet sand. "You're too close to the water. The tide's going to wash it away," she told him.

"You promised you'd teach me to swim," Frankie said, not looking up.

"Okay. Come on." She held out her hand.

"But don't take me out too deep."

As Debbie led the little boy into the water, she thought briefly about the strange man. Maybe he really was a pervert or something. Ever since she could remember, she and her friends had been warned about men in the bushes, men with candy bars, men unzipping their pants.

Had he been kidding about meeting that night? He was okay-looking, in a dorky way, but he had to be almost as old as her father. Well, not *that* old, but almost thirty at least. Much too old for her. Maybe she shouldn't have said that stupid thing— "You keep it for me." What if he took it the wrong way?

Wait till she told Colleen. And Lisa! An older man, asking her out. Lisa's boyfriend didn't even have his driver's license yet. But maybe she wouldn't tell them. Lisa would be sure to have something smart to say. Didn't she always.

★ ★ ★

33

Joyce watched her older daughter lead Frankie through the calm water. The girl was slight, like her father, and Joyce knew that Debbie despaired of her boyish form. She thought her daughter lovely, though. And so lucky. Frank was all jutting angles and quick, awkward movements, but Debbie had a coltish grace about her. Where the girl had gotten it, Joyce couldn't imagine.

There were many parts of her own past that Joyce was having trouble recalling. So far, her childhood and adolescence existed in tumbled disorder, with shadows obscuring vast stretches of time. One thing she was reasonably sure of, though: She had never been coltish.

That morning while Frank showered, Joyce had flipped through the heavy pages of their wedding album. Some of the faces had been immediately familiar. She could recall the most insignificant details of a dress, the exact words on a gift card. Other faces had left her puzzled. Had she really known all these people? And the bride. That pretty eighteen-year-old girl with the waving blond hair. Almost, but not quite plump. The only thing Joyce found familiar about the girl in the white gown was her forced, uncomfortable smile.

"Mommy. Look, Mommy! I'm swimming!"

Frankie was squealing and kicking as his sister lifted him over the gentle waves. The girl was smiling, her eyes narrow against the sun. There Joyce could see a resemblance. Debbie had her mother's deep blue eyes, and when she laughed her lips tilted up the way Joyce's did.

That was something Joyce was going to try to do more of—laugh. And get to know her older daughter. And lose weight. And maybe find some kind of part-time work to get her out of the house.

The sun had moved and the circle of shade from the umbrella no longer shielded her. The baby's feet were exposed to the glaring sun. Joyce moved him to the deep shade, giving quiet thanks that he didn't wake. Shifting her legs until they again rested in the shade, she lay back on the orange and white striped towel. A moment later, Maryann was bending over her.

"I'm tired of watching television."

"What's Daddy doing?"

"He fell asleep."

"Do you want to go in the water?" The child shook her blond curls. "No. I just want to stay here with you."

Joyce made room on the towel for her pudgy little girl. Of all the children, Maryann most resembled her. Just out of the delivery room, a nurse had remarked, "The baby looks just like her mother." God help the poor kid, Joyce thought as she lay at the edge of sleep.

It was several minutes before Ronnie trusted himself to move. He didn't want to risk losing the good feelings. When he finally fell back onto the blanket, he was weak with pleasure. He placed himself next to the spot where Deborah had lain, and imagined her still there, beside him. He was suffused with the sensation of her: her clear skin, the way it was just turning pink; the way her knees sank into the blanket. Something of her seemed to cling to the crevices she had left in the sand.

"Deb-or-ah," he whispered, weak with the sound of her name on his lips. Opening his fist, he dropped the necklace onto his chest and wiggled it along by its chain.

The Shark hadn't come out while she was there. More and more when the girls at the laundry teased him, it felt like the Shark was going to come out and lunge at them. Rip their evil smiles off their made-up faces—that's what the Shark thought he should do to those girls. With Deborah, there hadn't been any sign of the Shark. That was a good sign.

"You keep it for me," she had said. Ronnie experienced a sudden tightening in his groin, the beginnings of sexual arousal. His momentary misgivings quickly gave way to his excitement. She was such a sweet young girl, but he'd be careful this time.

35

He'd be sure of her love before anything happened between them. Grasping the shark's tooth necklace tightly in his hand again, he rolled onto his stomach until he lay on the imprint Deborah had left in the blanket.

Chapter 3

AFTERNOON shaded into evening, and evening into another night when the moon was a thin sliver of light. The shoe store, the bakery, the pet shop all closed before the sun finally disappeared. And later, the family restaurants hung out their CLOSED signs and rang up the day's sales. In the residential east and west ends of the town, shades were pulled. At Emma's, Little Ned saw the last customer out the door, turned off the last light, and locked the front door after himself.

And when the night sky grew so dark that you could pick out the constellations in it, Commercial Street came to life once again. A population scarcely seen in the day's bright light began filling the street. Neon lights shone over alley doors the day crowds never opened; laughter rang from second-floor windows and the backs of shops.

At the Shipwreck Restaurant near the wharf, in a back courtyard, an edging of Japanese lanterns swayed in the faint night breeze. Under them, on a plank stage beneath a trellis hung with red roses, a singer, a milk chocolate man in a blue strapless gown, sat at a piano and sang, in purest.tenor, of lovers—lovers lost, found, mourned. As the night grew late, his tenor grew husky and his lyrics bawdy, and the laughter from the audience—the men in well-cut summer suits, the boys in tight jeans who rubbed shoulders and whispered in each others ears—spilled from the courtyard out to Commercial Street.

Ronnie followed the laughter down the curving alley, stopping in the shadows where he could see and hear. As he watched, the singer dallied over the lewd phrases and the audience swayed with the tunes, mouthing lyrics with painted, girlish lips. Ronnie moved out of the shadows into the light of the lanterns. The singer, turning to the side, fluffing his red wig, looked at Ronnie. Dropping his feather boa off one shoulder, he batted his eyes suggestively. Ronnie was held captive by the spiky jeweled lashes that traced a feathery shadow across the dusky skin. Another face turned to Ronnie. A crew-cut, mustached man crooned to him with a kiss on his lips. The man's hand beckoned.

Needles of perspiration broke out across Ronnie's forehead. The air turned leaden, too sweet, so heavy with moisture, it was hard to breathe.

Once, not too long before the bad time, some of the boys on the swim team had talked about spending a weekend there. On the chance he might be included in their plans, Ronnie had mentioned the trip to his mother. Provincetown, Ronnie? That's not the kind of place where good boys go. Not boys who love their mothers. This had been a long time ago, before the Shark ever came to Ronnie. He had questioned Mother's wisdom then—not out loud, of course—but he saw now that she had been right.

Finally reeling, Ronnie rushed back to the safe dark of the alley. Their boy-girl voices, ripe with dirty ideas and evil laughter, followed him—"Yoo hoo, sweetie. You are sooo cute"—and chased him into the milling anonymity of Commercial Street.

The street was thick with them—the weirdos, the roller-skating, smooth-shaven boys in tight red shorts, the women in studded black leather, all of them flaunting their filthy bodies and minds. He passed a small theater. Under the marquee, a shirtless boy and a girl in shorts embraced so tightly, they seemed to meld into one obscene lump of squirming flesh. The girl raised a bare leg, wrapping it around the boy.

Fear and disgust assaulted Ronnie. This was a deviate place, where women wore crew cuts and roller-skating men danced in a daisy chain. He tried not to stare as the crowds swept by him, not to let their eyes catch hold of his again and trap him. He was buffeted, though, touched and pushed until he swayed off balance.

"Damned grotesque," a harsh voice said from behind him, and for a moment Ronnie felt as if the words were for him, defined him, and he was the strange one here, the grotesque. Then something at once soft and hard was pressing against the back of his legs. He staggered forward and then spun in a weak-kneed panic, ready to scream at his attacker.

"Come on, Robin," the harsh voice said. The big Labrador lumbered away from Ronnie and followed two men in plaid shirts through a weather-beaten door in the side of a nondescript frame building.

Retracing his steps, Ronnie pressed his face into a dirty window of the Fo'c'sle Tavern. Inside, the light was dim and the air thick with smoke. Men sat around the bar and surrounded the pool table. Not men like the ones on the street. These were working men with lined faces and rough clothes. There was no singing; laughter was restrained.

If eyes lifted when Ronnie walked into the bar, it was with the vague, drink-dulled curiosity of men who have worked hard all day. Their eyes dropped as quickly as they lifted—no questions, no problems.

Ronnie bought himself a beer at the bar. Since Mother's death, the Shark sometimes had talked Ronnie into buying whole six-packs of beer. He would have only one or two tonight, he swore to himself. Otherwise, he'd have a headache in the morning. That was something else Mother had been right about.

He carried his beer to a small corner table at the back of the room, a table almost untouched by the Fo'c'sle's weak lights. An undercurrent of blurred voices, the *click click click* of billiard balls glancing off one another, the soft thumps as the balls fell into pockets, the muffled grunts of the players. "No weirdos," Ronnie said to himself. He could finally relax, think about Deborah. Or maybe he could get to that quiet place where the Shark would come to him. Ever since he'd met Deborah on the beach, the Shark hadn't come out. Resting his head back against the wall, Ronnie's lids dropped over his eyes.

The street door opened and for a moment the Fo'c'sle was filled with street noise. With the slamming door, that noise was gone and there was a new sound. Ronnie heard men's muffled greetings, then the woman's voice, hard, whiskey-wrapped, carried across the room. She shattered the mood of the Fo'c'sle, coarsening the atmosphere. Voices at the bar grew louder, the woman's always rising above the others. She intruded on Ronnie's quiet, and in his mind a face began forming to match the voice. An ugly woman. He didn't have to open his eyes to see that. Ugly, loud. His thoughts drifted back to Deborah. A clean, sweet little girl. Had she really liked him? Her words returned: "You keep it for me."

For a girl like that, you needed a nice place. Would she like his house? Mother's room was the best one, but he quickly put that thought out of his head. It wouldn't be right. No. He should take Deborah somewhere that was new to both of them. A sun-washed room, with a porch, maybe, or a balcony that looked over the water. He'd have to find a place like that before he . . . This was so confusing. What if her parents tried to break them up? He had to take her to a place where her parents couldn't find them.

"Up yours, Ned." The woman's words carried back from the bar. Ronnie tried to push her voice away. She sounded like the girls in the laundry. When they got loud, they always ended up teasing him. He hated them. Deborah would never be like that. Her words would be like the feel of silk against his skin.

Again, rough voices broke through.

"Hey, Bobbie, you shouldn't be flashing around a wad like that."

"Plenty more where that came from."

"Like hell. The only thing you got hidden under that shirt's no secret around here. And it ain't money."

"Aw, go stick it, Ned."

Ronnie opened his eyes in disgust. He was right about her. Big, tall, bushy-haired . . . bitch! That was what the Shark would call her. Bitch! Perched on a bar stool and dressed up like a damned Indian! The Shark would have some things to say about her. *What a pig! Oink oink.* A mocking grin twisted at Ronnie's lips. He looked right at the woman. *"Oink,"* he whispered.

The woman's eyes were on him. She smiled boldly back. Without lowering her gaze, she pushed a wad of bills into a leather pouch hanging on a cord around her neck. Sliding from the stool, she walked to the table in the shadows.

"I saw you throwing me that kiss. Guess you won't mind me joining you." She pulled out the chair across from Ronnie and sank onto it.

What was she doing? He'd been getting into that quiet place where the Shark lived. If she sat down, she'd ruin it.

"Free country," Ronnie said. Cool, like the Shark would have said it.

Grinning broadly, the woman patted the place where the leather pouch was hidden by her blouse. "Better one if you've got a little bread in your pocket. My name's Bobbie. Haven't seen you in here before. Where you from?"

The Shark stared frankly at the spot where the leather cord disappeared beneath her fringed vest. "Around."

"Around where?"

"I've just come up from the Caribbean."

Something strange was happening. Ronnie was flustered by it. The Shark had always existed in a place no one knew about. No one had ever heard the Shark speak. Yet the Shark had just spoken to this terrible woman. This woman was making the

Shark come out of the quiet place. What could that mean? Ronnie wasn't sure, but he knew one thing: Whatever happened was her fault. She was asking for it. Pig!

"Oh yeah? It's easy to score dope down in the Caribbean. Bring anything back with you?"

He gave her a nasty look. "I was on a diving job. Serious divers don't use drugs."

"Tell me another one." Still smiling, she nodded at his beer. "Doesn't look like diet soda to me. So you're a diver. Join me in something stronger?" She pulled the leather string and the pouch reappeared. An intricate design of tooling and beads covered its surface.

The Shark nodded at it. "That's nice."

"Thanks. It's a medicine bag. I make them. This one's special. I keep my magic in it." She tugged on the leather cord and withdrew a couple crumpled bills. "First of the month, I like my scotch. How about you? Scotch and water sound like a diver's drink to you?" Her eyebrows went up, questioning him. When he didn't answer, she walked to the bar, clutching one of the bills from her medicine bag.

The Shark's fingers edged across the table and straightened the other bill. A hundred dollars, just lying there. Dumb broad! The Shark stole things. Little things—candy bars and gum from the drugstore where Ronnie got Mother's prescriptions filled. Glancing up, he saw the bartender looking his way. He pulled his hand back from the bill.

Bobbie studied herself in the mirror over the bar. Through the smoky air, her coarse-pored skin seemed finer; her wiry black hair with its few strands of gray looked as if it was made of softer stuff. She leaned in closer and rubbed at the dark circles under her eyes.

"Bobbie, your drinks." The bartender bent toward her and lowered his voice. "If I were you, I wouldn't leave my money laying around. Lots of strangers in town."

"It's all right. He's a friend of mine. A deep-sea diver." Using her thick, strong fingers as a comb, she quickly gathered the uncontrolled mass of hair and twisted it into a loop in front of her shoulder. When she backed away from the mirror and half-closed her eyes, beautiful Bobbie Yellowfeather looked back at her.

"What's with the Indian getup, anyway?" the Shark asked when she set the glasses on the table.

"It's no getup. It's my roots. My great-grandfather was a full-blooded Cheyenne chief. He kidnapped my grandmother from a wagon train. She was the daughter of a Confederate general."

The Shark's lips twisted.

"It's the truth," she said, petulant.

"Yeah. Right. And my grandfather was a great white shark. My roots are in the ocean."

"Up yours."

"I'm serious. You should see me swim."

"Yeah? Breaststroke, right? That's an old one."

The Shark smiled and lifted his glass.

"Okay, so you swim," Bobbie said. "Big deal. Anybody can swim. One time, I made myself this bikini, out of deerskin. You should of seen—"

"They can't swim like I can. I was on the U.S.A. Olympic team in 1978."

"You putting me on?" She leaned back in her chair and looked at him, at his brown hair falling over his ears and his gray-green eyes. "You know, I can see it now. You look like a Californian. You make a living at swimming?"

"Diving, like I said. For sunken ships. I look for treasure. They call me the Shark, because I'm fast and mean. Nothing gets in my way."

Bobbie pulled her chair closer to the table. "Isn't this something. An Indian princess and a shark." Tilting her head coquettishly, she added, "You know, we'd make a good couple."

"How's that?"

"I know a lot, like where you could dive around here. You

want to find treasure, you don't have to go down to the islands. There must be two dozen shipwrecks just off P'town." She moved nearer, a conspirator. "I could show you places no more than a half mile offshore. You have your diving gear with you? I'll take you on my boat."

"You don't have a boat."

"Sure I do," she replied, indignant. "A nineteen-foot Rhodes. It's tied up at the marina."

"So what kind of treasure could you take me to?"

"You been out to Dromedary Point, on the Atlantic side of North Truro?"

"Dromedary Point?" He shook his head. "No, but there's nothing out on any of these points but old lighthouses."

"Right, sucker." Bobbie tapped the table with her finger, then looked at the empty table behind them. "There's more than a lighthouse on Dromedary Point," she said softly. "Couple hundred years ago, there used to be a tavern out there. A rough place. Dutch pirates tried to put in there during a storm, but their ship broke up on the rocks. Most of the men were lost. The captain and a couple others dragged chests full of gold up to the shore. Men at the tavern saw where the pirates buried their gold."

Dumb, dumb pig, thinking she can get over on a guy like me with this story. "So why didn't the men at the tavern dig up the gold?" he asked.

"Slaughtered by Indians. All but one of them, and he was afraid to go back there."

The Shark took a long swallow of his drink, then set his glass down. "These the same Indians who kidnapped your great-grandmother? Lady, I never heard such a crock of shit." He pushed his hands against the edge of the table.

He was going to leave. In a minute, he'd slide back his chair and stand up and leave. A hot flash of dread swept over Bobbie. She could take anything. Men could hit her, kick her, curse her, rob her. They had. All of that, and more, and she'd taken it. She could take anything but being left alone. She put her hand over his. "You want to talk sharks? I'll tell you about sharks. Out on Dromedary Point, there's a fossil of a twenty-five-footer, hidden in the rocks. Indians used to worship it. During full moons, they had ceremonies for their dead out there. Sacrifices. In Indian lore, it's a sacred place. You can make out where the teeth were. Eight, ten inches long. Make that thing you're wearing around your neck look like it came from a guppy."

The Shark disappeared so abruptly, it was as if he hadn't been there at all. Ronnie pulled his hand away from the woman's and rested it over the necklace. "This belongs to someone special." *Deborah*. She'd slipped out of his mind. This woman had made that happen. He had to be very careful with this woman. There was something tricky about her. If she knew half the things she said she knew . . .

"What's wrong? How come you've got your eyes shut?"

He hadn't realized that he did. Opening them, he took a swallow of his drink, and another, giving himself time to think. "Twenty-five feet, you're telling me that fossil is? So how come somebody from some museum hasn't hauled it out of there?"

"Because the only people who know where to look have too much respect for those sacrificed Indians to tell the museums," she said.

Ronnie stared at her over the glass. He wasn't used to hard liquor. A tingling sensation was building at the back of his neck. His arms felt weak.

"You've really seen this shark?"

"Not actually, but I know exactly where it is," she said. "I know where the tavern was, too, and the Dutch ship. And that's not all that's out there. You ever hear of the dune shacks?"

He shook his head.

"They belong to the National Seashore. Only special people—artists and writers—are supposed to stay in them. There's a dune shack out on Dromedary Point. Furnished and everything. The most romantic place you ever saw. Right at the shore of the Atlantic. Looks like it's at the edge of the universe." She rested her hand over his again. "You interested?"

45

What she had said gripped his imagination: ". . . most romantic place you ever saw . . . the shore of the Atlantic . . . the edge of the universe."

When he ignored her hints, Bobbie became incensed. "So forget I mentioned it. And forget the shark, too." She stared morosely down at her glass.

"How long would it take to get out there in your boat?" he asked after a moment.

"Depends on the wind." Her flirtatious smile returned. "Knew you were interested. You like the idea of us sleeping over in that dune shack, don't you? We'd be better off going out in the morning, though. Where are you staying?"

Ronnie shrugged. "Nowhere special." He'd slept on the beach that afternoon, and when he'd awakened his thoughts had been so filled with Deborah that he'd forgotten his promise to his mother. He hadn't even thought about getting a room.

Bobbie ran the tip of her tongue across her upper lip. "You could crash at my place. I have lots of room. Even have a water bed."

A mass of conflicting emotions, complicated by alcoholic haze, carried Ronnie over the threshold, past the repulsion he felt for this woman. For a time, his barriers dropped. The Shark returned, so strong and real that, for the first time ever in the company of another human, Ronnie ceased to exist. He was only a conduit for the Shark, sharing the Shark's adventures with another person. For years, the Shark had been a secret part of Ronnie, but with this woman the Shark was alive.

Ronnie never considered that, for the woman, there were no conflicting emotions. This was foreplay for her, a kindling and heating of desires. She remarked more than once about the green flecks in his eyes—the color of the Caribbean, she said—but he paid no attention. Her fingers drifted across his hand and played with the lines on his palm. He was oblivious to her touch. She made other trips to the bar and put more drinks on the table. At some point, a full bottle appeared. The woman drank heavily. Ronnie drank more than he ever had. Fantasy mingled on top of fantasy. Bobbie's stories of wagon trains and scalpings, war paint and bloody initiation ceremonies grew fuzzy. The Shark's, of swim meets and record times, of deep-sea diving and underwater battles, became clearer as the night passed. Each detail added to his being, sharpening it.

Each time Bobbie returned from the bar, her chair inched closer to his. The casual bargoers saw the two huddled, heads together. And the moment came when she was right next to him, her body pressing against his, as close as she could get.

He'd been talking about Barbados, and a mako shark. He paused, midsentence, when her fingertips flicked across his earlobe. For the second time that day, he began feeling sexually aroused.

Bobbie smiled, a lopsided, drunken smile: "Did anybody ever tell you you have bedroom eyes?"

Bad, bad. This was a bad girl, putting dirty thoughts in his head. Ronnie was jolted into an intense, frightening awareness of his excitement, and of her—her vaguely animal-like smell, that terrible hair, the blunt fingernails on the hand that cupped her glass. If Mother ever saw him with this bad woman, she would know the kind of thing he was thinking.

He felt her other hand crawling up the inside of his leg. She was looking right into his eyes. His skin prickled with excitement and fear. Forcing his knees together, he twisted his body to the side.

"Stop that. I have to go now." He pushed his chair away from the table.

"What? I thought you were crashing at my place. Where you going?" Bobbie's voice rose sharply.

"I'm tired."

"So?" Bobbie stumbled from her chair. "I told you I've got lots of room." She quickly grabbed the beaded bag from the table and looped it over her head. "I've got a whole house to myself. And"—she gripped his arm and put her mouth to his ear—"I've got a stash of Colombian. And in the morning, we can take the boat. . . ."

47

"I told you I don't use drugs."

Catcalls followed the couple as they left the Fo'c'sle. When the door slammed behind them, Little Ned Mayo nudged his companion at the bar.

"You see that, Ephraim? Bobbie's in love again. Told me she picked up a deep-sea diver."

Ephraim Tucker studied the foam across the top of his beer. "Didn't notice," he said after a moment. "I never mind anybody's business but my own. That's a rule of mine. And I never loan money. That's another rule of mine. You owe me for two beers."

"Pious son of a bitch," Ned said, digging into his pocket.

Chapter 4

BOBBIE trailed him to the municipal parking lot, pleading all the way. When they reached his car, he slid behind the wheel and slammed his door.

He was leaving her. She could have screamed with frustration. They always left. Banging at his locked door, she shouted, "We can get my boat out tonight, if you really want. You listening?"

The car started rolling forward. Bobbie trotted alongside, frantic. "I know the exact spot where that shark fossil is because I've seen it."

Finally, Ronnie slowed and unlocked the passenger door. Bobbie hurried around the car.

"Stay on your own side," he warned as she climbed in.

"No problem. Cut back to Bradford and then left at the A&P. My house is the last one on Standish Street."

When he looked at her, she ran her tongue over her lips again. She was trying to trick him. Maybe there wasn't any shark fossil, or any dune shack, either.

"I thought we were going to your boat," Ronnie said, heading west on Commercial Street.

"Why can't we just go in the morning?" She slumped down, resting her head against the back of the seat. An almost empty bottle of scotch was propped between her legs.

"Turn here," she said. "Here! Now you missed it. Where are we going?"

"To the marina to get your boat."

"Oh, man." She banged her forehead with the heel of her hand. "I forgot. They lock the boat yard up at night. We'll go to my place, get some sleep. . . ."

Infuriated, Ronnie pulled to the side of the road. "In that case, you can get out now."

"No way, José," she said lightly. She slid across the seat and put her hand on his thigh. "Come on, honey, why are you being like this? I thought you liked me. If you're nice to me, I'll tell you another way we could get to the point. Across the sandbar."

Ronnie was having the dirty thoughts again. His feelings about this woman seesawed. He wanted her to go away. At the same time, he knew she had power. Her magic had forced the Shark to come out. No one had ever done that. She knew special things, too. She knew a special place where he and Deborah could go and no one would ever find them—a place on the edge of the universe. In the bar, the Shark had laughed at this woman's magic, but out here in the dark at the side of the road Ronnie knew her magic was real, as real as the Shark's. He had to protect himself from her, but he needed to learn the things she knew.

Ronnie pried her fingers from his leg. "You've got to stay on your side if you want to ride with me."

"You've got it, lover." Bobbie slid across the seat.

"I'm not driving my mother's car through wet sand in the middle of the night," Ronnie warned.

"Your mother's car?" She hooted. "Well, I sure wouldn't want to get Mom upset. We'll drive as far as we can. There's a sandbank. Even at high tide, it's barely to your knees. Tide's out now. We can drive most of the way, then walk across the narrows. The Park Service guys do it all the time. They keep the road up."

Ronnie took a deep breath to calm himself. That was the thing. Stay calm. Cool.

"I'm cool."

He had said it out loud.

Bobbie started giggling. "You're funny, too. Hey, gimmie the bottle."

"You've already got it." Pulling back onto the road, Ronnie turned south.

The wind was high when they reached Dromedary Point. On the western end of the Point, where at low tide its sloping beach connects to the land mass of Cape Cod, surf ripped the shore. Ronnie turned off the Chevy's engine at the place where the Park Service's packed gravel road disappears into the sand.

"Creepy out here, huh?" Bobbie said. "I didn't tell you, but a long time ago sailors called it Nightmare Point rather than Dromedary Point, because it was so hard navigating these waters. Probably doesn't seem so rough to you, though, after all the places you've been diving."

He stared at the sky, not responding. A million stars glittered down at him.

"See a falling star, you get your wish. Bet I know . . . what you're wishing for."

He looked across the seat. She had raised the bottle to her mouth again. In the faint light, he saw a thin trail of liquor trickling from the corner of her mouth.

"What do you mean?" he asked. "How could you know what I'm wishing?"

Bobbie lowered the bottle and wiped her mouth with the back of her hand. "I can read men's thoughts."

She was telling the truth. Ronnie was sure of that, and this certainty made him shiver. Her horrible blunt fingers were probing the recesses of his mind, feeling their way into his most secret thoughts. He couldn't let himself think about Deborah, not while this powerful woman was here. The Shark might have been able to handle her, but the Shark was gone.

"How do we get to that fossil?" he asked.

"Huh?"

"The shark fossil you were telling me about."

"Can't remember. Have to think." Bobbie tossed the empty bottle from the car window. It shattered on the gravel beside the Chevy.

"I hope you haven't been putting me on," Ronnie said, trying to sound tough, like the Shark. "I don't like girls trying to put me on."

"No, no. Maybe somewhere over by the big rocks on the other side of the sandbar." Bobbie glanced out the window. "Looks like I was wrong, though, doesn't it? About the tide. It's coming in. We'll get wet if we . . ."

"I'm going to take a look."

She was on Ronnie before he opened his door. Her sour breath assaulted him as she whispered a bedlam of erotic suggestions and endearments in his ear. One hand clutched at his belt; the other was around his neck, pulling him closer.

"You remind me of this guy I used to live with. Over a year we were together. The best man I ever had in my bed, only I didn't know it then. I hoped someday I'd find someone like him again."

She was strong for a woman. He fought her hands away, but they came back. Her fingers pulled at his shirt.

"Stop that." His voice was shrill with panic. He stretched his arm into the place beneath the seat where he kept the knife.

Bobbie stared at him, her eyes brightening with tears. "What's wrong? You worried your mom's going to find out you made out on her plastic upholstery? You a momma's boy?" Turning her head toward the window, she started to cry. "Maybe you're gay or something," she sputtered. "You walk into the wrong bar by mistake? If you're not into women, why didn't you just say so?"

Thoughts were banging around in Ronnie's head. There had

been too much for him that day, with Deborah, and then the queers and perverts on Commercial Street, and now this Indian woman saying such filthy things. A bad woman. The kind of woman bad boys went with. *Bad bad bad, Ronnie. You're a bad boy. I saw you looking at those girls. I know the kind of thing you're thinking.*

And on the tail of that memory came another one, a far worse one. Mother is wearing a dress as gray as a rain-laden sky. She walks from the hospital, with her eyes straight ahead. One of her hands is bandaged. Ronnie knows what's under the gauze. She made him watch while the doctor changed it. The flesh is raw, shining with ointment. Two of her fingers are drawn tight like a bird's talons. "I burned for your sin, Ronnie," she says when they're in the car. "I burned for what you did to that little girl.

A whimper of anguish and dread escaped Ronnie. Bile rose in his throat. He had to get away from these thoughts, away from this woman who was making these bad things come back. Quickly, while Bobbie's back was turned, he pulled the knife from the floor. When it was tucked under his shirt, he opened the car door.

"Where you going?"

Her face was wet with tears, but she had stopped sobbing. "I'll be back in a few minutes," he said.

"Call of nature?" She sniffled. "Wait for me. I'm not shy. Let's go up on the dunes to where those bushes are."

Her door slammed. Ronnie started moving faster through the sand, trying to put distance between them.

"Oh shit," she yelled. "Now my fuckin' foot's bleeding."

At the water's edge, he stopped and looked at the lighthouse on Race Point to the north, sending its beam over the dark ocean. If he looked the other way, beyond the sandbar, Ronnie could see the black outlines of huge boulders rising from the surf. He took a breath of cool night air. He'd be all right. He just had to keep from thinking about Deborah while he was with this woman.

"Is the fossil over where those rocks are?" he asked as he slipped off his shoes and rolled up his pants legs.

"No. It's past them, way out on the Point. Fastest way is across the dunes, but I'm getting wet. You don't really wanna . . . Oooo. . . ." She was right behind him, slogging through the rising water.

"What's wrong with you?"

"I cut my foot on that damned bottle."

"Where's that dune house you were talking about?"

"Shack. Dune shack. That's what they're called. Farther up the dunes in the scrub pine. Is that where you want to spend the night? You have any blankets in the car, 'cause if we're going to crash there . . ."

When Ronnie reached land, he turned away from the shore and started up the dune. She stayed behind him, but the sound of her cursing and panting as she made her way up the mountain of sand was dulled by the crash of waves. Hurrying over the first dune, he climbed onto another. The top was wide and flat, covered with scrub pine. He searched the dark landscape for any sign of the dune shack.

"Honey," Bobby said, struggling to catch him, "this sucks. Why don't we just go to my place?"

"What's over there?" Ronnie said, pointing to lights in the distance.

"Ephraim Tucker's place. He has hookups for trailers. He was sitting at the bar tonight. One of the old guys. Guess you didn't notice. You had your mind on other things." Staggering, she clutched his chest. Ronnie pried her fingers loose and backed away.

She grinned and held her hand toward him.

"Look what I've got now. You said it belonged to someone special. Now it does. It belongs to me."

The shark's tooth necklace hung from her fingers. For a moment, Ronnie was numbed by the sight. By the time he lunged for it, she had dropped to her knees. He watched in horror as she crawled into the deep cover of the scrub pines.

He had to get it back. Had to! This filthy woman couldn't keep Deborah's necklace. "You give that back," he said weakly. Stooping, he strained to see through the dense growth. She was on her hands and knees. He saw her feet and, beyond them, her head lowered into her hands. As he crouched at the edge of the pines, she started gagging. In seconds, the smell of vomit reached him. She had Deborah's necklace in her hands, and she was vomiting all over it.

There was a second when he couldn't even think of what to do, then the Shark was there and fury blotted out every other emotion.

"You dirty pig. You whore." He aimed a vicious kick into the bushes. He connected with Bobbie's leg, and a searing pain shot through his bare foot. "Either you give that back or I'll take it back the hard way."

"Bastard. You want it, you come down here and get it."

She grabbed his ankle. He kicked at her with his free leg. Missing, he fell and crashed into the thicket with her. Burrs scratched his flesh and tore at his clothes. The woman crawled up over his body. "I'm sorry, honey. I still love you," she was moaning. "Once I get my bearings, I'll remember where the shack is. We'll spend the night there. We don't need blankets. We can keep each other warm. Body heat." This time, both her hands gripped his belt. As she fumbled with the buckle, she buried her head in his neck.

Her putrid smell made him gag. Forcing her off, he pushed himself to his knees and drew the knife from his shirt.

"Give me the necklace if you don't want to get hurt. Understand?"

Bobbie stared, openmouthed. After a moment, she thrust the shark's tooth at him. He put it in his pocket. He was crawling toward the opening in the thicket when her powerful vomit-covered hands closed around his throat. He twisted and tore at her fingers, struggling to free himself. Her legs gripped him as a python grips its prey. Her nails ripped his chest. "Bastard," she was saying. "Bastard, bringing me out here and then trying to leave me." He freed his neck of her hands. Her teeth sank into the soft flesh under his thumb. The pain was so great, he let the knife fall from his other hand. Like wild animals, they grappled under the scrub pines. She pulled him down on the sand next to her, rolled him into the vomit, cursing him, cursing old lovers in her confusion. Her power astonished him. He felt for his knife in the sand. Finally grasping it, he sank it into her abdomen. Once, twice, and again, using all his might. Her moans and curses turned into a bubbling groan.

His strength was gone. His arms shook and his heart crashed into his ribs. Why wouldn't she get off? Warmth flooded through his shirt. It was a moment before he realized it was her blood. It pooled on his chest and trickled down his ribs. He gave a massive push and Bobbie toppled over. A sound came from her—a shuddering breath being expelled. Then she was quiet.

He lay gasping on the sand beside the body. Every part of his body ached. Finally, when some time had passed, he rose on his heels and stared down at the lifeless body.

Hell! She had asked for it, hadn't she? You don't push a guy. Not a guy like the Shark.

"What a pig." He gave Bobbie's still body an angry shove with his foot. His hand scraped the front of his shirt and came away wet with blood. "Filth."

Bobbie's medicine bag had fallen to the side of her neck. He wiped his hand on his pants, then grasped the pouch and tugged the cord over Bobbie's head. When her closeness and her putrid odors became too strong to bear, he dug a shallow trench next to where she had fallen and buried Bobbie in the cover of the pines.

The Shark followed the shore back to the narrows. The tide was high now, completely obscuring the sandbar that lay between Dromedary Point and the Chevy. He couldn't see the path, couldn't even see where the path began. The Chevy, even the land where he'd parked it, seemed to have been swallowed up by the dark water.

Dropping to the ground, he stripped off his clothes, bundled them, and tied them around his shoulders. Then he plunged into the sea.

It had been a long time since he'd swum anywhere but in his imagination. Though Dromedary Point sheltered the cove, the surf was strong and the bundle of clothes dragged at him. It took him a while to get his rhythm right. Finally, it came back, and he had nothing to fear from the waves. The Shark was the best. His arms stretched and pulled like a powerful machine, harder and harder still. He pressed forward, his legs pumping and crashing through the whitecaps. The roaring of his blood began pounding in his head. Then he could hear the screams of the crowd cheering him—Shark, Shark, Shark—and with each inch he gained the chant rose louder. He swam fast and smooth. Only when his lungs ached did he stop and tread water.

He'd swum out the wrong way. Now he could see the landmass rising from the water. The Chevy was a distant shadow nestled into a cliffside. When he had gotten his breath, he swam slowly to the far shore. By the time he climbed from the water, the Shark had gone and Ronnie was so weak that his arms quaked.

He rinsed his clothes in the surf and wiped his knife on the ocean's sandy bottom. The night air bit into his skin, and the tensions of the night evaporated as if by magic. Ronnie felt cleansed of the scum that had soiled him. He pulled a change of clothes from the suitcase in the back of his car. As he dressed, he looked toward the far end of the Cape. He couldn't see Provincetown, but he could see where its lights brightened the sky. Somewhere over there, his girl, Deborah, lay asleep. Maybe she was dreaming of him.

Chapter 5

ON her second night at the Cape, Joyce Neuhauser experienced the dream's terrors again. She saw the same impassive face, and felt the pressure of the smothering blue water. She woke fighting for breath. That passed in an instant, and in the next instant she was staring at her sleeping husband, praying that Frank wouldn't wake. He didn't. If I have the nightmare again, she promised herself, I'll call Dr. Weisman.

For the next three nights, she slept soundly and woke refreshed, and the terrible dream faded from Joyce's thoughts. Other things occupied her. Memories, for one. Sometimes, they would gather in force—faces, names, a high school dance, the birth of a child—but out of sequence. Other times, the sequence would be whole, but it was so dim, so fleeting that even as Joyce grasped it, it had already slipped away.

In all, though, the vacation was turning out to be a good one. After the first night, Frank adjusted to the unfamiliar condominium and the teeming beach town, and relaxed. Joyce's confidence grew—by inches, not miles, but that clearly had an effect on the children. Maryann seemed less eager for attention, and Frankie less likely to burst into tears at the least provocation.

And Andy, the baby? He was a darling, sleeping through the night, hardly crying, spending his waking time examining his toes and cooing happily. It was almost as if a charmed atmosphere inhabited the condominium.

It was only with her older daughter that Joyce experience the old anxiety. For the first several days, she weighed whatever she said to the girl, hoping to find the right tone. It never worked. No matter what she said or did, Debbie responded with either a grimace or a sigh of irritation. The last few months had been hard on the girl, Joyce knew. At thirteen, she had been forced into the role of housekeeper and baby-sitter. She had also become—and Joyce had almost laughed at Frank's old-fashioned expression—a woman. Not that she had volunteered the information to her father. He had found the evidence clogging the upstairs toilet.

One afternoon, after days of picking her way cautiously around her daughter, she found Debbie and Andy on the bed in the smaller upstairs bedroom. The baby slept peacefully. Debbie was wearing her headset and tapping her toes. Grains of sand clung to the girl's feet, occasionally sifting onto the bedspread.

Until that moment, Joyce and her older daughter had spent their vacation always separated by someone or something: a crying child or a meal to cook or a diaper to change or an errand to run. Joyce knew herself well enough to know that she'd welcomed those separations, those things that kept her from having to deal with this pretty, sullen girl. She herself had grown up in a home where silence was the norm, where many things were left unsaid and most gestures unmade.

Joyce's parents were such a perfect match that she often wondered how two people so alike had managed to find each other. The couple had been comfortable in their childlessness, contentedly, quietly moving into early middle age, when the appearance of their rather large baby girl shattered the quiet in their rigidly ordered home. Unable to cope with this noisy, messy intruder, her parents had withdrawn from Joyce in all but the most essential ways.

Joyce had learned to play noiselessly by herself, not to slam doors, not to leave her toys in the living room, not to have friends over or have friends who phoned too late or too often. She learned to keep anything vaguely disturbing to herself. She had lived her first eighteen years like a trespasser, quietly hiding on the fenced property of her parents. Joyce felt sure that the couple had breathed a joint sigh of relief when she married at eighteen.

Joyce didn't want that for her children. She wanted them to be comfortable talking to her, asking her questions—Even advice, though Joyce couldn't imagine what kind of advice she might give Debbie in the unlikely event that her daughter decided to share confidences with her.

Debbie had never been easy. The cranky baby had turned into a stubborn toddler. After that had come the little girl who cried every morning when the school bus came, or threw up, or developed rashes. At ten, after a fight with her daughter over something Joyce had immediately forgotten, Debbie had spent the night in a friend's garage without bothering to tell her parents. At twelve, it had been even worse. The girl had disappeared for two days before she turned up at Frank's parents' house in Connecticut, tearful, swearing she would never do it again.

Joyce stared down at her daughter. Debbie had glanced up when her mother walked into the room, but she said nothing. The silence was heavy and looming. Maybe now was a good time for some gesture of . . . what? Friendship, and parenting. After all, Joyce reassured herself, I *am* the parent.

"Would you like to go for a walk, Deb? I feel like getting some exercise." Ridiculous, but she almost felt as if her voice might shake as she spoke.

"A walk?" Yawning, the girl sat up and yanked off the headset. She nodded at the sleeping baby. "Where to? Are we going to take Andy?"

"We can take him in the stroller, or we can leave him with Daddy. Maybe that would be best."

"Eh," Debbie said. "I'd rather just hang out here."

"I understand that you had your first period a few weeks ago."

"Oh, no." Debbie groaned. "Do we have to talk about that?"

Joyce saw a faint flush developing beneath Debbie's tan. The girl refused to look at her.

"No, we don't, but if you want to . . ."

"Well, I don't."

Joyce sank onto the bed next to her daughter. "I hope this vacation is fun for you, Debbie."

Staring up at her mother, Debbie repeated the word, "Fun?" as if it was new to her vocabulary. "Yeah. I guess it's all right," she decided.

Joyce held her arm next to Debbie's. "Your tan looks wonderful. You're lucky. I always peel."

The girl eyed her arm critically. "It's okay. Nobody will even notice it, though. Not with my school uniform." Looking down, she ran her fingertips over the bumpy chenille ridges of the bedspread.

"Well, there are still some warm weekends left. If you'd like, we could walk up Commercial Street now, do some window-shopping. Maybe you'll see something. . . ."

Debbie narrowed her eyes suspiciously. "You mean I could get some new clothes?"

"I think we could manage that, if you see something you like," Joyce said.

Debbie got up from the bed. "That would be really great," she said, not exactly animated but not scowling, either. "There's this one store where I saw a denim jacket and skirt with these patches. . . ."

Mother and daughter left the condominium a few minutes later. Walking on Commercial Street, with the late-afternoon sun warming them, Debbie chatted about the outfit she wanted. She smiled at her mother as she described the colorful print of the patches that covered the denim. The girl's languor and boredom disappeared, at least temporarily. As for Joyce, she knew she was guilty of bribery in the name of mothering, but what the heck! It worked better than anything else she'd tried lately.

Gus Debrito, Provincetown's police chief, learned about the body in the dunes late that same afternoon, while he was making dinner for himself.

The Debrito's kitchen was at the back of the house. A wall of windows overlooked their terrace and the bay. Gus always found the kitchen the most pleasant room in the old house. Since his wife, a nurse, had started working nights at the hospital, he'd come to think of the kitchen as his domain. And what a domain! If he stretched a little and pretended the new wharf wasn't there, Gus could see the curving shoreline almost all the way down to Truro. Looking the other way, he could see people walking across the rock jetty that stretched out to the lighthouse at Wood End. All in all, about as good a place for dinner as an average man was likely to find in this world.

Dinner, on the other hand, was reaching new depths—or was it heights? he wondered. New heights of absurdity, new depths of taste, maybe. Putting the bottle of beer he'd been drinking onto the kitchen table, he read the frozen package with exaggerated care, then ceremoniously dropped its contents—two plastic bags—into boiling water.

When that was done, he settled down at the table and began studying the shoreline beyond his backyard. That was something he did a lot these days; it guaranteed almost instant depression. It—the shore—was moving. Gus had spent forty-seven years on the Cape, all of them in the same house, all of them watching the bay fill in, just a half inch or so a year. It hadn't mattered during his self-absorbed youth. Later, there had been a young family to support, and who could pay attention to inches of sand with the price of milk soaring? But lately—forty-odd inches were a lot of inches. Low tide was noticeably lower this year; high tide farther out. Every couple of years, the city brought out the big yellow dredges and had a go at it, but still the sand pushed west, wind and tide driving the whole peninsula farther into the bay. Someday, someone's going to be able to step off my property and walk all the way to Boston without getting wet above the knees, he thought.

This disheartening line of thought was interrupted by the slam of a door and the muffled pounding of rubber-soled shoes in the hall.

"Dad, you home?"

Gus unconsciously braced his shoulders for the moment when the kitchen door would swing open violently and slam into the bruised wall behind it. "In here, Mike."

The crash came. Gus groaned and looked at his son.

Mike was lounged against the door frame, bouncing the door with the toe of a threadbare sneaker.

"What are you making for dinner?" Mike lifted the lid on the pot. "Oh. That. Two little plastic bags bopping around in a pot of water."

"There're more pouches in the freezer if you want to join me," Gus said. Taking the box that the boiling pouches had come from, he read, seriously, "Cooked spinach macaroni product, low-fat milk, moisture-reduced part-skim cheese, vital wheat gluten, reduced iron, partly hydrogenated soybean oil. . . ."

His son shook his head. "Groovy, but I think I'll grab a pizza. Times in this kitchen are hard. I'll be glad when Mom's back on days."

Gus had just turned off the burners when his phone rang. Mike grabbed it before Gus could. When he'd listened for a second, he handed the receiver to his father.

Gus's expression grew grave when he heard what his caller had to say. He responded in the Portuguese so many of Provincetown's natives spoke.

"So much for dinner," he said to Mike when he hung up. "I have to go. A body's been found out at Dromedary Point."

"Isn't that closer to Truro?"

"Yes," Gus said, "but unfortunately the body belongs to Provincetown."

"Whew. Old Bobbie hasn't been spraying perfume in here, has she?"

Gus winced. Deputy Perry had a way with words—always the wrong one at the wrong time. Gus turned his head up, trying to breathe something other than the sweet-sour fumes from the corpse. An army of sand flies and mosquitoes, their feast disturbed, attacked the soft exposed skin on his neck.

There was no telling how long she had been in the sand. There was the heat and the moisture, not to mention the bugs. The only thing the doctor was reasonably sure about was the jagged wounds in her side and chest and the deep, gaping one in her abdomen—Bobbie Yellowfeather had died violently.

The body was faceup in the sand. It was hard to believe this had ever been a living woman. To Gus, Bobbie's flesh resembled the remains of a rotting soft-fleshed fruit, a plum tossed into the air and lobbed with a tennis racquet.

There was a groan from Deputy Perry. He'd slapped a mosquito on his arm. He was staring, wide-eyed, at the streak of blood. Suddenly, Perry bolted toward the bushes.

"Looks like I'm not the only one," Gus said to the doctor.

"I've about had it myself. This is enough to make the coroner lose it. I'm going to get the guys with the stretcher." The doctor followed Perry out of the pines.

Gus looked once again at the body. His first impression stayed with him—she had been so angry. Her lips, purple and caked with sand, were drawn back over blackened gums. Eyes like dull brown stones glared angrily from their sockets. Bobbie's arm, bent at the elbow, had caught on a low branch and her hand, that bloated claw with its braided leather bracelet and silver rings cutting through the flesh, might have been raised in a threat. Over the stomach, her blouse was stained with an almost-perfect dark brown circle.

The ambulance was parked back on the road. It wouldn't take

the attendants long to get there with the stretcher. Drawing a breath through his mouth, Gus left the bushes at a crouching half run.

Deputy Perry was standing by the bike path with a group of hikers and sunbathers. He looked a lot better than he had a few minutes earlier. In fact, he appeared in his glory, with bystanders hanging on his every word. Gus called him over.

"Where are the people who found her?"

"They're standing by my car. A young couple."

"Did they mention why they were crawling around in the bushes?"

"Honeymooners. Had a blanket and a bottle of wine and all. Bet they cooled off fast when they found Bobbie."

Gus and Perry watched the ambulance attendants carry the stretcher off the dune. The late-day sun cast long shadows over the sand, and the body on the stretcher seemed to approach forever. A black body bag had been draped around Bobbie's corpse. As the procession crossed the bike path, a strand of matted black hair escaped the plastic and was lifted by the stiff ocean breeze. The crowd stepped back as if on signal.

A line of cars had collected along the gravel road. There were three black-and-whites now, and cars belonging to reporters from the two local papers. There was a vanful of fishermen and two of the green pickups that the Interior Department fellows drove.

"Should have sold tickets," Gus said to no one in particular.

He spoke briefly to the couple who had found the body. Whatever shock had affected them initially was gone, replaced by excitement. They wanted to talk, in graphic detail—more detail than Gus wanted to hear right then. When he finally got into his own car and glanced back through the mirror, he saw that they were leaning against one of the black-and-whites talking to a reporter. The young woman was nodding eagerly as her husband traced a circle on his abdomen with his fingers, again and again.

★ ★ ★

It was 8:00 P.M. that same evening. The red ball of sun had just fallen over the horizon, and in the gray light Standish Street was a poor, dingy place. It was actually more an alley than a street, one of the places tourists seldom wander into. No shops, no restaurants. No beach; no view. The street was partially unpaved. Gus parked where the asphalt ended and followed the sandy ruts leading between straggling hedges to the house at the end.

The house Bobbie had lived in leaned away from the sea on its foundation. To Gus's eye, familiar with what salt air can do, it hadn't been painted in decades.

The forensics crew from Orleans would be meeting him there soon. Gus fit Bobbie's key into the lock. It turned easily; a careless lock, even in a town where break-ins were infrequent. "Anybody here?" he called as he stepped into the small foyer. A damp quiet answered. Turning left, he walked into the parlor and switched on the lights.

A recent rain had washed through one of the open windows at the house's side, and an old turquoise shag rug moldered under his feet. A damp, smoky odor remained in spite of the open windows. It might have been built into the foundation. The furniture was the kind of thing Gus saw on the streets on trash day at summer's end—bright, cheap furniture built to be discarded. It had not, could not have, acquired a patina of age.

Gus walked into the kitchen. Week-old dishes were jumbled in and around the sink. A greasy, fetid bag of garbage rested against a cabinet door. He opened the closet drawers absently, knowing that what he wanted, if it existed at all as anything but a part of his memory, would not be in the kitchen. Back in the parlor, he paused at the foot of the stairs. Up there, that's where it would be. The steps creaked under his feet as he climbed.

He had been in a dozen houses like this one. He headed right for the bedroom. Bobbie had turned it into a Mideast fantasy of sooty gold brocades and faded red velvet pillows, of etched brass trays and fat green Buddhas. On the floor, a worn Oriental runner covered a threadbare rug.

Gus began at the big bureau, methodically opening and searching drawers, through faded blue jeans and frayed shirts, through yellowed pieces of nylon, through crazy things—a matted brown teddy bear, a collection of broken periwinkle shells. A jumble of brightly colored glass beads swept back like the ocean when he opened a shallow side drawer. He slammed it shut, sending the beads crashing against the wooden front. In the deep bottom drawer lay uncured hides. Their smell escaped into the room. He quickly shut it out. The built-in shelf in the water bed's headboard yielded a couple of empty vodka bottles, a stack of yellowing paperbacks, and little else.

At the bedside was a small table with a single deep drawer. A long time ago, Bobbie, or maybe a previous owner, had painted it bright, almost neon, purple. The paint was chipped now, and light circles, tales of a hundred wet glasses, swirled over the surface. Gus lowered his face to a drinking glass. A residue of sour liquor thickened in its bottom. Pulling on his leather driving gloves, he opened the drawer and began searching through the clutter.

There, on the bottom, he found what he was looking for: a small cardboard-bound book—the kind from the five-and-ten, with the pebbled black and white cover. He opened it carefully, holding it by the covers, and scanned the contents. It was a chronological log, the first entry some eleven years earlier, the last, less than halfway through the book, dated five years back. These last entries were hardly more than illegible scribbles. Laying the book aside, Gus reached back into the drawer. There was another log, an older one, its black and white cover faded into hues of gray. The rubber band holding it disintegrated when he touched it.

The handwriting in this book, though faded, was clearer, the contents coherent—too coherent. Gus shuddered as his eyes skimmed the pages. A wave of memories washed over him. Without intending to, he sat on the edge of the bed and remembered a summer long ago.

Summer 1972

For several years now, songs have been telling the young police-man that this is a special time, a new age of freedom, of throwing off the old ways and setting new boundaries. The six o'clock news shows him people, not just kids but people his own age, discarding jobs, uniforms, families, bras, countries. It is a time of movement, of slogans and of songs sung by people who are making changes. They move to the country, to the farm. They meditate on mountaintops in Nepal and backpack through Europe.

Gus DeBrito, twenty-seven, a newly promoted sergeant in the Provincetown police department, lives in the same house his father was born in.

He stands in front of the courthouse watching the Commer-cial Street traffic. It is July, late afternoon, and the sun burns so hot, the sky appears bleached white. His uniform blots the sweat pouring down his back. He moves into the shade and glances at his watch. Half hour more on the shift and then he'll be sitting in his air-conditioned den with a can of cold beer. His wife will bring him a kid to watch while she finishes making dinner. Gus's boundaries have long been set.

Someone catches his eye. Bobbie Yellowfeather walks out of the grocery store across the street.

She is exotic in a way that stirs Gus's fettered spirit, tall, graceful, with a dark tan and the straight shoulders of her Puritan ancestors. She calls herself an Indian, and her newly opened leather shop 'Great Plains Leather.' Her hair is worn in thick dark braids that swing across her back. A convertible full of boys stops. Their eyes lock on the woman passing in front of them: a halter of fringed leather, cutoff jeans, wide, swaying hips, and a very warm smile. She walks across the sun-drenched sidewalk onto the worn path through the grass and toward the shade of the elm trees. Gus struggles to lift his eyes from the place were a tiny leather knot fastens the halter. For a moment, it is quiet—time and place are suspended and Gus feels only the woman's presence. She passes him. He keeps his eyes ahead and smiles to himself. Another close call averted. Back to reality. Noise and time return. Then he hears her voice.

"Sergeant Debrito. I wonder if you could give me a hand with this."

A hand? Everything, lady. He turns. How does she know his name? She had asked someone about him, she says. "My boy-friend's gone off to a gig in Boston for the night. Could you help me carry this bag upstairs?"

He follows her up the back steps to the big sloppy apartment over the store where they sell the homemade fudge and saltwater taffy. He's uncomfortable at first, with the poster of Jimmy Hendrix and the water bed in the middle of the floor, and leaves as soon as the bag of groceries is on the table. At the end of his shift, though, he returns.

He sits on the one straight-backed chair. She gives him a glass of cold jug wine, then another. He relaxes. The uniform shirt is too warm then, the shoes too confining. Soon the chair is too hard, too straight. "Sit here with me," she says. The water bed is just right. Bobbie draws the shades and pulls the beaded leather thongs from her hair so that it falls down her back in an inky cascade. When she returns to the water bed, Gus unties the knot in the center of her halter.

They see the sun dim between the slats of the blinds. He raises on his elbows. His mind is urging him to leave. "Don't go," she says. She has something in her hand. A small bottle, like the pharmacist gives you. As he watches, she lays two small pink squares in the palm of her hand. A dark dot, not much bigger than a pinhead, is in the center of each. Gus has seen LSD before. He has arrested people carrying it. Fear seizes him. "It's a great high," she says, extending her palm to him. "What are you afraid of?" she asks when he hesitates. He can't define his fear. Then it doesn't exist, she says. He looks away from the hand and into her face. She seems to possess some primitive, knowing quality, something that has bypassed Gus. He stays.

In his delirium, she is a goddess, he a god. Their words, their smallest gestures have layers of meaning. Only they can understand them. When he looks down at her during the night, her hair has formed a black halo around her face.

Sometime in the night, he realizes that she is writing in a black and white notebook. "It's a history," she says, taking the book out of his hand. "My personal history." She rolls to the side of the water bed and places the book on the table.

"You're not going to put me in there, are you?"

"What makes you think you're important enough for my personal history?" As she moves across the water bed toward him, he knows that he is going to regret all this later. But later will wait.

Gus arrives home in the early morning. His wife throws a glass of orange juice at him. Five hours later, she goes into premature labor and at midnight gives birth to their third and last child, a tiny boy with a cleft palate and a harelip.

Gus is not an overly superstitious man, but he only half-believes when their obstetrician and then later a plastic surgeon in Boston tell him the cleft had been formed months earlier. He cannot shake the idea of divine retribution exacting its price for his act of infidelity.

The surgery is successful; his child is fine.

Avoiding Bobbie proves easier than Gus had imagined. They move on the same sidewalks but not in the same circles. He crosses the street to avoid her. He falls into the habit of taking a quick look toward her apartment before he leaves the courthouse. But when summer is gone and the sea air is fresh and the trees around the courthouse have lost their leaves, he falls out of that habit. Retribution has been paid, and Bobbie Yellowfeather's importance in Gus's life vanishes.

Tires spinning in a sandy rut and then the sound of men's voices brought Gus back to the present. The blurred lines on the page began drawing together. Bobbie had meant it: He wasn't important enough for her journal. Quickly—there was a single rap on the door—he pushed the book back into place and quietly closed the drawer. Then he removed his gloves. There were more knocks. The flimsy door rattled.

"You in there, Chief?" Perry called. "The forensic guys are here."

"Coming," Gus shouted, walking toward the stairwell.

Chapter 6

"MONEY," Denis St. John said to the two policemen, "and not nouveau, either. Our girl Bobbie came from old Boston money. Her real name was Roberta. Roberta Adams."

A row of minuscule diamonds pierced the art dealer's ear, following a quarter-moon around the outer curve from the point of his lobe. Deputy Perry, try as he might, couldn't keep his eyes off them.

"It hurt much to get that done?" he finally asked.

St. John pointed a well-manicured fingertip to his ear and raised a well-shaped eyebrow. "Hurt?" He smiled quizzically at the deputy. "A little, perhaps, but well worth the pain, don't you think?"

Perry's mouth turned down in disapproval.

St. John's shop had been next to Bobbie Yellowfeather's Great Plains Leather eight years, he told Debrito and Perry, adding, "Kind of a longevity record around here." St. John was not a tall man, but, by tilting his head back, he managed to gaze down his nose at the policemen.

"Must be the product," Gus Debrito replied.

St. John straightened and looked closely at the chief, searching for a trace of ridicule in the other man's expression. Debrito returned a look as bland as one of St. John's paintings.

St. John's Fine Arts consisted of a sliver of a front room facing the street and an even smaller office behind that room. In the front gallery, paintings were suspended from every available surface, including the ceiling. When the door opened, they flapped in the breeze like strips of flypaper.

In the back office where the three men sat around a cluttered desk, canvases were stacked a dozen deep against the walls. Gus's untrained artistic eye picked out three themes: surf breaking on the sandy shore, storm-tossed ships at sea, and bearded ancient mariners. The smell of drying oils was conspicuously absent. "Simply can't bear that odor," St. John had explained to the policemen. "They're done on consignment in the Far East—I suppose a seacoast is a seacost, wherever you go."

"You were talking about her family," Gus said. "Was there anyone she was particularly close to?"

"Are you kidding? There wasn't one of them she could stand. I suspect the feeling was mutual. As far as I know, the only thing Bobbie had to do with them was to cash their checks. That's how she kept going. You know how she was always talking that sixties mumbo jumbo—back to the land and nature takes care of its own?"

Gus nodded.

"Well, in Bobbie's case, nature got a nice shot in the arm from the old family trust. She had accounts everywhere. The bills went straight to her father. I used to wonder why they would finance something like Great Plains Leather. Not exactly blue-chip, you know. They must have figured having their daughter in Provincetown was cheaper than keeping her in an institution."

"If the bills went to her father, that must mean she didn't carry a lot of cash."

" 'A lot.' " St. John shrugged. " 'A lot' is relative. Once a month, Bobbie got an allowance check—about eight hundred bucks or so. She cashed it and then carried the cash with her in that beaded leather pouch she wore around her neck. She called it her 'medicine bag,' because it made her feel good. Anyway, she'd throw money around like a sailor on shore leave for as long as the money lasted. She usually finished out the month borrowing from me or anyone else she could find."

Gus nodded thoughtfully and made a mental note to check on the leather pouch. He hadn't noticed it when he'd seen Bobbie's body, and couldn't remember it appearing on the list of items found around the murder site. "She was killed near the first of the month," he said to St. John. "You think she could easily have had a couple hundred on her?"

The dealer nodded. "That might have looked pretty good to someone. Especially some of the types Bobbie hung around with."

"Meaning?"

There was a moment of hesitation on St. John's part.

"Well, I don't like to gossip, but I suppose I'm not telling any secrets when I tell you Bobbie played around a lot. I mean, you name it, she did it. Or else she wished she was doing it. I don't know if you remember, but Bobbie used to be hot stuff. Terrific-looking."

Gus shook his head. "I don't recall that."

"Well, she was. She could have had her choice of men. Even eight years back when I moved in here, she looked good when she got her act together. Not that I'm much tempted in that direction," he added, "but people should keep their options open."

His gaze moved to Perry. The deputy shifted uncomfortably in his seat. St. John continued. "The last couple years, though, Bobbie really hit bottom. There were a couple guys—I mean, we're talking street types. But even they haven't been around for a while."

"You remember their names?"

"No."

"What about business associates? Do you recall her mentioning any problems there?"

"Business associates?" St. John gave a wry smile. "Poor Bobbie hardly had enough business to have associates. Some months, she couldn't make the rent here. Thank God for Daddy. Once—it was over a year ago—she had a falling-out with one of her suppliers. He made a delivery when she was closed and he left the hides on the doorstep. It rained and the skins got soaked. They had a big fight over the bill. I could hear them screaming through the wall. But that was all it amounted to—a lot of noise. After that, she changed suppliers. You think Bobbie got killed over a pile of wet skins?"

Ignoring St. John's question, Gus asked whether the other man knew the supplier's name.

"No, but she kept records—about like I do."

All three men glanced at the chaotic pile of papers on the desk. "If you look through them . . ."

"Did *you* find Bobbie a good neighbor? Easy to get along with?"

"Sure. She was okay most of the time. Especially at first— sometimes when business was slow we would spend time talking back here. I have a burner"—he nodded toward a counter behind him—"and sometimes we'd fix a pot of tea and just shoot the breeze. Big stuff, like the meaning of life and how you know when you've found Mr. Right. That one was good for both of us." Again he smiled at Perry. "Strange, you know, but Bobbie had some awfully conventional ideas for one of those free-love types. I used to kid her—tell her underneath all the tie-dye and love beads she had a Republican soul."

"You ever go to Bobbie's house?"

"Oh, no. She invited me a couple times, but you know how it is."

St. John averted his gaze, and Gus understood that the art dealer felt guilty about this. "The sad part is, Bobbie probably thought of me as one of her closest friends."

"Did you ever hear anything about drugs?" Debrito asked.

"Drugs?" St. John rolled his eyes. "Perish the thought. Seriously, Bobbie did a lot of talking—you know, talking about the time she was tripping on this and the time she was stoned on that—but, frankly, I think Bobbie's main drug these days came in a bottle."

A bell over the front door rang as two couples entered the shop. St. John rose. "My public awaits."

On the way out of the office, Deputy Perry paused in front of a painting—a fishing boat floundering in rough seas, its terrified crew clinging to the collapsing hull.

"You sell a lot of these?"

St. John nodded. "You show me a tour bus from Montreal and I'll show you a month's rent. Hideous stuff, isn't it?"

"I don't know. Doesn't look that bad to me," Perry answered. "Of course, I couldn't draw a straight line myself."

"Personally," St. John responded, "I loathe anything straight."

"I think he liked you," Gus said to Perry as they returned to their car.

"That's disgusting," the younger man replied.

Little Ned Mayo had a bad hangover. Gus Debrito knew the signs well. The old man's eyes were webbed with red, his hands shaky. His renowned Yankee reticence was in full force.

"A beard? A beard. Em." He rubbed his chin, as if this was the first he'd heard about any beard. Then he tilted his head toward the fluorescent bulb lighting the ceiling of Gus's office and raised his shoulders. "Well, I'm not saying for sure he did have one, and I'm not saying for sure he didn't." With that, and a self-satisfied nod, Little Ned crossed his arms over his chest and waited for the next thing the chief might throw at him.

In a corner of the room, a young police artist from East Orleans sat poised over his sketch pad. Deputy Perry watched over the artist's shoulder. At first, the policemen had enjoyed the boozy line of witnesses from the Fo'c'sle, with their slow, thoughtfully muddled answers. After four hours of them, though, the three policemen were just plain bored. The artist stretched his legs and yawned. The gesture was catching; Little Ned raised his hand to cover his yawn.

"Ned," Gus said, "I'm not trying to put words in your mouth. . . ."

"No danger of that, Chief. No one ever put his words in my mouth. Emma, she's been trying for years."

"But I would like to read back your initial description." Gus picked up a typed page of notes and read purposefully. " 'An okay-looking white guy, medium brown hair, worn longish, light eyes, not clean-shaved.' " His voice rose on the last words. "Now tell me, Ned, what is 'not clean-shaved'?"

"Chief, it's like I said, it's so dark in the Fo'c'sle, a fellow's got to feel his way round. Suppose they can't afford no electric lights. Only place on the Cape still drawing dollar beer. Not a bad place, son," he said to the artist. "You ever been there?"

The young man shook his head.

"You want to come around some night. I'll buy you a cold one."

"The beard, Ned."

Ned gave the chief an exasperated look. "Just trying to be social. Anyway, looked to be a bit of stubble at the time. Not like he was growing a beard. More like he hadn't shaved for a few days. Like a lot of those fairies around here—they like a little stubble on their face."

"You think he might have been gay?"

"Of course not." The old man drew back in his chair, visibly insulted. "You don't find none of them prancing around in the Fo'c'sle. That's a man's bar."

"How about this, Mr. Mayo?" The artist flipped his tablet and held it up. Ned leaned forward and studied the drawing.

"You're close, son, but he was sneakier-looking. Little light eyes. Never trust a guy with light eyes, I always say. Remember this one time I was working this trawler. Captain was this French Canadian. Blue-eyed bastard. Cheated everybody blind."

Gus continued reading from his notes. "Fairly tall, you said."

"He wasn't any midget, if that's what you mean."

"It's not. About how tall?"

Ned thought hard, his eyes narrowing and focusing on an invisible spot on the wall. "More tall than short," he said finally.

Gus stood up. "Taller than me, Ned? Or shorter?"

Ned stared up at the other man's five-nine frame. "Taller by an inch. About."

"Weight?"

"Weight? Cripes, Gus, you want me to tell you if the guy had a wart on his behind? Sure, Chief, I went to the head with him, saw he had a name tattooed on his pecker."

"Male or female?"

"What?"

"The name," Gus said. "A girl's name or a guy's?"

The old man laughed. "Damned if you're not just like your granddad. Always quick with the comeback." He turned to Perry and the artist. "Bet old straight arrow here never told you two about the night his grandfather—that was old Captain Debrito—had the Coast Guard chasing him. Back in Prohibition. Captain Debrito ditched his cargo of bootleg right in the bay. Bottles floating around far as the eye could see."

"They're not interested, Ned."

"Not interested? Hell of a lot more interesting than this picture drawing. Christian Debrito was the last of the great captains around here." Ned scooted his chair toward his audience. "Anyway, here we are, coming around Long Point one night, holdful of booze and the Coast Guard on our tail. I'm just a boy. . . ."

Gus interrupted. "Tell them later, Ned. You said you were sitting at the bar the whole time Bobbie was in the Fo'c'sle. Is that right?"

"Right, Chief. Right."

"And you don't remember this man walking up to the bar at any point? He didn't pick up drinks for them?"

"Can't recall if he did. Recall old Bobbie bellying up a few times, like I told you. Primping herself in the mirror, making like the debutante. Poor gal. 'Bobbie,' I said to her, 'you don't have to bother fixing yourself up. The guy's got to be blind as a bat.' Told you what she said then."

"Tell me again."

The old man groaned with annoyance. "Don't understand why I have to keep saying this. You got it all written down in your book there. Anyway, Bobbie stops fluffing that mop of hers and kind of beats it down. Then she says to me—and she's looking at me serious—'Fuck off, Ned. I've got a real man here. An athlete.' Well, I come back: 'Only athlete you've got is on your foot.' Riles her up. She starts telling me she's picked herself up an Olympic swimming star. A shark, she calls him. Well, I'm getting ready to come back with something else, but then the bartender's standing there with a bottle in his hand, waiting for Bobbie to pay. She had some wad of bills, too. Stuffed into that pouch she wore around her neck. That had to be what the guy was after."

"Would you say Bobbie and this man were drunk when they left?"

"I'd say Bobbie was feeling no pain when she got to the Fo'c'sle. Drunker when she left. Him, can't say. Looked to be kind of nodding off before she sat down with him. Guess he had to be drunk if he left with her. No amount of money was worth going off in the bushes with Bobbie." Ned loosened his upper plate and let his toothless gums flash in a pink grin.

Gus's sense of humor was shot. "All right, Ned," he said brusquely. "That's it for now. Thanks for your help. You'll be around in case we need you?"

"Been here for seventy-five years. No place else to go. No big boats going out anymore. Nothing but pansy tour boats left. You need me, leave word with Emma. And you young fellows," he said to Perry and the artist, "you want to hear the rest of that story, you come around to the Fo'c'sle. That way, we won't have Mr. Straight Arrow here interrupting all the time."

Gus closed the door in the old man's face. Standing over the artist's shoulder, he looked at the sketches.

"Now what happens?" he asked.

"I go back to East Orleans, plug all this into the computer, and come up with a composite."

"In time for tomorrow's paper?"

"Don't see why not."

"And it really works. That computer?" asked Perry.

"Well," the artist answered, "it will give us a okay-looking white male with a couple day's worth of beard, medium brown hair. . . ."

"And sneaky light eyes," Gus added.

Chapter 7

THE *Provincetown Progress* was delivered to the police station at the back of the town hall late the next morning. Gus scanned the headlines quickly, flipping the first page and then the next ones. Restaurant and hotel advertisements, bulletins about the tides and runs of fish, schedules for harbor tours and nature walks.

"Nothing but the good news," he grumbled. So far, there was not much to go on in Bobbie's murder. The murder weapon was a sharp knife with a five-inch shaft. Forensics had turned up some strands of brown hair in her hands and traces of B-positive blood under her nails. There was no sperm in her vagina, and, indeed, no indication that sexual activity of any kind had taken place.

Gus found the story and sketch at the bottom of the seventh page, tucked between an notice about an upcoming church supper and an article about dune erosion. The headline, LOCAL MERCHANT FOUND SLAIN, and the paragraph that followed it were inconspicuous almost to the point of fading into the columns around them. The sketch, fortunately, was surprisingly sharp. Unfortunately, Gus realized, it looked like no one he knew, yet it had a strangely homogeneous quality. With minor modifications, it could have resembled almost any average Caucasian male between twenty-five and forty. Lighten the hair and give him a shave, he could have been Gus's next-door neighbor. Add ten pounds and a haircut and you had the mayor.

There was a knock on the office door. One of the department's clerks was standing there. A pretty dark-haired woman in her midtwenties, she had been born and schooled in Provincetown. Gus motioned her in.

"Annie, take a look at this character. Does he resemble anyone you know?"

The young woman picked up the newspaper and looked at the sketch carefully, turning her head from side to side.

"Come on," Gus said. "Humor an old man. Tell me you went to the senior prom with him."

She dropped the paper onto his desk. "Sorry, Chief. Don't think I know him. Sort of looks like a lot of guys, doesn't he? Too bad he doesn't have elephant ears or crossed eyes or something. The guy who took me to the prom did."

Gus lifted an eyebrow. "Then we can scratch *him* off the list."

She grinned at the police chief, then her expression darkened. "It's sad about Bobbie, but I can't imagine *any* guy going up in those dunes with her. Even elephant ears. Can you? He had to be either drunk or crazy."

Gus surprised himself by wanting to defend Bobbie. Something in him wanted to tell this young woman how appealing Bobbie had once been. He didn't.

"Maybe both," he said.

"Maybe. What I came in to tell you is, there's a lady out front at the counter to see you."

"What about?"

"I don't know. She wouldn't tell me. She said it was personal."

"Personal?"

"That's what she said."

Gus grunted and pushed back his chair. "Probably selling

magazine subscriptions or condominium time shares or something."

Gus followed the clerk out the door. Down the hall, a trio of teenage boys huddled over a form on a bench outside a door marked CITY CLERK. Otherwise, the long corridor was deserted. From inside one office came the sound of unhurried typewriters, from another the raised voices of people talking about baseball scores.

"She was here a minute ago," the clerk said. "Maybe she's gone to the women's room."

Gus shrugged. "I'm going to get some lunch. If she comes back, ask her to wait a few minutes."

From the window on the second-floor landing of the town hall, Joyce Neuhauser had a clear view of the sidewalk. She saw the dark-haired man leave by the side entrance. When she heard a uniformed patrolman call him Chief, she quickly moved away from the window. Shaken, she lowered herself onto a step. Taking the newspaper from her purse, Joyce once again turned to the page with the sketch.

In the dingy coffee shop a few hours earlier, the sketch had made her heart race. Now, though the bright noon light coming through the window put the face in sharp relief, Joyce's reaction to it was dulled. The face in the police artist's composite was that of a stranger. Joyce traced the sketch's flat planes with her finger as a blind person follows a braille outline, then reread the article. A woman who ran something called Great Plains Leather, last seen in the company of the man in the sketch, had been killed. That was sad, but that was all it was. Joyce experienced nothing now—no jolt of recognition, no fear. The mist of cold sweat that had appeared across her forehead when she first saw the man's picture did not reappear. Her only anxiety now was the anxiety of having almost made a colossal fool of herself. She had been only words away from ruining everything good that had happened that week.

It had been a good vacation. A little rough at the start, maybe, but a fine finish. Sure, the sand fleas had eaten Frank alive, and none of her clothes had fit, and Maryann and Frankie had had their spats, but things hadn't been awful—not in the old, devastating way. Sand fleas always bite, kids always bicker, and one overweight lady looks like another overweight lady in her too-tight clothes.

No. It hadn't been devastating. Even things with Debbie were smoother. After their shopping trip, Joyce's older daughter had remained, if not consistently cheerful, at least reasonably civil. Bribery had its place. Over the last few days, Joyce and her daughter had managed another long walk—this time without Joyce dangling the carrot of new clothes in front of Debbie. The day before, the two had actually jogged together on the beach and ended up splashing in the water.

And then, this last morning on the Cape, Joyce had opened the paper and seen the sketch, and almost finished the week in a fit of crazy paranoia.

Below her, Joyce heard the fall of feet on the lower steps of the building. What if it was the clerk? What if she was recognized? She tried to stand, but a numbing anxiety pushed her down. She could only stare dumbly when, seconds later, two middle-aged women passed her on the stairs and disappeared into the ladies' room.

God—suddenly the thought of what she had almost done made her stomach churn. She had been right on the verge of telling the chief of police some wild nonsense even she didn't understand. The vacation, the fresh start for all of them, could have ended in shambles. And over what? She looked at the sketch again. Again the face of a stranger stared back. Shaken by her close call, Joyce pushed the newspaper to the bottom of her plastic beach tote and pulled herself up. Before she had taken a step, the big front door on the lower level swung open. An old woman entered and walked briskly toward the offices at the back of the building.

Joyce stared down at the woman. Another familiar face? This couldn't be. She had to stop this lunacy. It was one thing to try to remember the past, another to let her imagination run wild.

She glanced at her watch: quarter after twelve. They'd packed that morning. Frank was probably loading the car already. And here she was, trying to hide from the chief of police on a public stairway. As soon as the sound of the woman's steps faded, Joyce hurried down the stairs.

She controlled her urge to run away from the town hall. It took her fifteen minutes to make her way through the shoppers on Commercial Street and past the Coast Guard station. On the way, she stopped to buy saltwater taffy for the neighbor who had collected their mail. At the drugstore, she put a nickel in the big old-fashioned scale. The white band with its black numbers spun and stopped on a number that brought a smile to Joyce's face. Five pounds less than a week ago, and that was without even dieting!

By the time she got to the row of condominiums, Frank had pulled the station wagon to the door. Joyce found him struggling with their luggage, trying to make it all fit. Beads of perspiration dotted his forehead.

"Where were you?"

Before she could answer, Maryann and Frankie burst through the condo door. "Our seashells, Daddy," Maryann cried. "We almost forgot our shells." In her arms, she held a big yellow shopping bag.

Frank rolled his eyes. Taking the bag from his daughter, he shoved it into a tiny crevice. "I can't believe how much stuff we have. Is this everything?"

"I'll look around," Joyce said, starting for the door. Her husband's next words stopped her.

"You know what? I kind of hate to leave," he said. "We've had a pretty good time."

She looked back at her husband. He was smiling.

"We have, haven't we," Joyce agreed.

It was after one o'clock when Gus returned to the police station.

"Long lunch for a public servant," Emma Stone said when he

walked to the bench where she was sitting. "I've got better things to do than warm this seat." She rose briskly to her feet.

"What can I do for you, Emma?"

"Nothing," she said, stooping to dig into a carryall. "I can do something for you. This guy"—Emma held up the morning paper, opened to page seven—"the one in the sketch. I think he may have been in my store last weekend."

"You recognize the man?" Gus put an eager arm around Emma's shoulders and escorted her into his office.

Emma sat, ramrod-straight, on a wooden chair. "I don't know him from around here. Could be the same guy, though. He was in on Saturday morning. Just that one time. Bought . . ." She hesitated. A sly smile crossed the old woman's face. "Just picked up a couple things."

Gus cocked an eyebrow. "What kind of things, Emma? You selling something you shouldn't be?"

"A soda, and . . . one of those shark's tooth necklaces. You know, the ones with the gold plate. . . ."

"I know the ones."

"There's a sucker born every minute," Emma said defensively. "Might as well give his money to me as some bartender."

"Was Ned in the store at the time?" Gus asked. "Ned saw the guy Bobbie left the Fo'c'sle with. He didn't mention seeing him at the store earlier."

Emma shook her head. "I asked Ned, but he couldn't remember. This fellow might have stopped in while Ned was doing some work in the storage room."

"Did you notice anything unusual about the man?"

Emma shrugged. "Didn't seem any stranger than most of the summer people. I can't remember what he was wearing, but I wasn't paying much attention to him. There was this family in the store at the same time. Now, there was an odd bunch."

She went on to tell Gus about the woman who had knocked down the brooms, about the baby and the husband and the other children. "Weedy husband. Skinny half-dead-looking thing. Wife was just the opposite. She looked like she was about to have a stroke. Carrying too much weight around. A shame. Couldn't have been much more than thirty. Blond, pretty face, if she lost some of that fat."

Emma tapped her forefinger on the sketch. "Cute-looking kids, though. If I'm remembering it right, the older daughter talked to this guy for a while."

"Older daughter? Tell me about her."

"I know what you're thinking," Emma said hastily. "You're thinking he was interested in the girl. For a minute, I thought that myself. Couldn't be, though. He was a grown man. Thirty, I'd say. She wasn't any more than twelve. Just a little kid." She regarded Gus with sharp, unblinking eyes. "The kind of degenerate that picks up Bobbie Yellowfeather in a bar isn't going to be the same kind of degenerate that goes after little girls."

2
Autumn

Chapter 8

RONNIE had waited for over an hour, his body tense, eyes closed, ears pitched, listening through the darkness. He was so still that he could count his heartbeats as they echoed through the sagging spine of his mattress. A thin mist of icy perspiration covered him. For more than an hour he had lain rigid, hardly letting himself shiver.

From across the room, the hands on his clock hummed, creeping toward dawn. He let his sleep-starved eyes open to a slit. The luminous dial glittered at him: quarter after five. He almost allowed himself a relieved sigh, but that could be dangerous. The Indian woman could still be there. She had been there before. He'd lost count of how many times during the past three weeks she'd crept into his room, sneaking, trying to dig through his thoughts, trying to find her bag of magic.

Soon a thin streak of light would outline his drawn curtains, cutting through the dark, and he would hear the sounds of the world returning to life—car doors opening and closing, cold engines idling, the garbage men with their clangs and shouts. A little longer, just a few minutes.

He hadn't slept, or if he had he wasn't aware he had drifted out of consciousness. In the early hours of the night, time had passed quickly, filled with a waking rapture. His girl had come to him and they'd swum together out beyond Dromedary Point. And later, filled with happiness, they'd wandered hand in hand back to their house on the dunes.

Whenever his waking dream had edged toward something that wasn't nice, it had grown purposely hazy. He wouldn't allow himself those dirty thoughts about Deborah. Deborah: The name caressed his thoughts, a silken whisper. He recalled every small detail of her from the time they'd spent together on the beach. Her small, even white teeth, her blue eyes half-closed against the beach light were drawn indelibly for him. Sometime, though, in the eerie hours before daybreak, Deborah had begun fading. He'd grasped after her, trying to harden the blurring edges and force her outline into focus, but she had gone, leaving Ronnie emptier than if she had never been there at all.

Maybe here he had slept; he didn't know. What he did remember was the moment when a noiseless terror startled him from a black void, stunning him into this fearful night watch. The Indian woman had been there. She hadn't had a physical substance. Oh, no. She was too tricky for that. She was a vapor who crouched in the shadowy corners of his room. Ronnie had sensed her presence in the same skin-sharpening way the Shark could sense a strong competitor. He had waited then, knowing that a tremor of his hand or the shifting of his head on the pillow would alert her to him, and those coarse dirty fingers and foul breath would touch him again.

Each time she stole into his room, it was worse for him. He could no longer bear not confronting her, and he planned how he must grab the knife under his pillow and leap into the shadows and confront her. Now, his thoughts told him. Now.

The clang of a garage door opening shattered the silence. There was the grinding of an engine, then the quickly muted blare of a car radio. The familiar sound of his neighborhood waking up broke through Ronnie's terror. In a moment his own alarm clock would jangle on the table next to his bed. A sigh escaped him. He ran his blankets across his sweat-slick skin, then clutched them tightly. Finally, Ronnie opened his eyes wide and peered into the lifting shadows. Squares of morning light brightened the wall around the curtains. The Indian woman had gone.

There was one thing he had to do, to be sure everything was all right. Sliding from his bed, Ronnie knelt beside it and stretched his arms under the springs. His hands searched the linoleum. Wedging his shoulder farther, he reached until he held the familiar plastic grip of a suitcase. Sliding it out, he lifted the lid and, in the dim room, took inventory.

There was a faded burgundy banner—an elongated triangle with gold letters—laid out neatly on the bottom of the case. LINCOLN HIGH SCHOOL, the gold letters read. On that banner, displayed like jewels in a museum case, lay Ronnie's treasures. There was a trophy—a swimmer poised to dive. The shark's tooth necklace lay nestled into the banner, its gold chain coiled neatly around it.

The small leather pouch was there, filled with the Indian woman's magic medicine. Ronnie had looked in the pouch the first night he was home: several hundred dollars, in tens and twenties, in a messy roll. It wasn't just money, though. Ronnie knew the money was for something special for Deborah.

And there one other thing: a torn pair of child's shorts. The cloth was green, patterned with pink leaping frogs. It was a pattern for a little girl.

He picked up the shorts and ran his fingers across the fabric. At the elastic waistband, the fabric was dark and twisted. The shorts had been partially burned in the fire. After he'd gotten Mother out, he'd gone back into the house, but he'd only been able to save a couple of things. *Look at my hand, Ronnie. I burned for your sin.*

Placing the shorts carefully back onto their banner bed, he picked up his newest treasure—a page torn from a Boston area phone book. Folding it carefully, Ronnie stuffed it into the beaded pouch. The roll of bills took the page's place on the banner.

He should do something soon, before the Indian woman found out where her magic medicine was hidden and took it back.

As Ronnie draped the pouch around his neck, a massive accumulated fatigue overtook him. Turning off his alarm, he slid back under the blankets and closed his eyes. A few minutes rest.

The next time he looked at the clock, it was 7:50. Jumping up with a start, Ronnie made his bed and then raced efficiently through his morning routine. On the area rug that lay next to his bed, he did four sets of eight push-ups and four sets of eight sit-ups. Standing, he stretched his hands high, then touched his waist, then his toes. Four sets of eight. When he'd done, he balanced on his bathroom scale. One hundred and sixty-four pounds. Ten pounds more than high school. He'd been getting lax lately, eating the junk food the Shark liked. He had to watch that, he thought as he stepped into the shower.

The cool water washed across his face again and again, rinsing away what remained of the night. There was no question of what he would wear to work. One of the two blue overalls hanging in the closet went on mechanically. He took a blue cap with a white visor from the shelf.

For breakfast, he had cold cereal and milk, with banana sliced into it. No sugar. Whole wheat toast and orange juice. He swallowed a multivitamin with the juice. When he had washed the dishes and set them on the rack to dry, he went into Mother's room and lifted her shades up to the middle sash of the window, the way she liked them. Her quilt was straight and neat over her bed, and the pillows were rolled into tight cylinders. It had been a while, though, since he'd dusted in here. A light film of dust dulled the shine on Mother's dresser. It was getting harder and harder for him to keep things the way Mother liked. Tonight, for certain, he'd clean.

He slid open the top drawer of Mother's dresser. There was still an almost-full bottle of the sleeping pills she'd taken after the fire. *For the pain, Ronnie.* When the pain subsided, she'd stopped taking the pills, but she'd never thrown them away. "Just in case," she said to him once, and she'd looked at him almost fearfully, as if she expected the bad times to start again.

Ronnie examined the label on the plastic bottle. The pills had expired years before, but he decided to keep them—just in case.

Before leaving the house, Ronnie examined himself in the bathroom mirror. His hair was cut short, and he'd shaved close. Except for the faint puffy circles under his eyes, he was pleased with his reflection. It showed a face not hardened by years or beaten by liquor or drugs. He looked younger than lots of the kids at the laundry, though he was older than any of them. They didn't live right. They didn't take care of themselves.

He adjusted the cap on his head. VITTUCCHI's, the patch across it read. The flap on his uniform pocket bore the same logo.

It was almost 8:30 by the time Ronnie backed the white van up to the side door of the cleaning plant. Sal Vittucchi had the van's back door open before Ronnie was out of the cab.

"How many times I gotta tell you, Ronnie. Eight o'clock means eight o'clock. This is a business I'm running here, not some welfare agency."

Ronnie looked down at the pavement. "I'm sorry. There was lots of traffic coming through town."

"Yeah. Yeah. Always sorry, always traffic." Sal spoke with his hands, waving them in the air for emphasis. From the door of the plant, two dark-haired girls watched, giggling.

"Hey!" Vittucchi motioned to a brown-skinned young man. "Come on, Carlos. Help me and Ronnie get this thing loaded."

The big cigar-chomping man thrust a sheet of paper Ronnie's way. "Here's the list. You got probably a dozen deliveries and pickups to get through before noon. Okay? Ronnie, you hearing me?"

Ronnie nodded. His eyes swept across the list: letters, words jumbled together. None of it meant anything anymore.

"And—Hey, Ronnie, I've lost you. You're out there in space again." Vittucchi's open palm waved in front of Ronnie's face, causing the younger man to flinch. "This is important," his boss continued. "You got the clean towels for the municipal pool in there. This is gonna be a big weekend for them. End of season. You drop these off and pick up the dirties early so they can set up. You got that, kiddo?"

"Yes, Sal."

"Yes, Sal," the other man aped. "That's what they all say."

"Yes, Sal," a girl's voice singsonged from the plant. Sal ignored her. "You finished loading, Carlos? Okay, Ronnie, it's all yours. And, Ronnie, you get back here in time, you get to take the new van home with you. I'm taking delivery this afternoon."

Vittucchi walked back toward the laundry's door.

Ronnie took a step toward the van's cab, then turned to his boss. He had to do it now or it would be too late.

"Sal? Mr. Vittucchi?"

"Yeah? What is it?"

"Remember what you said—that as soon as the new van came in you'd see about me buying this one from you?"

"Oh, yeah?" Vittucchi shrugged. "Sure," he said finally. "But you remember what else I said. I take no responsibility for what happens to this thing once she's yours. She's got a lot of hard miles on her. 'Cause of you. Hot-roddin' around."

Seeing Ronnie's stricken look, Vittucchi instantly relented. "What do you want with something this big, anyway? Single guy like you? With your mom passed away now, there's no need for you to hang on to her old Chevy. It's in good shape. If you was to trade it in, you could get yourself a nice sporty job. Impress the girls."

Ronnie's stare dropped to the pavement again. He studied its oily splotches as if they might give him words he could say to stop Vittucchi's questions.

"Hey, Sal," Carlos said with a voice full of laughter. "Maybe Ronnie wants the van 'cause he's gonna put a mattress back there, really impress the girls."

From inside the plant came the sound of girls laughing. Vittucchi grinned. His moment of sympathy disappeared.

"What about that, Ronnie? Plan on playing a little hide-the-salami back there. Or"—the other man's eyes glistened—"or maybe you already been getting it. Hey guys." Vittucchi swung his body toward the plant door. He was playing to a full audience now, loving it. "Maybe that's why we're having such a hard time getting the sheets clean lately."

Ronnie felt heat rising past his collar. What did Vittucchi know about nice girls—that vulgar slob. Ronnie had thought, briefly, that he would bring Deborah there and show them all. They would be so jealous—a filthy-minded man and a bunch of Puerto Ricans. But then a terrible vision had followed: Vittucchi touching his girl. Ronnie knew how it would happen. Vittucchi would pretend he was joking around and he'd rub her hair and maybe even touch her the way he touched the girls in the plant when he thought no one was looking. It sickened Ronnie to think about it.

He climbed into the van, red-faced. He could never bring Deborah to Vittucchi's. He and Deborah had to go away, like he'd planned.

Sal Vittucchi watched the van pull out of the driveway. "You see his face turn red?" he said to Carlos. "Sometimes you gotta wonder if old Ronnie's ever been with a girl in his life."

"Ronnie's been with a girl, all right," Carlos said. "A little girl."

Vittucchi regarded his employee shrewdly. "What are you saying?"

Carlos was quiet for a moment before he motioned for the older man to follow him away from the plant door.

"I don't want to be spreading rumors or anything, but when Ronnie was on vacation and I did his route, I got to know some of the lifeguards at the municipal pool in Lincoln. Seems like one of them has this older cousin—he's about Ronnie's age."

"Yeah? And?"

"This older cousin, he was a lifeguard back twelve or fifteen years ago. He says that Ronnie got in deep shit for messing with some guy's little sister. I mean little like—a kid. Ronnie ended up getting beat up and . . ." Carlos shrugged. "I don't know the whole story, but there was all kinds of big trouble."

"Big trouble." Vittucchi repeated the words softly. "Kind of hard to believe that of Ronnie, isn't it?"

Unload the clean, pick up the dirty. Always be polite to the customers. Ronnie followed Vittucchi's rules and Vittucchi's list diligently. He worked more quickly than usual, and pulled the van into the lot alongside the municipal pool before the lifeguards got there.

The pink stucco building looked soft in the morning sun, and the blue-green water was still as a mirror. A tart chlorine smell hung in the air. It was a smell that Ronnie knew so well that sometimes, even in his own bed with his arms crossed over his face, he would smell it as if it was seeping from his own flesh.

As he waited, Ronnie's hand slipped under his shirt where the beaded leather pouch rested against his skin. The Indian woman's magic—her crumpled bills—was gone, replaced by his own magic. His fingers tugged at the opening and withdrew the folded sheet he'd torn from the phone book.

An old Honda turned into the parking lot. Rock and roll blared from its open windows. Ronnie quickly pushed the folded paper into the bag and hid the bag under his shirt.

The lifeguards disappeared through the doors at the far end of the building. Ronnie watched them going through the motions he knew so well—joking with each other as they unlocked the snack bar and set the umbrella over the raised guard chair. Finally, one of them walked through the locker room door.

"Hey, Ronnie! You got the clean towels?" When Ronnie didn't answer, the kid slapped the side of the van with a flat hand.

"Come on, man. I've got a lot to do. Big day today."

"Okay." Ronnie climbed from the van and walked to its rear.

"We're closing for the season tomorrow," the lifeguard said. "You should come out and watch the races this afternoon. You used to be pretty fast yourself, didn't you, Ronnie? One time I heard some of the older guys talking. . . ."

The words hit Ronnie as painfully as a kick in the stomach. For a moment, it was almost as if he could see through the pink stucco walls into the locker room. He saw a boy on the concrete floor, on his side, legs drawn to his chest like a fetus, trying to protect himself from the slashing kicks of the other guys.

The lifeguard was still talking, lips moving as he shouldered a tied bundle of towels, but the sounds meant nothing, just jarring interruptions of a meaningless present on the ugly reality of the past. Ronnie tried to force himself to listen, to shake the terrible images. As he crawled into the back of the van, the boy's voice finally broke through. "So what was your time in the five hundred meter, anyway?"

"I thought you were in a hurry," Ronnie answered. Grabbing one of the stacks, he began to work silently.

By skipping lunch and pushing through his afternoon deliveries, Ronnie was able to finish before three o'clock. Vittucchi didn't expect him before 4:30. At a red light, he studied the torn page from the phone directory. Three names were circled in blue pen. All three had addresses near Lincoln Township. The first, a L. D. Neuhauser, was the farthest away. Ronnie had already decided to save that one for another day if neither of the others worked out. When the light turned green, he turned in the direction of Salisbury, where a Joseph Neuhauser was listed at 916 Tenth Street.

Ronnie's teetering spirits dropped even as he approached the area. It wasn't houses; it was apartments—the kind of unadorned six-story brick buildings in poor neighborhoods everywhere. There were many brown faces, few white ones. Nine sixteen Tenth Street was a corner building. As Ronnie slowed the van in front of it, a group of black teenage boys followed him with their eyes. He stared back, as unafraid as they were. An old black woman began walking toward his open window, mouthing something that sounded to him like gibberish. Her stockings were down around her skinny ankles. There were sores on her legs. Disheartened, Ronnie pulled back into traffic.

It was close to 4:00 P.M. when he finally turned into Old Covered Bridge Estates.

Chapter 9

JOYCE Neuhauser tugged the skin from the last piece of chicken and laid it on the counter with the others. The recipe called for three pounds. She had a little more. It was okay, though, she decided absently. Increase the other ingredients, that's all. Then, struck by the way she had decided—absently—she smiled.

During the first few days at home, Joyce had been her own worst enemy, double-checking each thought and movement, poking through the dusty edges of her mind for eccentricities. Then, the big question had been, Will I be able to handle it? Now, three weeks after their return from the Cape, it was, How well am I handling it? And the answer, as far as she could tell, was, Not badly. There had been none of her former, numbing depressions. Stresses had been minor, easily dealt with. A few blank places in her memory still bothered her, but every now and then something would suddenly fill in one of the blanks. A little more time and maybe all the blanks would disappear.

Tilting the magazine so that it would catch the afternoon light coming through the window, Joyce read aloud: "Three-pound chicken, boned, twelve mushrooms, eight ounces egg noodles, one medium onion, chopped." At the bottom of the page, she saw, for the first time, a small note: "For a special finishing touch, dot the top of the casserole with chopped black olives before placing it on the center rack in the oven."

She hadn't noticed that when she planned the meal. Olives certainly hadn't been on her shopping list. "Special finishing touch." She mulled the words over. That was something Frank might say. No. He wouldn't say those words, not like that. But he might think them. Frank had the second-largest office in his company. On his desk was a silver pen and pencil set given to him by his boss, on which these words were engraved: "To Frank Neuhauser, Who Always Gives That Extra Ten Percent And Always Goes That Extra Yard."

That's what she had to do, Joyce decided. She had to take this chicken that extra yard.

The clock on the kitchen wall read 4:15. Debbie was at choir practice, Maryann was down the street with a friend, and Frankie junior and the baby were in the family room next to the kitchen. Joyce looked over the dividing counter at the two boys. Frankie was lulled by the television. His face was inches away from the screen. His eyes were fixed on the frenetic cartoon characters; his lips were open. On the floor next to him, Andy slept, a half-empty bottle at his side.

Joyce could leave the kids next door with Gloria Collins for a few minutes, but over the last few months Gloria had been imposed on so many times. Her neighbor had never said no, but there was a limit.

Joyce stared back at the pale yellow chicken. Next to it was the casserole dish with its mushroom sauce and noodles. The meal suddenly seemed bland and unappetizing, the careless effort of a person who didn't care enough to give it that special finishing touch. If she hurried, she could get to the store, pick up the olives, and be back in plenty of time to have dinner ready when Frank walked in at 6:30. Making a quick decision, Joyce hurried into the next room, grabbed her purse, and picked up the baby.

"Come on, Frankie. We've got to run to the store."

The little boy took his mother seriously. "Are we really going to run there?"

Joyce smiled at him. Since their return from the Cape, Joyce had been jogging every day. The first day, she'd walked ten steps for every three she ran. By now, the figures had been reversed, but she still wasn't ready to run to the grocery store. Not with a four-year-old and an baby in tow.

"No. We're going to take the car."

"I wanna stay here."

There was no time for an argument. "I'm sorry, honey," she said, tugging his hand, "but you have to come with Mommy."

The little boy lifted his knees so that he hung from his mothers arm, a deadweight.

"Only if you let me take my cars."

"All right, but hurry." As Joyce walked toward the door, Frankie stuffed his pockets with plastic cars.

Old Covered Bridge Estates was not old. It had been built in the early 1970s. Nor were the homes estates: The forty acres of played-out apple orchard had been divided with neat economy into eighty-by-one-hundred-foot lots that not even the most pretentious resident could call an estate. As for the covered bridge, it was only a memory. It had burned in the same Fourth of July fiasco that had cost the only mature trees on the property. A utilitarian iron bridge now spanned the stream that ran between the development and the highway.

Streets through the Estates were plumb line–true, and houses lined them like pastel-clad soldiers at attention—no less than twenty-five feet of front lawn, no more than thirty, sliced at even intervals by blacktopped driveways. Every house boasted a full basement and a two-car garage. Grass seldom showed brown spots; it seldom grew longer than three inches. Untrimmed edges outside were a clear sign of trouble within.

New visitors to the Estates often experienced a peculiar disorientation. Oak, Elm, Cedar streets—they all looked so much alike that drivers felt as if they were going through a maze. Like the other residents, Joyce had become accustomed to cars moving at slow motion, their confused drivers peering hopefully at the tastefully minuscule house numbers.

Joyce settled Andy into the corner of the backseat. "Now, Frankie, you sit in front of him so he doesn't roll."

"Why don't you put him in his car seat?"

"Because I forgot and left his seat in Daddy's car. And we're just going a few blocks." She paused as she backed out of the driveway to let a slow-moving white van go by. When it had passed, she pulled into the street.

The sun had beaten on the station wagon all afternoon, and she held the steering wheel gingerly. At the corner, Joyce turned and looked at the children. The baby had dozed off again. Frankie was kneeling on the floor, running his cars over the hills of the backseat. When she had made the turn, Joyce saw the white van at the edge of her vision. The diver had made a U-turn and was now coming back down the street. Another lost deliveryman, she figured.

In middle of the next block, Joyce realized the van had followed her around the corner, that it was still there, drawing closer. When she pulled up to the big intersection at the blinking red light, the white van was right behind her.

"I can't stand it when people tailgate like that."

From the backseat, Frankie made motor sounds, competing with the noisy van engine. The combination began making Joyce nervous. "A little quieter please, honey." She looked left and right. Traffic moved steadily in both directions. She glanced in the rearview mirror. The van moved closer. The grating motor noise was louder now. How annoying—impatient drivers who tried to edge you into traffic before you felt safe to go. Especially with children in the car. Surely, he could see the kids.

"What a smart aleck." Curious, Joyce leaned forward and looked through the rearview mirror, at the same time loosening her grip on the still-warm steering wheel. An ordinary white delivery van. If she could see the company logo, she just might complain to someone. Sliding down farther in her seat, she adjusted the mirror enough to bring the driver into focus.

Joyce froze for a second, not believing what she saw. Then uncontrolled reflex took over. Her foot slammed onto the accelerator. The station wagon exploded into the intersection. From both directions, tires squealed. Horns blew. As Joyce cleared the traffic and shot into the shopping center parking lot, the tires on the passenger side bounced off the curb.

"Mommy, what are you doing?" Frankie yelled from the back. Andy's screams began as the car came to a bouncing stop.

Joyce jumped from the car, opened the back door, and picked up the shrieking baby. Tiny droplets of blood had begun seeping through an inch-long scratch on his temple.

Frankie picked himself off the floor. "Look what you did," he yelled. In his hand was a small red car. Its front wheels dangled by a sliver of plastic. "You made him roll on my favorite car and break it."

"Just shut up for a minute," Joyce shouted angrily.

Her little boy's eyes widened, then filled with tears. His lips quivered. Oh, no. She couldn't deal with two crying children.

"Oh, honey. Don't cry. Mommy's sorry she yelled at you. Would you do something for Mommy? Would you hand me a tissue from my purse."

She dabbed the scratch gently, crooning soft words to quiet the baby. After a moment, Frankie leaned on his mother's lap and touched the baby's face. "Wait till Daddy sees that."

Joyce's unfocused distress crystallized to one awful thought. Under no circumstances could Frank find out about this. It was bad enough that she had taken Andy in the car without his seat, but to roar through the intersection. . . .

"Sees what, Frankie?" she said calmly. "Children get scratched all the time. Like when you fell on your knee and Mommy kissed it better. Do you remember?"

Frankie watched the oozing cut on the baby's skin. "Can you kiss that better."

"Sure I can." Joyce patted the tissue on the cut again, then pressed her lips to the baby's forehead. Thankfully, the child's tears had stopped. She pulled him up onto her shoulder, and as she did her eyes skimmed the parking lot. No white van in sight.

She smiled at Frankie. "You see? He's all better."

"Okay," the little boy said. "What are you looking for in the parking lot?"

"Oh, nothing. I thought there was someone I know."

"Is that why you drove so fast?"

"I wasn't driving fast, honey. The car jerked because the accelerator sticks. We'll have to get that fixed."

"What about my car?" Frankie asked. "Can I have a new one? A racing one?"

Joyce took one more look at the cars in the lot, and then contemplated her son. She had only a few dollars in her purse. The olives would be little more than a dollar, but she doubted whether she had enough for Frankie's car, too. She looked down at the baby. The bleeding had stopped, leaving only a thin scratch. Even in the bright sunlight, it hardly showed. In the house, Frank might not even notice it. More parenting by bribery, but a three-dollar plastic car was a small price to pay if it would take Frankie's mind off the incident. As for the olives— the casserole would be just fine without them.

Joyce's fifty-minute session with Dr. Weisman was almost at an end. Ten minutes left. Her fingers plucked at the well-worn upholstery on the couch as she wondered whether, after the *success* of the past three weeks, she wanted to end this appointment by telling her therapist about the man in the white van. She began apologetically.

"I can't tell you how foolish I feel, mentioning this other thing," she said finally.

"What other thing is that, Mrs. Neuhauser?"

"I think there may be a man after me."

A rather long silence followed her words. She resisted her impulse to turn her head and look at the doctor. The impulse was always there, every time she said something she thought would astound him. Whenever she gave in to it, she invariably found his expression impassive. He had yet to look astounded by anything she said.

Realizing that her words could be misinterpreted, she corrected herself. "I mean, someone who would want to do me some harm. Not a man *interested* in me."

"Tell me about this man," Dr. Weisman said.

"I'm not sure how to begin."

"At the beginning?"

"That's the problem," Joyce explained. "I don't know where the beginning is."

She told Dr. Weisman about the man on the highway near the Bourne Bridge, and her vague feeling that she had known him before. She told him about the artist's sketch she'd seen in the Provincetown paper, and about her aborted visit to the police station. And she talked about the dreams she'd had on the Cape, the dreams she woke from gasping for breath.

"Is there anything particular you recall from your past that reminds you of this dream?" Dr. Weisman asked.

"No. I've gone through some old photos and my wedding album. There's . . ." She shook her head. "Nothing."

A brief silence. "What makes you think this man is after you now?"

"I saw him yesterday. I *think* I saw him yesterday. He was in my neighborhood. In fact, he slowed down when he passed my house."

This time, there was no hesitation from Dr. Weisman. "Why do you feel foolish telling me this?"

"It's crazy enough, isn't it? And besides, yesterday he was in a van, not a brown car."

"Mrs. Neuhauser, you've never experienced any paranoid delusions before. Why should you start now?"

She shrugged, embarrassed. "You told me that sometimes the benefits of electroshock therapy are only temporary and people have to have further sessions. I remember you saying that."

"Yes, I did say that," Dr. Weisman agreed. "But a return

of anxiety and depression has nothing to do with paranoid delusions."

"But . . . I wondered if the electroshock treatments might have done something to my mind."

Dr. Weisman hesitated before speaking. "The treatments may do many things to a patient's thought processes, but if they've given you paranoid delusions, that would be a first."

He shifted in his chair. Joyce recognized the sound. The session was over.

Her therapist's reaction had a mixed effect on her. She drove home with a feeling of elation, at the same time laughing at herself for that feeling. What a wonderful thing, she mused, to be reasonably secure in the knowledge that I'm not having paranoid delusions. A suspected murderer really is after me.

Later that afternoon, while the baby and Frankie were napping, Joyce descended the stairs to the basement, green plastic trash bags and a few boxes in her arms. On one side of the stairs was the laundry area. On the other, past the lawn mower and garden tools, was the room she and Frank had tiled and paneled when they moved into the house. They had intended it as a playroom for the children. As far as Joyce knew, not one of the children had ever played there without being encouraged by bribes or threats. It was their Siberia. The room maintained, despite all efforts and expense to the contrary, a year-round temperature of about sixty-two degrees.

It had become the junk room, the room where every now and then the sliding door was pushed aside and another carton was added to the pile. Joyce had occasionally made halfhearted attempts at cleaning it. Frank had attacked the room a couple of times in fits of energy that stirred the dust and his temper and not much more.

Joyce pushed back the room's sliding door. Here, she sometimes had the feeling of time standing still. Lining the inside wall were cartons of old clothes, abandoned dolls, and discarded games. Under the window stood the white bookcase she had brought with her when she and Frank were married. Next to it was a jumble of outgrown tricycles and bicycles waiting to be grown back into.

Where to start? Shaking her head at the enormity of the job ahead of her, Joyce pulled a three-legged stool to the bookcase. How easily she remembered the day she had painted the piece of furniture white, all the coats of white paint it had taken to cover the knotty pine finish. Funny, she could still see her small childhood room with the blue flowered bedspread on the bed. She could still see the newspapers spread over the floor as she added another coat of paint. The paint was chipped now, and grimy from dirty fingers.

Not much worth keeping, she thought as she peered across the shelves. Debbie and Maryann had already taken what they wanted. It wasn't likely Frankie and the baby would want many of the other books. In the open box at her side went a couple of old math books. As she sifted through the books, she sifted through her past. Some things were vivid. Others were obscured by time and eclipsed pieces of her memory. Her high school yearbook, the one thing she thought might make some order out of her jumble of memories, wasn't on the shelf. Maybe in her old cedar chest. Joyce made a mental note to look for it later.

She threw a geography book from twenty years earlier into the box. And there was eleventh-grade biology. That one brought back memories. Poor Mr. Finney, who lived across from the school with his father. Joyce couldn't remember which of the boys it was who finally sent Mr. Finney running from the classroom in tears, and she couldn't remember what the boy had said to push the teacher over the edge, but she remembered the defaced poster of the human reproductive system, and how some of the kids had howled with laughter while others sat in embarrassed silence. Her own response was lost to her. She could have gone either way, she knew. She had been shy, easily tongue-tied, but she had also been dazzled by the kids who weren't, the bold ones, the ones who manipulated the rest of them. What had been that one boy's name? Football quarterback, captain of the swim team. Pete Robbins.

Tag ends of things came back. Pete Robbins, tan and muscular, occupying as only he could the lifeguard's platform at the public pool where many of the kids spent their summer days. He had a reputation for being a little wild, and Joyce, already dating staid, dependable Frank Neuhauser, had been tantalized by stories of Pete's exploits—women, cars, six-packs of beer, marijuana. Pete was invited to every party, knew everyone, tried everything at least once.

That summer before their senior year, she'd worn a new red bathing suit and Pete Robbins had smiled approval down from the lifeguard's platform. Oh, the fantasies that smile had started. They had remained fantasies. Pete Robbins's girlfriend's name escaped her, but she had been the prettiest girl in the senior class. That, Joyce was sure of.

Something else plucked at her memory then. There had been rumors around school those first weeks of their senior year. Whispers, lowered voices. Something serious. Joyce closed her eyes, trying to gather the filaments of the memory into a tight knot. It had been bad; she knew that much. Even now, fifteen years later sitting in her basement storage room, she knew that this thing had been serious. Pete Robbins had been involved. Drugs, maybe? She didn't think so, but it had been the seventies. Drugs had been everywhere.

Joyce rubbed her temples, but this stubborn recollection remained buried.

Whatever had happened, Pete Robbins had emerged unscathed. Senior year, he'd been voted class president and, later, king of the senior prom. Joyce dropped the old biology book into the box of discards. Wasn't life strange: The humiliations of eleventh-grade biology thrust onto poor, strange Mr. Finney, and a perfect tan bestowed on Pete Robbins by the first of June every year.

Chapter 10

DURING the next few days, things fell into place for Ronnie, so neatly that the possibility of failure, even the possibility that there might be another way to do things, ceased to exist for him. Having seen Deborah's mother coming out of that house—and so now knowing where Deborah lived—propelled Ronnie into action.

On Monday, he gave Vittucchi a downpayment on the van. His boss pocketed the money and asked no more questions about what Ronnie planned to do with the vehicle. After work that day, Ronnie left the van at a drive-in paint shop. When he picked it up late the next afternoon, it was black as night.

Ronnie had envisioned a deep, reflective ebony. The old finish, though, had absorbed the coats of paint, and the van was now a flat black—so dull, its surface would absorb a spotlight at midnight. Disappointed, Ronnie spent hours that evening waxing the paint, trying to force a shine where none existed. That night, the flat-black paint lay like a shroud across his fantasies until he convinced himself that the paint job wouldn't matter to Deborah. What mattered to her was their love.

At a Western Auto store in a nearby shopping center, Ronnie

picked out opaque shades for the van's windows. He chose an island scene, an orange sun setting over the water, glimpsed between fringes of palm trees. That evening, he spent hours meticulously cutting the shades and pressing them into the windows. They gave the van's bare interior a cool, secretive look.

Arranging the Chevy's sale was easy. Carlos, the Puerto Rican kid from Vittucchi's, stood in the weedy lot next to the laundry, running his hands over its surface and kicking the tires.

"Yeah, man," the kid said, slamming the door so hard that the window rattled. "I'll pick it up payday. A deal?"

"Sure," Ronnie answered, ignoring the boy's extended hand. At one time, the whole process would have disgusted him—this foreigner treating Mother's car like some piece of trash on a used-car lot. Now, though, the Chevy meant nothing more than quick cash to Ronnie. When Carlos paid him for the Chevy, he could pay Vittucchi for the van.

Only one thing was important now: Deborah. She dominated his thoughts, taking most of his time. Not like a thief who takes away something, but as someone who is entitled to something possesses it and nourishes it.

On Friday, twelve days after Ronnie found Deborah's house, he found Deborah.

He was driving Vittucchi's new van, a big medium blue Ford with a white logo like the one on Ronnie's uniform. He'd been past her house once that day and many times during the days before without seeing her. She wasn't the kind of girl who would hang out on the streets, but it had been too long. He had to find her.

It was almost four in the afternoon when Ronnie drove to Our Lady of Mercy. The school was situated on a grassy knoll off one of the secondary state roads. At one side was pastureland. On the other, a quiet street separated the school from the narrow band of woods that ran behind Old Covered Bridge Estates. Ronnie pulled the van onto that side street as the final bell of the day rang. Then he waited.

The exodus began with a trickling of girls filing rapidly

through the school's double doors. The girls all were dressed in plaid skirts and white blouses. Some of them wore dark blue sweaters. The trickle grew heavier, turning, for a few minutes, into a flood. The girls were so much alike that the sight of them stupefied Ronnie. How would he even know her? A chorus of bright young voices carried across the school yard into the van's open window. Ronnie adjusted the sun visor to shield himself. He then began searching the young girls' faces, trying to focus for an instant on each one before moving to the next. There seemed to be hundreds—hundreds of the same noses, the same eyes, the same hair. There. Or there? Was that Deborah? He leaned against the window frame, straining to distinguish one girl from a dozen others before she disappeared into the crowd.

At the end of the sidewalk that led from the school door, the group thinned. Some of the girls got onto a waiting bus; others climbed into cars parked at the curb. And suddenly, magically, Deborah filled Ronnie's vision, so sharp, standing out so clearly from the rest that she might have been the only girl there. She walked with two other girls, a yellow canvas bag swinging on her shoulder. At the corner, the three girls turned toward the van.

A rush of fear blotted out all Ronnie's other feelings. He wasn't ready to speak to her, not yet. Settling back into the seat, he bent his arm around the window frame to shield himself from the sidewalk. As she walked toward him, talking with her friends, he recognized her voice and her laugh. A second later, the girls veered into the street and passed directly in front of the van without looking at it.

They entered the woods on a wide, cleared path. Before Deborah disappeared into the trees, she turned her head and seemed to stare directly into Ronnie's eyes. His heart leapt and he turned away. Had she seen him? Could she look at him like that and not know him? Had her eyes locked on his, sending him a secret message? Of course! His fear gave way to such excitement that even after the girls were gone from his view he remained breathless.

Minutes passed before he was able to start the van, before he trusted himself to drive. And he couldn't trust himself the other way, either. As he pulled onto the state highway, he knew he wouldn't be able control himself that night. He would do that dirty thing he had promised Mother he wouldn't do again. Mother had been so angry when she called the strange number that appeared on their phone bill.

The phone sat on a small table in the hall, between Ronnie's room and his mother's. Ronnie made sure the door to Mother's room was shut before he dialed.

"Dream date," a soft female voice at the other end of the line said. "Tell me your dream and I'll make it come true for you."

Ronnie knew what she looked like, this husky-voiced woman. He'd seen her picture, or pictures of women just like her, on the television late at night. She wasn't the kind of girl he liked, but she knew where to find those girls for him. She'd done it before. She'd done it three times when Mother was alive, and dozens of times since Mother died.

Ronnie hadn't called the woman since he'd met Deborah, and he worried that maybe the girl he liked was gone. "There was a younger girl there. I want to talk to her."

"Susan is here," the woman said. "She's seventeen, and she'd love to talk to you."

"No," Ronnie said sharply. Glancing at the door to Mother's room, he lowered his voice. "Younger."

Ronnie's dream date that night was Candy, age eleven, she told him. And yes, she said, she did remember him from the last time they'd talked. She'd thought about him a lot since then. Candy told him what she looked like, and that she was pretty and no, she would never wear makeup.

"Is your hair still long?" he asked.

"Is that how you like it? Long?"

"Yes," he said hopefully.

"Well, it's still long. Way down my back."

The way she described herself, she reminded him of Deborah.

114

He knew, of course, that Candy wasn't really a nice girl like Deborah. Deborah would never talk to men the way Candy finally talked to him. Guilt cast a small shadow over his pleasure. He could never let Deborah know about this dark, secret thing he did.

One morning the next week, Vittucchi rode Ronnie nonstop for five minutes. As Vittucchi ranted, Ronnie could feel the Indian woman's medicine pouch rubbing against his chest. He carried Deborah's shark's tooth necklace in it now, along with the page from the phone book. Knowing these things were there made him feel better, helped him remember that nothing Vittucchi said meant anything. They were just loud words. They had nothing to do with Ronnie's world. He gave back "Yes, Sir"'s automatically and meaninglessly.

"I got the nursing home on my back, 'cause, Ronnie"—Vittucchi stabbed the delivery list with his stubby forefinger—" 'cause yesterday you forgot them. The thing is, Ronnie—"

And then his boss did what Ronnie hated the most. Vittucchi put his arm around Ronnie's shoulder and leaned over until his ugly red face was inches from Ronnie's and it was impossible to escape from the older man's cigar breath.

"Like I always said about you, I know it isn't no attitude thing. You always had a good attitude, Ronnie. The customers like you. I like you. What you got to do is start paying attention to what's on the list. Seems like you're slipping lately. Like the last few months, you don't seem to care no more."

"Yes, sir."

"You upset, maybe, 'cause I made Carlos assistant manager? That it?" Vittucchi asked, his voice dropping. Without waiting for an answer, the big man took Ronnie's arm and led him away from the plant door. "You got to understand how it is. Carlos, he's a Puerto Rican. I don't promote him, I got the EEOC on my back. Hadn't been for the EEOC, you would of had the job. You understand that, Ronnie?"

The promotion? How could Vittucchi be dumb enough to

think Ronnie would want some stupid promotion. For the first time in twelve years on the job, Ronnie had a sudden desire to laugh at one of the jokes he'd heard around Vittucchi's plant. Only this time, he was the only one who knew the joke. "Yes, sir," he said.

"You're my front man, Ronnie. My public-relations guy. Remember that. And try to stay on the ball."

Ronnie took care of all the customers that day—the nursing home with its pale, shrunken old people and its pee-smelly sheets, the café with its greasy tablecloths—bundle after putrid bundle piled in the back of the van. It was minutes before four o'clock when Ronnie pulled up at Our Lady of Mercy. Parking far back, so that the van could be mistaken for one of the vans delivering to the school's cafeteria, he climbed from the door that faced away from the school's windows and hurriedly crossed the street.

The dirt path into the woods was wide and well traveled. Weeds had been trampled down along its edges. Ronnie walked purposefully, hardly pausing along the path's unfamiliar curves. There would be a perfect place, he knew, because everything else was perfect. Through the thin cover of trees, the houses of Old Covered Bridge Estates were visible on his right. On the left, the trees were denser. When the path veered to the right about fifty feet into the woods, Ronnie stopped.

He examined the trees around him carefully, then the low bushes. Just beyond the curve, a low-hanging branch of a young maple tree jutted into the path at about the height of his chest. At the top of a slight rise on the left where the growth was thicker, there were trees mature enough to conceal an adult.

He tested the maple branch. In the distance, the school bell rang. He had to move quickly now.

Ronnie lifted the leather pouch from around his neck. Pulling apart the ties, he took the shark's tooth necklace from the pouch and draped its thin chain over the low branch. He pushed the branch with his fingers; the shark's tooth bobbed up and down, tantalizingly. She had to notice it, and when she did she would

116

understand he was trying to reach her. Shoving the leather pouch carelessly into his pants pocket, he stepped into the heavy bushes on his left.

The undergrowth was denser than he'd thought. Branches slapped at him. A vine, its tentacles lined with barbs, scraped his exposed forearm. Ignoring the stings, Ronnie climbed to the top of the rise. He shoved his way beyond the big trees and positioned himself behind one of them. Stooping, he pushed an opening in the branches so that he had a clear view of the curve in the path.

Though the leaves were now tipped with the red and gold of autumn, the afternoon was warm. Insects buzzed through the thicket. Ronnie brushed something away from his neck. Seconds later, a dozen bugs swarmed around his eyes. He rubbed his arms together noiselessly. The cuts from the barbs had started to itch. Finally, from up the path, he heard girls' voices. It sounded like at least two of them. He saw the flick of the first plaid skirt at the bend, the sleeve of a white shirt, bright against the foliage. Then Deborah's yellow canvas bag swung into view. Ronnie moved to one side, trying to see their faces. A branch snapped across his leg, and he tensed until he was sure they hadn't heard.

He stretched until he could see the three pretty young-girl faces shining briefly when the sun hit them, then shadowed by leaves. Deborah walked between her friends. She was by far the prettiest of the group. Her hair was in a ponytail that swung as she walked. She had a blue sweater draped over her shoulders. Ronnie smiled. She was so lovely that for a moment he forgot why he was there. He could just watch her forever. Then an unfamiliar voice carried up the hill.

". . . going to the mall Friday night," the tallest girl was saying. "Are you going to meet us there?"

"If I can, Lisa, but I'll have to sneak out," Debbie answered. "My mom and dad are going somewhere and I've got to baby-sit."

"Again? Yuck! We're going to Pop's Pizza. Some boys from Central High are going to meet us there. There's this one guy you might like. He's getting his license. . . ." The girl paused midsentence. "Look. What's that?"

The maple branch bobbed, then lashed into the air. Ronnie held his breath as the girl named Lisa picked the necklace from it.

It seemed to Ronnie that Debbie was transfixed. "This is utterly strange," she finally said.

"What's strange about it?" asked the third girl.

Deborah looked at the other girls, and Ronnie knew she wanted to tell them about him. She wanted to brag, to tell them she had this new boyfriend.

"It's just . . . you know . . . weird," she said, "the way it's hanging over the branch."

"Oh, sure. Weird," said the tall girl. "Rad! I bet those sixth-grade boys put it here. They're so retarded." She balanced the tiny white trinket in her palm. "Plastic. I can tell."

"Let me see it, Lisa." Debbie took the chain in her hand and stared at it. Finally smiling, she hung the chain over her finger and began swinging the tooth in front of her friends. "You're getting sleepy. Your eye lids are growing heavy."

The girls squealed with laughter. Debbie was the last of the three to turn down the path. As she disappeared around the corner, Ronnie saw her drop the necklace into her sweater pocket.

Ronnie couldn't move. His confusion was too great. Again, too many thoughts were slamming around in his head. Why had she done that—pretended she didn't know he had left the shark's tooth? The necklace meant so much to both of them. Why had she used it to make her friends laugh like that? And why had she said it was weird? His confusion gave way to rage as an idea rumbled up from deep inside him: Had somebody been telling her lies about the bad time?

Everything that had been so clear suddenly clouded. Ronnie slumped against the tree, trying to think.

Deborah had taken the necklace with her. That meant that she wanted it. And if she wanted it, she wanted him. She hadn't told her friends about him because she knew how friends could turn on you. Deborah couldn't know about the bad time. Only the Indian woman had known Ronnie's secrets, and he had been careful not to let her find out about Deborah.

With the falling shadows, the air around Ronnie was cooling, but he was drenched in sweat. Reaching into his pocket, he pulled out his handkerchief and mopped his brow. Unnoticed, Bobbie Yellowfeather's leather medicine bag fell to the ground behind him. He fought his way from the thicket, ignoring the barbs that grabbed his arms. As he made his way down to the path, his toe caught the leather pouch and knocked it through the undergrowth onto the steepest part of the hill.

To Ronnie, the atmosphere where the girls had stood seconds earlier seemed charged with life. He ran his fingers tentatively along the low maple branch. He and Deborah were connected. He experienced it as strongly as if he was holding her hand in his. The good feeling stayed with Ronnie until he was back in Vittucchi's van.

"Friday night . . . the mall." That was Lisa who had said that. The wild girl. The one who was always getting into trouble. And the boys from Central High—Lisa wanted Deborah to meet one of those boys. Ronnie thought about what that boy might want to do to Deborah, and a prickle of cold sweat ran down Ronnie's spine.

He'd waited long enough, Ronnie told himself as he started the van.

Debbie waved good-bye to her friends and crossed the field into her yard. She'd never mentioned the man on the beach to anyone. With the way Lisa was—always so smart about everything, always making fun of the two younger girls—she was sure to have something nasty to say if Debbie told them about the man.

Anyhow, there was nothing to tell. It was just coincidence. Why would a grown man do anything so stupid as hang cheap jewelry over branches in the woods. Her father would never in

119

a million years do anything so dumb. As she walked through the kitchen door, she fingered the shark's tooth necklace in her sweater pocket. There was no way it could be the same necklace. Just no way.

Chapter 11

ON the highway side of the iron bridge, partially hidden by the sign for Old Covered Bridge Estates, is a big dusty lot where teenagers gather in the evening, gunning their engines and playing their radios. Every now and then, a county police car comes along and shines its light across the parked Cameros and young faces, but it is understood by everyone, even parents, that nothing too bad ever happens there. On school nights, the crowd usually breaks up by nine.

That October evening, one car remained after the others had gone. The passengers, a boy and a girl, argued. The girl jumped from the car, slamming the door angrily. The boy gunned the engine and roared off in a trail of dust.

The girl was small for her age, her body lean and strong as a dancer's. With a defiant glare after the disappearing taillights, she walked to the shoulder of the highway and put out her thumb.

Anxiety pulled at Ronnie that night. He'd already cleaned Mother's room and straightened the rest of the house. Carlos was picking up the Chevy the following day. Ronnie's old life was almost over. With his new life drawing close, the walls of the house he'd shared with Mother seemed to be pulling in, imprisoning him. He decided to drive by Deborah's house.

He drove much faster than he ordinarily did. A light rain had begun falling, and the Chevy sometimes felt as if it were skimming through the air. At a slight curve, Ronnie hit the brakes. His heart pumped with fright as the rear wheels spun out. For a moment, there was only the sound of the wind and the wheels sliding across the dark, slick pavement. When he brought the car under control, he was shaking. Approaching Old Covered Bridge Estates, he slowed.

Suddenly, beyond the arc of his headlights, someone was there—a one-dimensional figure at first, flat and ghostly against the dark. It was a girl, with long light brown hair and a bag hanging loose over her shoulder. As the girl came into focus, something about her shook Ronnie's senses. She had a scarf over her head, but her hair hung in damp strands over her shoulders. When his headlights were fully on her, she stood frozen and Ronnie was reminded of a stilled doe. The girl was not Deborah, but she was very much like Deborah—young and sweet. The thought of Deborah standing in the rain filled Ronnie with sadness. He pulled to the shoulder ahead of her and waited for the girl to catch up.

"Are you going to Yorkville Heights?" Her voice was small and breathless.

"I'll take you."

She bent and peered through the car window, staring frankly. A good girl, cautious about getting in a car with a stranger. Ronnie was touched by that. When she hesitated for a second before opening the door, Ronnie leaned across the seat and pulled the handle for her. "I live near there."

She bounced into the car. Pulling off her scarf, she smiled across the seat at him. The overhead light shone on her face, deepening faint crevices on her forehead and darkening blue shadows under her eyes. For a moment, she looked astonishingly old. Then she slammed the door. The light extinguished and she was young again. Ronnie pulled back on the road.

"What are you doing out here alone?"

The girl lifted her hair away from her shoulders and twisted it behind her neck. "My boyfriend and I had a fight. The creep left me in the rain. I'm glad you stopped. I was afraid I'd never get a ride."

He looked at the girl from the corner of his eye. She had her face half-turned, half-resting on the window frame. The anger in her chin had softened and Ronnie saw a sweet childlike delicacy in her expression. She gave off a faint perfume, the smell of flowers. She excited him, and for an instant, before he realized that she was doing something bad, he enjoyed the way she was making him feel.

When he looked at the girl again, she had turned toward him. She smiled, a sly cat-faced smile, and Ronnie's growing excitement was suddenly tinged by fear.

Bad, bad, a ghostly voice said. This wasn't a good girl. She was putting these bad thoughts into his head. Deborah would never do that. This girl might even be trying to tempt him away from Deborah. The knowledge hit him hard and his stomach knotted.

Ronnie looked straight at the girl. She had slumped against the door again. There was a gentle shadowy curve to her neck, and something frail and almost sad about the way she held herself. She was all right now. But she could change—good to bad to good. He had just caught her doing that. He had to stay alert.

The girl noticed that he was watching her. Her smile was slight and quizzical. Ronnie looked back at the road. Ahead, it was straight and clear.

"Clean car you've got," the girl said. "It's an old one, isn't it? Like from the early eighties?"

"It's my mother's," he said.

The girl rubbed the upholstery on the seat between them. "The inside's in good shape. My boyfriend drives a Taurus. It's his father's, actually. It's really hot." Leaning toward him suddenly, she reached up to the dashboard and turned the radio on. "Let's have some music."

Ronnie clenched his teeth and tightened his hands on the wheel. Her nearness had caused a tidal wave of dirty thoughts to wash over him. He was afraid to look at her again. If he did, she would make the feelings worse.

The girl had settled back into her seat.

"Nice girls don't hitchhike," Ronnie said.

"Jesus!" the girl snapped. "What are you? My old man? This sure isn't my day. Why is everyone giving me such a hard time? You can let me out up here at the intersection. I can walk from . . ."

Such bitches, all of them, like this one, with her sly cat face, her girl cat's teasing face, leading him on. All of them trying to make him think about things he shouldn't think about, trying to get guys in trouble. There was something wrong with this one, too. A voice in that hidden part of Ronnie's mind that knew which girls were the bad ones kept telling him about this girl. The Shark knew how to handle these girls, but the Shark hadn't been around in a long time. Ronnie had to take care of this girl himself.

The Chevy shot through the yellow light. Ronnie glanced at her again, unable to help himself.

She had huddled against the door. Her eyes were wide and white showed all around their edges. Her lips were pressed together and when she opened them to speak, her voice trembled.

"Look, mister. Why don't you pull over anywhere and I'll get out."

In the dim light, her shadowy features ran together before his eyes, reforming themselves, for a second, into something grotesque, something old and bloated. The half-hidden, half-formed thing that had hovered out of his reach came to him then.

"She sent you, didn't she?"

"Who?"

"The Indian woman."

"What are you talking about?"

Ahead of him, two circles of red light drew closer. Ronnie

124

lifted his foot from the accelerator as he approached a slow-moving car, then inched out to pass it. Headlights bore down on him. He pulled back into his own lane. The car ahead slowed and its left turn signal began flashing.

Ronnie saw the girl's move only after she had started it, when her hand had already gripped the handle and the Chevy's door was opening. A blast of cold damp air whipped through the car. The tires swerved wildly as Ronnie made a wild one-handed grab across the seats. For a second, the sleeve of her jacket was in his hand, then it slipped away. She jumped. The door slammed violently behind her. When Ronnie looked back through the mirror, there was no one at the roadside.

She left him shaken. He didn't know why, but he knew the Indian woman had sent the cat-faced girl. Should he wheel the car around and chase her? A new, grim thought struck him: The girl with the cat face was running through the night toward Deborah's house. She was going to tell Deborah terrible stories about him.

A half mile down the road, Ronnie pulled off at an all-night convenience store and waited impatiently for a couple of boys to get off the public phone. When they'd finally gone, he stepped into the booth and deposited his quarter. This wasn't the first time he had gotten this far—put his coin in and hesitated, fearful, with his finger poised above the dial. Though every secret signal Deborah gave him said she loved him, he hadn't been able to overcome the fear of her rejection. Now, though, he had to reach Deborah. He wanted to tell her the truth about the bad time before the cat-faced girl got to her.

His hand was steady as he dialed the familiar number. There was the first ring, and then another. The third ring was cut short when a woman answered.

"Hello?"

He knew the words. He had said them often enough to himself: Is Deborah there? He thought them now, so clearly that it seemed almost certain they could travel through the wires.

"Hello," the woman's voice said again.

He mouthed the words into the receiver—Is Deborah there?—straining to make himself heard, but no sound came from him.

There was a click on the other end. The phone went dead.

Ronnie cradled the phone and slumped against the wall of the booth. A wave of despair washed over him. He was going to lose Deborah if he didn't do something soon.

Joyce heard the soft click of the receiver falling into place. She thought there had been someone on the other end, but she wasn't sure. "Another hang-up call," she said.

She looked into the den at Debbie and Frank. Frank was dozing on the recliner. Debbie sprawled on the sofa, books and sheets of paper surrounding her. Neither of them looked up. "Maybe it didn't even ring," Joyce said to herself. "Maybe I really am crazy."

Sometimes she was sure she was. She had seen the man again, the day before. She had glimpsed him behind the wheel of a blue van as she emerged from the car wash. Or had she? Her windshield had been streaked with a film of water and the man's face had been distorted. By the time the attendant had dried the glass, the van had disappeared.

Sitting in the chair by the phone, Joyce tried recalling the face again. If she could once catalog it—give it a name and a place and a time—the man would stop haunting her. But surrounded by the normalcy of the house, the sound of the television and the dishwasher running in the kitchen, the face eluded her.

She got up with a sigh and picked her daughter's blue sweater from the chair.

"Bedtime, Debbie. And take your clothes up to your room."

"In a minute."

"And pick up your papers, too."

"All right! I'm coming." Debbie kissed her father's cheek— "Night, Daddy"—before she gathered her papers. As she walked toward the kitchen, she took her sweater from her mother. Something dangled from the pocket, then dropped and

126

hit the linoleum floor with a *ping*. Bending, Debbie absently picked up the shark's tooth necklace.

Joyce's conscious seemed to explode with fragments of the stranger's face—light gray eyes, smooth sunburned skin, glistening with water.

"Night, Mom," her daughter said.

"Where did you get that?"

Debbie stopped at the foot of the stairs, her sweater and the papers bundled in one hand and the shark's tooth dangling from the other.

"Get what?"

"That." Joyce's hand shook as she pointed at the necklace.

Debbie raised her hand until the necklace swung in front of her face. "I found it in the woods."

Joyce took a deep breath, knowing she was close to losing control. "Please, Debbie." She tried to keep her voice low, but she couldn't. "Don't lie to me!"

Frank appeared at the kitchen door. "What's going on?"

"She's losing it again," Debbie snapped. "That's what." Throwing the necklace into the kitchen, Debbie ran up the stairs.

Frank turned to his wife. "What the hell was that about?"

Joyce slumped into the chair by the phone and rubbed her temples. "I don't know." With an angry kick, she sent the necklace sliding across the kitchen floor. It disappeared under the refrigerator, unnoticed by either of them.

"I know Debbie can be difficult, but maybe you could try to be a little more patient with her," Frank said, shaking his head. When he had switched off the television, he followed his daughter up the stairs.

That night, Joyce's nightmare was back—more vivid and more terrifying than before. The pressure pushed at her again, deeper into the water this time, forcing her life from her. She fought against the swirling blue around her, waking with a stifled scream when sleep became too terrible.

Joyce took a deep breath, then another. Her skin was damp,

as if she had been caught in a sea mist. A breeze ruffled the bedroom curtains and passed over her, raising cold bumps on her skin. Around her, the house slept. She was only vaguely aware of Frank's breaths rising and falling. The panic left slowly, but, when it was gone, she left the bedroom, quietly closing the door.

At vacation's end, her plastic beach tote that held the Provincetown newspaper had been stuffed into the back of the hall closet. A few minutes of rummaging and Joyce had the Provincetown paper in her hand. She retreated to the kitchen and, for the first time since that morning when she'd hidden on the steps of Provincetown's town hall, she examined the inky outlines for a clue to whatever it was that was haunting her. The face kept its secret.

She glanced at the clock over the stove. It was almost 1:00 A.M. She had already arranged to leave Frankie and Andy with Gloria the next morning so she could get to a conference with Maryann's teacher. Then there was her weekly appointment with Dr. Weisman, and then some grocery shopping, and then, then, then, well into the evening. She should try to get some sleep. She'd been trying to do without any pills, but maybe a glass of milk would help.

Taking the carton of milk from the refrigerator, Joyce carried it to the sink. As she picked a clean glass from the dish drainer, she glanced through a gap in the yellow and white kitchen curtains.

Someone was there! For a shocking moment, she thought there was a man moving across the backyard. A blink of her eyes and the figure was gone, lost somewhere in the shadows between their house and the Collinses'.

With a soft cry of panic, Joyce dropped the glass back into the drainer. Her first thought was that it was the man who haunted her; her second thought was to wake Frank. She stopped herself. What if it was nothing? What if it was Bill Collins? He'd been working in his yard that afternoon. Maybe he'd left something outside and was retrieving it from the light rain. There had already been one uproar in her house that night. She had to be certain before she caused another one.

Joyce opened the back door and stepped onto the flagstone path that ran along the back of their house. The half-moon was obscured by gray clouds, and the space between the two houses was full of shadows. The boxwood hedge that bordered the Neuhausers' garage looked dark and sinister. The two willow trees she and Frank had planted when they moved in shimmered ominously.

"Bill?" Joyce called softly. "Is that you?"

There was no sound, and no movement. At the Collinses' house, all the lights were dark except one shining through a back window. Their den. Of course! Bill had been watching a late movie and he remembered he'd left one of his garden tools outside.

A clanking noise from somewhere near their neighbors' garage told Joyce she was right.

"Bill?"

She had taken a couple steps toward the garage when suddenly her hand slipped into the mechanism that held the coiled garden hose. "Oh," she cried as the three-pronged metal sprinkler fell onto her foot.

When the pain passed, Joyce focused her gaze across the neighboring lawn. Nothing. There was nothing at all. She chuckled softly with relief. This was ridiculous—nothing but her overactive imagination at work. What would Frank say if he found her out here? Frank didn't believe in sinister shadows.

Ronnie drove home slowly and carefully. Two hours crouched behind the shrubbery in the Neuhausers' backyard had left him cold and wet but had taken the edge off his anxiety. He'd watched the house carefully, seen the rooms downstairs darken and the lights go on upstairs. By midnight, the entire house had been dark. The cat-faced girl hadn't ever appeared.

Ronnie had been on his way back to the Chevy when Deborah's mother opened the door. Why had she been out there, stumbling around in the dark and crying out and then laughing? Had she spoken to the cat-faced girl? And who was Bill? Ronnie knew he had to get Deborah and take her away from this place.

It was near dawn, with the veil of dark lifting in the east, when he fell into an exhausted sleep.

Before daybreak, the predicted heavy rain fell. The cold, hard downpour washed away the heat that had hung on so long and signaled the coming of cooler weather. Leaves, parched by the long summer, dropped into the path that ran between Our Lady of Mercy and Old Covered Bridge Estates. Tiny rivulets made their way through the dust, carrying the leaves along the path's sides, blending shapes and textures until original forms were obscured. Bobbie Yellowfeather's medicine bag was caught in a minuscule mud slide. When morning's light broke up the clouds, the pouch rested in a damp mulch at the base of a rotting log.

Chapter 12

FRIDAY evening, the Covered Bridge Mall was crowded with shoppers—middle-aged couples, women pushing strollers, an endless parade of wandering teenagers. It was the teenagers Ronnie watched: their clothes—tight, faded jeans slashed uniformly across the thighs, bright vests, leather jackets—their horseplay, and their laughter.

He had walked through the wide main doors, feeling intoxicated by anticipation. His mind buzzed with thoughts of Deborah. As he moved into the crowds, though, a cloud of confusion descended. There were so many girls. What if she wasn't even there? He'd spotted the Pop's Pizza sign on the outside of the mall, but inside, in the maze of shops and kiosks, in this place of miniature playgrounds and fake waterfalls, he couldn't find an entrance to the restaurant.

Ronnie followed the crowds around the inside of the mall, past stores where blank-eyed mannequins stood in tortured poses, neon lights bouncing off their hard angles. He remained alert for that special smile Deborah had, for the bell-like quality of her voice. Several times, he thought he had found her. His eyes would seek out the face that went with shining brown hair or with a sweet, chiming laugh. He would find himself staring into a stranger's eyes.

After half an hour, he edged toward a side exit, stopping near a couple of uniformed security guards. He didn't want to talk to them. He had wanted this night to be a special one—just his and Deborah's. But what if he never found her?

"There are a lot of kids here," Ronnie finally said to one of the guards. The man nodded, scarcely looking at him.

"How do you get into Pop's Pizza from here, anyway? I'm supposed to meet my girl there," he added. *My girl:* He liked the way that sounded. And wouldn't this man be jealous if he knew how wonderful Ronnie's girl was!

"There's no entrance from inside," the guard said. "You have to go out and walk around."

Ronnie left the mall by the main entrance and followed the wide sidewalk to Pop's Pizza. When he pushed through the door, he was assaulted by the throbbing beat of rock music that blared from gigantic speakers mounted on the ceiling. The mall had been crowded; Pop's Pizza was crammed. Kids were everywhere—waiting in lines, packed two deep around tables. Four burly men worked the big ovens behind the counter.

The fog of disappointment that Ronnie had been moving under began to break apart. There were so many of them that she had to be here. He would find her for certain. If she hadn't eaten yet, he'd buy a pizza. He'd get her anything she wanted on it—anything. They'd get it to go. They could eat it in the van. Deborah would love the way he'd fixed up the van. He'd already packed. Everything they were going to need for their new life together was in the van.

He began at the back of the restaurant and worked his way forward. He moved from table to thronging table, examining each girl's face closely before moving on to the next. At one table, a girl stared back frankly, then said something to a boy beside her. "You looking at something?" the boy asked.

Ronnie turned away. When he'd examined all the tables, he wove through the tight lines of customers near the counter, watching for Deborah. He came up behind a girl and touched her hair lightly with his fingertips. It was shiny and fell down her back straight, like Deborah's. The girl turned briefly, then moved closer to her friends.

He had worked his way to the front of the restaurant when he felt the hand on his arm. For an instant, he was gripped by such a spasm of excitement that he couldn't catch his breath. Deborah. Deborah was here.

Wheeling, he looked into the flushed, angry face of one of the countermen. The man wore a white apron streaked with dirty red stains. When Ronnie tried to speak, the man's grip tightened.

"Come on, buddy. Let's you and me step outside."

The man pushed him out the door.

"Now let's get something straight," the man said as he steered Ronnie across the sidewalk. "People come in my place, they come in to buy pizza. They don't come in to harass the girls. I've had three complaints about you in five minutes."

Ronnie tried to explain. "I'm looking for a special girl," he said weakly.

The man jerked his arm so hard that it hurt. "You can look for your special girl somewhere else, you sick fuck. Do yourself a favor and keep away from these little girls. Get! Move! I see you around here again and I'm calling the cops."

Little girls! Terror gripped Ronnie. The man knew. But how could he? It had been another town, and so many years ago. Fifteen. Nobody could know, except for the Indian woman and the cat-faced girl.

"You listening to me, buddy?"

Ronnie nodded, mute with fear. As soon as the man released him, he hurried to the van and left the mall.

The chairwoman of the Old Covered Bridge Estates Home Owners' Association was an elementary-school teacher with a voice that could split logs. She leaned forward on the dias and said to Joyce, "I'm not sure I understand what you mean by 'more important things.' Perhaps if you speak up . . ."

Joyce felt every eye in the basement of the Congregational church turn toward her, every ear cock, waiting for her response. She could imagine what a curiosity she was in the neighborhood. It wasn't every day that a housewife from Old Covered Bridge Estates tried to OD on Seconal, much less underwent shock therapy.

"I meant . . . What I was wondering was . . ." For a moment, what Joyce had planned to say about the proposed plantings on the median strip became a jumbled mass of meaningless words. Again gathering her thoughts, she forced the words out. "I was just thinking that maybe the money set aside for plantings could be used for something more pressing. Some neighborhoods," she added, "have hired security services to drive through them."

"I'm not sure we have the crime problem here to warrant a security patrol, but . . ." The chairwoman shrugged, and fanned her face with the minutes of the last Home Owners' Association meeting. "Whew! The temperature outside drops a few degrees and they turn on the heat full blast in here. Does anybody have a comment about Joyce's suggestion?"

"I haven't heard of any crime problem," said a woman sitting in the back row. "The plantings will do more for property values than having a rent-a-cop drive through every few hours."

"Most of those guys are even older and fatter than I am," a man said.

Someone snickered. The chairwoman suggested a vote be taken. The vote was taken; the plantings won by a landslide. Joyce's hand was one of the few raised for a security patrol.

"That's settled." The chairwoman glanced down at her agenda. "Let's move to the drainage problem at the corner of Evergreen Terrace. . . ."

Joyce took a quick look at Frank, who was sitting by her side. His back hugged the rigid outline of the metal chair. His face was quite pink, whether from the overheated room or her voted-down suggestion, she didn't know. Was it enough to

134

make him blush, that his wife wanted rent-a-cops cruising the neighborhood? He hadn't looked at her since she'd raised her hand. She followed his gaze down to the floor. Late in the year for white shoes, but surely he wasn't studying her white pumps. Still, she couldn't help noting the greenish smudge that showed across one toe.

"Polishing didn't help," she began in a whisper.

"Shush!"

Joyce's outfit—her blue print dress, stockings, the white pumps—was the result of several days' on-and-off consideration, and several minutes' hurried preparation. She hadn't worn the dress since before her last pregnancy, and hadn't realized how loose it would be. Her weight loss—by now she was down almost twenty pounds—delighted her, but the way this dress hung on her slimmer frame did not. She had made do by cinching her belt tighter, and felt sloppy among her neighbors. The nylons had been a mistake, too. In the heat of the basement, they clung to her legs, tight, damp, and cloying.

The meeting went on, item after item, speaker after droning speaker: drainage, streetlights, twenty angry minutes when one owner threatened to deface the pastel landscape with red aluminum siding.

"Become Involved," Frank always said. "Think about something besides your own troubles. Keep busy." Joyce was trying. She had already decided that she would volunteer for a committee. The security patrol, her pet for reasons she had shared with no one but Dr. Weisman, was out, but there was always drainage or school-crossing signs or speed bumps along the stretch where the kids drag raced.

Finally, there came the welcome rap of the gavel on the table. Joyce looked at Frank as he stood, wishing he would stay there with her, knowing he wouldn't. Frank liked these meetings. He was at his best in the impersonal camaraderie that permeated them. He'd sold lots of insurance policies by working the room at these meetings.

135

She could do that. Work the room, too, though to what end, she wasn't sure. She started to rise.

"Joyce, Joyce."

A thin, well-dressed woman was coming toward her, arms outstretched. Joyce sank back onto the metal chair. The woman took the seat Frank had vacated, then took one of Joyce's hands in her own. The minister's wife? Joyce wondered. Or that pushy woman who ran the flower shop?

"Frank told me you'd be here. It's so good to see you again. You look so . . . relaxed."

The woman was smiling into her face. Joyce smiled back. Overweight people often look relaxed, she could have told the woman. The fat stretches out their worry lines so that you can't tell they're ready to pull their hair out by its roots.

"I've noticed you walking past my house," the woman said.

Oh, no. She must be the minister's wife, thinking that Joyce was wandering the streets aimlessly. Joyce moved as if to rise. The woman's cool, dry hands continued pressing Joyce's hot, damp ones.

"And now I see you're jogging," the woman continued. "There are three of us who jog three nights a week at the high school track. Why don't you join us? It's more fun when you have company."

"Why, I'd love to," Joyce said, betraying only the slightest surprise.

The two women arranged to meet the following Monday evening. When the other woman dropped her hand and stood, Joyce quickly got to her feet, too. Her metal chair rocked back on its legs. The other woman righted it.

"Meet you Monday at the track."

When the woman had gone, Joyce let out a quiet sigh of relief. She felt as if she'd passed a test. She might be a curiosity, but she wasn't a social leper. Now all she had to do was come up with the woman's name.

She looked for Frank in the sea of faces, but he was nowhere to be seen. The chairwoman, who was responsible for staffing the volunteer committees, was in the center of a knot of people, all of them trying to get her attention. Joyce took a step toward the group, then faltered. Across the room, toward the back, was a table holding cookies, soda, and a few bottles of wine. Feeling momentarily adrift, she fled to its consolation.

Her hand hovered over the soda bottle but then found its way to the wine. Just a sip, enough to get up her nerve to charge into that group around the chairwoman. A first plastic glass of wine downed, miraculously soothing, a second . . . safe in her hand. She leaned against a wall and looked around the room. In the mass of unfamiliar faces, she spotted first one, then another she recognized. There was her new jogging companion trying to do something with the thermostat that controlled the heat. And the husband of the chairwoman—that tall, stooped man?

She was feeling better. She saw Frank among one group, and then another, holding intense conversations with committee members, or maybe just trying to sell them insurance. The idea struck her as funny. She giggled quietly. His hands gestured, formed a lopsided square. Was it a drain? Or a piece of aluminum siding? Maybe a hedge.

The room was growing warmer. She rubbed a hand across her forehead; it came away wet. Couldn't something be done about the heat? Joyce tried to twist the handle of one of the shoulder-high casement windows. It held fast. The glass felt cool to her touch, though, and she longed for a deep breath of fresh air. She began to imagine how it would feel sweeping into her lungs, bringing her to life. She leaned closer to the glass, her eyes fixed on traffic moving through a cone of light from the street lamp.

A van, big and black, filled the space. The driver, caught in the streetlights' glare, looked like that same man. A small distressed cry escaped Joyce, but no one overheard. She tried to focus on the man, but the van rolled away into the dark.

Debbie's words from the night before came back to Joyce: "She's losing it again." Losing it again! It was true. She was, and that thought was as horrifying as a dozen strangers in a dozen

137

different vans. This time, she was absolutely, unquestionably going out of her mind.

In her purse was a bottle of antidepressants Dr. Weisman had prescribed. *Take one as needed,* the label read. Her hand shook as she pried the lid off the bottle. Keeping her back to the crowded room, Joyce quickly put two of the pills on her tongue and swallowed them with the remainder of her wine. Pouring herself another glass, she turned and searched for Frank.

She found him easily this time. He was talking to a woman in plaid slacks. They both had plastic glasses in their hands. Frank always claimed he couldn't drink cheap wine. "Instant headache," he would say, dramatically pressing the back of his hand against his forehead. But there he was, cheap wine in hand, animated, laughing. The woman threw back her head and laughed with him.

What on earth could he have said? Joyce wondered, taking a sip from her glass. Their marriage had been much better in the past few weeks. There had been smiles—many of them—but laughter? No. Not yet. Joyce slumped against the wall behind her. Maybe she should be jealous of this woman, but she wasn't. That was the beauty of having so many other things to worry about.

The pills were working, the weight of worry about the man in the various vans evaporating into nothing. Now, if she could just walk over to Frank and his companion and join their conversation, everything would be fine. That's what any normal person would do. And that's what she would do.

When Joyce pulled away from the wall, she discovered that her dress had molded itself to the back of her legs. She reached back to pull it away. The floor seemed to undulate beneath her feet, rise toward her, and then recede until it was impossibly far away. Straightening quickly, Joyce moved into the crowd.

She could have been in a foreign country where everyone spoke in booming alien tongues. Straining, she picked up snatches: "So I told him what he could do with his automatic sprinkler system . . . it seems to me that trash collection . . .

zoned for single-family . . . day care." Conversations all ran together, none of them making sense. Pressing forward, she tried peering over heads and between bodies. Her arms rubbed against backs and shoulders. A big man swayed into her, and the wineglass in her hand pitched against his arm. She saw him flick at the wet spot on his shirt. He stared at her, and when his mouth opened he spoke in unison with the rest of them. Mouths moved together and words blended into a chorus that pounded in Joyce's head.

She pushed farther into the crowd. There was Frank, with that awful woman from the flower shop. No, no. He wasn't there. He was across the room by the door, and then he was gone. Was that his voice behind her? She spun. A spray of wine followed her movement. No. As she turned back, the room spun the other way, faces and bodies swayed together and faces began to blur—faces a blotchy, pallid pink abstraction, hair a swirling monochrome. The mouths of Old Covered Bridge Estates were dozens of tiny circles blending, voicing soft noises at her. They moved toward her. She stumbled back. They kept coming, their voices growing stronger. Her knees crumbled. Someone must have turned off the lights. As she reached her hands to her eyes, the room went black.

"Give her air, for heaven's sake." The chairwoman's chain-saw voice carried over the others. "Now, Joyce, you keep your head down on your knees. You'll be all right in a minute. It's so damned hot in here, it's a wonder we're not all passing out."

Someone was pressing something cool and wet across her face. Someone else was wiping the back of her neck. Joyce looked up into the circles of faces around her. There was her new jogging companion. When Joyce focused on her, the other woman quickly looked away. Joyce's stomach lurched.

"I think I have to vomit," she said into her knees.

"Let's get you to the ladies' room fast," the chairwoman said. "If you do it here, they'll never let us use this room again."

As she and the chairwoman rushed from the meeting, Joyce saw Frank watching her from the other side of the room.

★ ★ ★

Debbie sprayed cologne from a sample bottle onto her neck. Dabbing a sample smear of blusher on her cheeks, she stared into the round mirror. The glass magnified her features, making the pores on her face look gigantic and oily. And God! The pimple on her chin was huge!

It was so bright in the department store. The vivid fluorescent lights made her feel exposed, as if she was outside in the sun. And here came that snoopy old saleslady again. Hair dyed orange. Glittery blue eye shadow and about a ton of mascara. Perfect for the cosmetics counter.

"We close in a few minutes. You're sure I can't help you?"

Shaking her head, Debbie stared back down into the glass case where the more expensive makeup was displayed. She couldn't look at the clerk. If she looked at the woman, she might start laughing. She couldn't look at the nail polish displayed in the rack on her left, either. That might give it away. And she definitely couldn't look over at the other side of the counter where Colleen and Lisa were pretending to sample perfumes. If she did, she'd break up for sure.

"In a minute," she said to the clerk.

As the clerk walked away, someone brushed against Debbie.

"Pardon me," a woman said.

Catching her breath, Debbie glanced over her shoulder. A short black woman with a shopping bag had moved down the aisle. Relieved, Debbie shrugged. "That's okay." She couldn't help it then. Her glance slid away from the makeup, past her oversized reflection, past the rack of nail polish, to the expensive perfumes displayed on the other counter. Her eyes met Colleen's, and Colleen's serious-shopper expression crumbled into laughter. Lisa didn't laugh. She examined a perfume bottle carefully, then dabbed a drop onto her wrist and sniffed delicately. When she glanced back at Debbie, she gave the younger girl a sly, knowing smile. "I dare you," she mouthed.

Debbie took a quick look at the clerk. The woman was at the

other side of the counter now, helping someone at the register. Lisa's lips moved again: "Dare you. Dare you."

Debbie's left hand began climbing the kaleidoscope of nail polish. Her nails were jagged, chewed raw. Dumb, she thought. I'm stealing something I don't even use. Her fingers inched cautiously across the plastic-capped bottles: Passion Fruit Pink, Kiss Me Tangerine. One more: Strawberry Frost. A fast, deft move and the three bottles were in Debbie's pocket.

The orange-haired clerk was still at the register. Stepping quickly away from the counter, Debbie stole a look at her friends. Something was wrong. Lisa was leaving, already moving toward the door that led into the central mall. And Colleen. What was she looking at? Why was she staring past Debbie's head. For an instant, Colleen's eyes locked into Debbie's. Debbie recognized the other girl's fear. She saw Lisa take her sister's arm and quickly lead the younger girl away.

"Young lady!"

The voice came from behind her, an aisle away. As Debbie turned, she looked at the exit—not the one that opened onto the bright mall but the side exit leading to the parking lot. There was no guard at the door.

"I'm speaking to you, young lady."

It was the black woman, the one who had brushed by her minutes before. The woman was staring at her, her eyes hard, unblinking. Then . . . What was that? Something in the woman's hand. A gun! No. A two-way radio. As the woman approached, she pulled at an antenna and raised the device to her face.

For an instant, Debbie was frozen by fear. A store detective. Oh no! Her mom and dad! They thought she was home babysitting. What if the Home Owners' Association meeting let out early? What if Frankie woke up or Andy started crying? What if Maryann told. Maryann could be so rotten sometimes.

She hadn't meant it to go this far, hadn't meant to stay gone so long. Damn Lisa and Colleen, probably at Pop's Pizza laughing their stupid heads off while she was being arrested.

Debbie bolted for the door to the parking lot. Heart pounding, crashing past shoppers, she raced through the familiar aisles past women's purses and small leather goods, past women's shoes. Shoving through the revolving door, she ran across the wide sidewalk and street, into the parking lot, never looking back until she was safely crouched behind a car.

The woman detective was outside the revolving door, talking to one of the uniformed security guards. They both stared out into the lot. When the detective pushed back through the door, the guard walked slowly around the outside of the store toward the front of the mall. A moment later, he disappeared around the corner.

Safe! As Debbie let out a deep breath, nervous giggles convulsed her, almost bending her double. Now that she was safe, it was so funny. Hilarious. Wait till she told Colleen and Lisa. Wait till she showed them the three bottles of nail polish in her pocket. She'd show them, and then she'd keep all three bottles for herself, because they'd both chickened out and left her.

A few late shoppers were leaving the department store. It had to be almost 9:30, but, if she hurried, Debbie had enough time to meet her friends, show them the polish, and still beat her parents home.

Getting to Pop's Pizza, though—that was a problem. It was all the way on the other end of the mall. She couldn't go around the front, not with that security guard creeping around. And there was absolutely no way she could go through the department store.

Darting between cars, Debbie headed toward the service road that led around the back of the mall. She could cut through, past the Dumpsters and trucks and the employee entrances, and be on the other side in minutes.

Ronnie had driven through the quiet streets of Old Covered Bridge Estates. Twenty minutes passed before the paralyzing fear and the bad thoughts the counterman had provoked left him. When they were finally gone, replaced by an almost unbearable frustration, he returned to the mall, driving slowly so he wouldn't attract attention.

He parked where he could just see the door of Pop's Pizza and watch the customers passing through it. He thought he glimpsed Deborah's two friends hurrying into the restaurant, but he was too frightened of the counterman to go in and look for them. After a while, he'd started the engine and circled the periphery of the mall, driving past the Dumpsters in the back. Again, he stopped the van near Pop's Pizza, leaving the engine running in case the man came back.

Minutes passed and the needle on Ronnie's gas tank began wavering at half-empty. When he turned in his seat and saw that the big lot at the front of the mall was emptying, he faced his disappointment. Deborah wasn't coming.

His thoughts were ragged and painful. The only constant was the Indian woman. That morning, he'd discovered her little leather pouch was missing. During the night, the Indian woman had come into his bedroom and taken it. She had her magic now, and she had Deborah's address, too. He'd never removed the phone-book page from the pouch. If the Indian woman told Deborah about the bad time, that was the end of everything.

Ronnie could hardly bear the thought of going home. The Shark had come to him the night before while he was packing. Ronnie wasn't sure whether the Shark's visit, his first in weeks, was related to the Indian woman's or not, but the Shark had done something terrible in Mother's bedroom. Ronnie would never be able to go into that room again.

He slipped the van into first gear and began moving. One more time around the side and back of Pop's Pizza. Then he'd cut through the service road around the back. That way, he could miss the traffic lights and get directly onto the road into Old Covered Bridge Estates. He would drive by her house again. There was a chance she was waiting for him there.

Suddenly, a small, thin figure darted past a row of green Dumpsters at the edge of Ronnie's vision. He slammed his foot on the brake. It couldn't be Deborah. In the dim light, it could be anybody, anything. But Ronnie caught his breath as he let his foot off the brake. The van rolled slowly forward. There was the figure again, edging closer to the Dumpsters. A girl. What was she doing? Trying to hide?

The big black van coming slowly toward her absorbed the thin light until Debbie couldn't tell anything about it. Except she knew one thing. It had to be a police van. It was going so slowly, the driver looking so carefully. Behind her, where she'd just passed, she heard employees beginning to leave the department store by the back door. She couldn't go that way.

Tears welled in Debbie's eyes. Crazy, just crazy. A minute ago, she'd been laughing. Everything was crazy. They'd called the police over three lousy bottles of nail polish. "God, let me get away," she prayed. "I'll never do anything bad again. I swear I'll never sneak out again. I'll bring back the polish. I'll baby-sit my brothers and Maryann every night."

Debbie looked around, frantic. One side of the service road abutted the stores' back doors and loading docks. Along the other, where she now crouched, the row of Dumpsters ran along a brick wall. The wall had to be eight or ten feet high. But on the other side of that wall was a field, then the highway. The traffic light where she could cross and—safety. Old Covered Bridge Estates. She could do it in ten minutes if she ran the whole way.

She peered around the edge of the Dumpster. The van had stopped. She could see the driver's dark form in the front seat. In a minute, he would be out there, looking between the Dumpsters. She didn't have a choice. She took a deep breath, and another, then pulled herself on top of the Dumpsters.

Who would have thought sneakers could make so much noise? She jumped from the first Dumpster to the one by the wall. The banging! She sounded as if she was wearing boots. Behind her, the van's door slammed. She flung herself at the wall. Her arms were over, her elbows scraping against the brick. She hoisted a leg up.

"Deborah? Deborah Neuhauser?"

He had her. Almost unconsciously, she let herself drop back onto the Dumpster. Her friends had told. The security guards had gotten Lisa and Colleen and they'd told. There was no point in running. Resigned, Debbie slid back onto the pavement.

The man had opened the doors at the back of the van. Oh, no. Was it like the kind of van they put real criminals in? He was walking toward her now. She couldn't make out his face.

Debbie's knees were trembling until she almost couldn't hold herself up. She started to cry again. "I'm sorry. I'm sorry." Reaching into her pocket, she grasped one of the bottles of polish and held it toward the man. "I'll put them back. All of them. I promise. I'll never do it again."

A second later, his face was in the funnel of light. It was only a second, and then she recognized the man from the beach, the one with the shark's tooth necklace. As his hand closed over her wrist, the bottle of nail polish she was holding fell to the ground and shattered.

There was scarcely time for her shock to register before he had pulled her around the side of the van. A desperate hope stayed with her. Maybe he's really a policeman. But then she saw the tropical print covering the van's windows and she knew he wasn't. She screamed, "No, no," and fought him, pulling away. The man's grip on her wrist tightened. He wrapped his other arm around her and put his hand over her mouth. As they struggled, he kept saying, over and over, "Everything's all right, Deborah. Everything's all right."

She bit down on his palm as he dragged her to the open door and tried to force her into the van. Bracing her feet against the van's frame, Debbie pushed herself away from the horrible dark interior. The man shoved harder. Her head slammed against one of the open doors. Darkness closed over her.

At the department store's loading dock, the store detective cupped her ear. Nothing now, but a second before a girl's voice had broken through the night. The woman took another drag on her cigarette.

"Did you hear that?" she said to a young man standing inside the door.

"Hear what?" The man stepped past her.

"Sounded like a kid screaming for help. A girl, I think."

"What was she screaming?"

The woman shook her head. "I'm not sure, but it sounded like 'No, no.' "

The two listened. The body of a forty-foot semitrailer blocked their view, but an engine was running on the other side of it, over by the Dumpsters. The engine faded. A moment later, a bright red compact car roared around the truck. It was filled with kids—three in the front seat, three in the back. As they passed the loading dock, one of the girls was squealing, "Slow down. Slow down."

The young man looked at the detective. "There's your lady in distress," he said, stepping back through the door. "You're taking your job too seriously. Come on. Watch me lock up, so I can get out of here."

The woman didn't answer. Dropping her cigarette, she ground it out on the concrete and followed the man into the store, pulling the door shut behind her.

"I'm trying to be understanding about this, Joyce," Frank said. "But . . . Christ! A double dose of tranquilizers and three glasses of wine! What were you trying to do?"

Joyce didn't know whether she should answer that or not. What was Frank going to think if she told him that a man who drove a variety of vans was haunting her? When she spoke, she managed a tired quip.

"I'm like that joke, aren't I? 'Can't take her anywhere.' "

Frank had no response, and Joyce had no desire to talk anymore. They were quiet until they had rounded the corner onto their block.

"Everything's been going so well," he finally said. "Most

146

of the time, you seem happier than you were. Things like to-night . . . they make me wonder what the hell's going to happen to us. I want you to be okay, you know."

She did know, and that knowledge brought a lump to her throat. She knew that Frank loved her, and that he was devoted to their family. He'd struggled with a situation he scarcely understood in order to keep the family together. But she also knew she was married to a conventional and unimaginative man, a man who valued the appearance of normalcy almost as much as he valued normalcy itself. And knowing that, she doubted she could ever make him believe in a man she hardly believed in herself.

"I will be okay," Joyce said as Frank pulled into their driveway. "I only took the pills because I saw something that upset me."

Before she could continue, Frank had given a disgusted groan.

"Would you look at this! Every light in the house is on! Those kids think money grows on trees! Debbie should know better."

Joyce climbed from the car. She was near the kitchen door when she saw a small pink-gowned figure fluttering across the space that separated their house from the Collinses'. For a moment, it seemed like an apparition, a ghostly little specter, light against the black of the backyard.

"Maryann?" But Joyce's voice was soft, easily overwhelmed by Frank's.

"Now what the hell is going on out here?"

Their youngest daughter raced across the grass to her parents. The little girl's face was pink with excitement.

"Debbie went out," she said breathlessly. "She promised she was going to be back before you got home, but she hasn't come home, and then Frankie got scared and wanted all the lights on and then Andy started crying and I couldn't make him stop. . . ."

The side door to the Collinses' house opened and Gloria Collins walked onto her patio. In her arms was the Neuhausers' screaming infant. Frankie junior remained huddled in the doorway with Gloria's own two children.

"And I couldn't get him to stop, so I took him to Gloria's house, and Frankie just wouldn't stay home. . . ."

As Joyce reached to take the baby from her neighbor, the yellow porch light deepened the questioning lines in Gloria's face. "Is everything all right?"

"Everything's dandy," Frank shouted across the yard. "Maryann! Get in here!"

"Everything's fine," Joyce said. "I'll see you tomorrow." Balancing the baby on her shoulder, Joyce took Frankie's hand. As she led him back to their house, Maryann caught up with them.

"I'll bet Debbie's in trouble now, isn't she, Mommy?"

Chapter 13

IT was the worst kind of bad dream. As Debbie drifted into a hazy consciousness, she wondered whether she was dead. Vague images and terrible loud noises tore through her sleep and then faded into the background. The bright lights at the mall. A tall display rack of colorful nail polish. Lisa mouthing her silent words: "Dare you." The parking lot, the dark alley where the Dumpsters lined the brick wall. And the man. The man from the beach. The black van.

Debbie's mind cleared, and there was one image pushing the others away: the shark's tooth necklace, swinging from its gold chain.

With time, images and noises receded and the pain in her head became an acute, throbbing headache and she knew she was alive. Something cold and hard vibrated along the length of her back. A dull rumbling noise went on and on, but she couldn't tell where it came from.

All around was darkness. Something was pinching her face, pulling her skin taut. She tried to move her hands to her face, but they were gripped hard behind her.

It wasn't a bad dream. This was something worse—a bad

149

dream that followed her into consciousness. Wakening fully, the real terror returned. She was tied up in the back of that black van. The rumbling came from the engine. Kidnapped. With the horror of that knowledge, there was nothing for Debbie but all–consuming fear, a fear so alien that a part of her kept saying that this couldn't really be happening. Except that it was. Debbie tried to scream, but the screams were stopped by binding that tore at her lips, and she choked on her own anguished howls. Her body thrashed in panic, head and shoulders beating into the hard metal floor of the van. Her legs were wrapped in something heavy and hot. The more she twisted, the tighter the wrapping became.

Time passed, and Debbie's convulsions subsided into tears. The sounds she made were muted whimpers, the sounds of a small trapped animal. Unconsciously, she drew up her knees and bent her head until it rested against her chest.

She slept fitfully then, waking in bursts of anxiety, unable to tell how much time had passed. At some point, moisture seeped through the heavy cloth wrapped around her lips. She woke with a start, realizing she had wet her pants. Fully conscious, she started crying again.

The van swayed sharply, throwing her against the metal side. It slowed and began bouncing violently. After a few minutes, the rumbling of the engine stopped. Debbie's heart had been racing. When she felt the floor sway slightly with his footsteps, it began beating furiously against her rib cage.

She knew he was near her even before he spoke. He made muted sounds as he moved around—cloth being folded, the sound of metal against metal. She heard a match struck. A thin light flickered and caught.

She watched him set a kerosene lamp carefully beside her. He reached for her and unzipped the heavy thing that had bound her legs. It was a sleeping bag. When he moved it away from her, the cool night air swept across her and she shivered. He touched her ankles. She gazed through the dim light in horror as he slowly shook his head.

"I didn't have enough tape for your ankles. I had to use some rope. You're going to get rope burns. We'll get something for your skin when we stop." He sniffed the air delicately. "It smells bad in here. First chance we get, we'll air it out."

His hand still hovered over her ankles. She yanked her feet away from him. He lifted his hand and scooted closer, until his face was only inches from hers.

"Deborah. It's me. Ronnie. Don't you remember? You know I'm not going to hurt you. If you promise not to scream, I'll take the tape off your mouth."

For a moment, she couldn't move. Finally, she nodded.

"Okay, now," he said. "I'll try to do this slowly so it doesn't hurt you."

His fingers were on her face, touching her hair. A surge of nausea swept her. The gag was off. She was breathing hard through her mouth, crying at the same time.

"I'm sorry you got hurt," he said. "You were struggling so much. I would have let you ride up front with me. I just wanted you to see how nice I fixed it up back here for us." He shook his head sadly. "I'm sorry I had to tie you up."

"Please let me go home," she said, sobbing.

He frowned. "I know you don't mean that. Remember how we talked on the beach that day? Remember how nice it was?"

"No, no, no!" She screamed the words and bucked her body against the unyielding side of the van.

He threw himself over her, muffling her cries with his body. "Please, please," he kept saying. "We're close to the road. Someone could hear you. It's going to be nice. You'll see. Please. I know where there's this place near the dunes. There's a little house. It's so peaceful there. We won't have to worry about anybody finding us. Your parents will never look for you there. Please, Deborah."

When her convulsions subsided, he straightened. Lifting his arm, he ran his fingers across his damp sleeve and then looked at her, puzzled. After a second, his eyes widened.

"Oh."

151

Through the thin light, Debbie saw his lips wrinkle with distaste. He scooted to the far side of the van. "I didn't think about that. I guess I should have, but with everything else . . ." He was quiet for a moment. "Would you like to change into something of my mother's? I brought some of her things for you."

The thought repulsed her. She shook her head.

"You can't just stay . . . like that."

Debbie fought for composure, prayed that when she spoke, her voice wouldn't betray her fear.

"Maybe we could stop and buy me something to wear."

He'd been sitting with his head down, as if he didn't want to look at her. She held her breath, hoping he'd agree to her suggestion.

"It's after midnight," he said. "Nothing's open."

"Maybe there's an all-night drugstore. Where are we?"

"North of Boston, off Route Ninety-five."

"I'm sure there's one that's open in Salem," she said cautiously.

After a few seconds, Ronnie nodded. "Okay, Deborah. But you have to promise me you're going to be good. Promise?"

"Yes."

As he picked up the kerosene lantern, Debbie saw his glance fall on the roll of black tape. Putting the lantern aside, he tore off a length of it. "I'm sorry to do this, Deborah, but . . ." Pausing, he stared directly into her eyes. "I don't know why you would scream, but I'm afraid you would. Once we get to the Point, you'll see how nice everything is. But now . . ."

She raised her head, trying to protest, but before she could say anything he clamped the length of tape over her mouth. "I'm sorry, Deborah. Just keep thinking about how much I love you." He zipped the damp sleeping bag around her.

Ronnie climbed back into the driver's seat and started the engine. He was chilled, repelled by what she had done. Gross. How could she? Right in her pants! And she'd smelled like sweat, too! And some sweet, sticky perfume. The sour-sweet stench in the back of the van had revolted him, turned his stomach.

It was a good thing she hadn't wanted to put on Mother's clothes. Ronnie hadn't been able to salvage many of her things after what the Shark did. He didn't want Debbie wearing any of Mother's few remaining clothes until she had bathed.

As Ronnie pulled onto the highway, he tried to talk himself back into his earlier elation. For just a second, back in the alley behind the shopping center, the Shark had almost come out. Ronnie had heard the Shark's voice. Hit her, the Shark had said. He was glad he hadn't listened to the Shark. Deborah would be fine. She was already acting better. Once they got her some clean clothes and she washed—

A sudden picture—Deborah taking a shower—filled him with pleasure. Maybe someday she would let him watch. Not right away—a good girl wouldn't do that—but someday soon. The chill left him. He would buy some nice soap at the store.

He found an all-night variety store off the highway and parked at the back of the parking lot that sloped down toward the store. Peering through the curtain that separated the cab from the rest of the van, he saw that Deborah's eyes were open.

"I'll be back in a minute. You'll be quiet, won't you?"

She nodded.

The moment the door had slammed and his footsteps faded, Debbie tried pushing herself out of the tangle of the damp sleeping bag. The thing gripped her tightly and she thought she might never get out of it, but she kicked and struggled with all her strength and her torso burst free. Within seconds, her legs were out. She lay breathing hard for a moment, then started inching her way across the floor toward the cab.

Her progress was agonizingly slow. There were things piled between the van and the cab: suitcases, duffel bags. Her body quaked with fear as she made her way over them. Finally, her head poked through the curtain into the cab. Though her hands were bound behind her, she was able to rise onto an elbow and rock back and forth until she was on her knees. From that position, she began trying to climb past the emergency brake onto one of the seats. If she could get the door unlocked, she could throw herself onto the pavement and roll toward the store.

The soap was easy—almost too easy. There was half an aisle of soap. What kind did she like? He should have asked her. His eyes scanned the wrappers: body bars with bath oil, with skin conditioners, with perfume. No perfume. Perfume was for the wrong kind of girl. He selected an expensive bar that advertised itself as pure and natural, dropping it into the wire basket he'd picked up at the door. It joined two rolls of black tape, the bottle of shampoo—*Gentle enough for a baby,* the label read—and a tube of hand cream.

He felt stupid about the other thing—the girls' underwear. He knew where it was. He'd wandered past it as he combed the store's bright aisles. He'd paused in front of the cellophane-wrapped packages, not daring to touch them. It had to be done, though. He couldn't stand having Deborah smell that way.

Ronnie strode by the checkout counter, where a young male clerk drank coffee and read the newspaper sports page. The one other customer, a woman, approached the counter with a box of cereal and a carton of milk. Ignoring them both, Ronnie passed the nylon stockings on their revolving rack and returned to the perplexing cellophane packages. It wasn't that there were so many, but to Ronnie's eye they looked rumpled and a little dusty. He shuddered inside at the thought that the first personal thing he bought her would be dirty. Still not touching, he read the wrappers. There seemed to be three to a package, in three sizes—small, medium, and large—and two styles—briefs or bikinis. Deborah was clearly a small, but which style should he buy? If he got the bikinis, she might think he had bad thoughts about her. He could feel blood rushing to his face as he chose a package of white briefs and put them in the basket.

"Hey, mister," the clerk called sharply. Ronnie looked up, startled.

"That your black van?"

Ronnie stepped toward the window where the clerk stood pointing, alarmed. The big van was lumbering slowly across the sloped parking lot toward the store's gigantic plate-glass window.

For an instant, Ronnie experienced a stupefying paralysis.

"You plan to do something about it?" the clerk shouted. Without waiting for Ronnie's answer, he jumped from behind the counter.

Ronnie ran to the door and shoved the clerk aside.

"I'll stop it," he shouted over his shoulder. Dropping the basket, he raced for the van.

It was moving slowly—maybe five miles an hour—when he reached it. Terrified, he flung himself at the door, trying to stop the big vehicle's progress by sheer brute strength while fumbling for his keys. Through the window, he could see Deborah's head, down between the two seats, directly over the emergency brake. Ronnie's fingers were slippery with sweat by the time he gripped the keys. He shoved the key at the lock. The key skidded across the door panel, scratching the new paint. The van was less than five feet from the plate-glass window of the store. He tried again. This time, the key slid into the lock. He turned it, yanked the door open, and pulled the emergency brake. Sliding into the driver's seat, he grabbed Deborah's hair in his hand and threw her back behind the curtain. The van lumbered to a stop.

"Close damned call, mister." The clerk was standing on the walk a few feet from Ronnie, shaking his head. The woman customer stared through the glass, her eyes wide.

"I forgot to set the brake." As Ronnie stepped out of the van, Deborah started making a high-pitched keening sound. He slammed the door, muffling it. Hurrying across the walk, he steered the clerk back into the store and quickly paid for his purchases.

★ ★ ★

He screamed at her as he drove, a torrent of rage and profanity. She sobbed as he called her every bad name she had ever heard of. She could hear him gasping, as if he were struggling to dig the words from some horrible place.

Finally, he fell silent. She lay rigid with fear as the van again turned off the highway onto a bumpy side road and the engine quieted.

He was going to kill her now; Debbie was sure of that. She had lost her only chance. As the weight of his footsteps rocked the back of the van, she closed her eyes tightly.

"Why are you making him hurt you, Deborah?"

His words were choked. She realized he was crying, too.

"I know you're not really all those bad things he said. I know you're a good girl."

Crouching at her side, he unzipped the damp sleeping bag. He took her bound hands in one of his and pulled until her back bent and her hands touched her feet behind her. Taking the roll of black tape with his other hand, he tore a long strip between his teeth. He bent close to her and bound her hands to her feet, bending her back so hard that she gasped with pain.

He leaned over and put both arms around her body. She started the high-pitch keening again without realizing she was doing it.

"It's all right, Deborah. It's all right. I just want to make you more comfortable." Lifting her, he forced the sleeping bag around her contorted body. "I know it's going to be hard in that position, with the bag wet, but I want you to try to sleep. I've got some of Mother's sleeping pills, but you better not take one tonight, since you hit your head. It's your own fault, Deborah. I don't know why you're making it so hard for us."

For a moment, his words were choked off by his own sobs. "There's this special place I'm going to take you, but I don't think we're going to go there yet. Not while you're acting this way. I want you to be happy when you first see it. Maybe we'll

156

just drive around for a while, until you understand how much we love each other.

Ten minutes later, as Ronnie drove north on the highway, his hands were still shaking. The Shark had come back. He'd called Deborah all those bad names. And he'd whispered things to Ronnie, too—terrible things. The Shark's words still reverberated through Ronnie's mind: Let her know who's boss. If you don't give her what she's asking for right now, she's going to walk all over you.

After that first night, when he finally removed the straps that bound her hands to her feet, a terrible pain shot through Debbie's back and legs. It eventually became a dull ache, and she fell into an exhausted, restless sleep. When she finally woke, he took the tape off her mouth and made her swallow a pill along with a carton of milk. He left her hands tied, and fed her cereal and fruit with a spoon.

For a time, the hours passed as one gray jumble. In her half-awake stupor, Deborah wasn't sure whether they were moving. The tropical print that blocked the windows showed light, but she was unable to keep count of time passing. Sometimes the trembling of the van's wheels over the road blended with her own trembling terror, and other times the van was still and quiet and she was sure he had gone, leaving her to starve.

He let her out of the van several times a day. Hands temporarily bound in front, and mouth taped, she relieved herself in the woods or under a bridge, then changed into clean underwear. He always turned his back, but she never felt awake enough to run. Whenever the fog in her head began to lift, there was another pill.

On the second morning, she spat one at him in a torrent of fury. He picked it off the van's floor and wiped it on his shirt. Then, to her horror, he reached his free hand around her head and grasped her nose.

"We can't waste these. They cost Mother a lot of money."

His fingers probed between her lips, and finally, gasping for air, she opened her mouth and swallowed the pill.

He didn't tape her mouth while he made her breakfast, and Debbie understood that they were somewhere where no one could hear her if she screamed.

"Are we going to visit your mother?" she asked nervously, hoping that the mother he mentioned so often could help her.

It seemed an age before he finally answered.

"Mother's dead." A frown clouded his face. "I can't show you her room, either. Something bad happened in there."

Shivering, Debbie worked her legs farther into the sleeping bag. He poured her a glass of milk, and then peeled the banana he would slice into her cereal. Bananas, milk: It was like being a baby. Moisture burned in her eyes. She missed the baby. All of them. Daddy, Frankie, even Maryann. And her mother. In a weird way, she missed her mother most of all.

And then she understood something and it made her feel better and worse at the same time. Her mother had known. Somehow, her mother had understood about this man, right from the start, from the moment he held that shark's tooth necklace in front of her in the little grocery story in Provincetown.

"They're looking for me, you know," she told him when he began to feed her. "My mother knows who you are. She recognized you in Provincetown."

He bent over the bowl of cereal and dipped the spoon into it. He didn't say anything, but Debbie could tell that what she'd just said worried him. He always tried to smile when he fed her, but this time his smile wasn't there.

"If you let me go now," she said, "I'll tell them you were nice to me, and you won't get in any trouble. I'll tell them I went away with you because I wanted to."

As he lifted the spoon to her mouth, he stared at her thoughtfully. Her heart leapt. He was really thinking about it, about letting her go. After a moment, he shook his head.

"But then we wouldn't be together anymore, Deborah. You wouldn't be my girl. Here."

He nudged her lips with the spoon. She opened her mouth and swallowed the cereal.

"Yes, I would," she whispered, afraid if she spoke aloud her voice would give away her excitement. "We could still date. I'd like that a lot."

He was quiet until she had finished her cereal.

"You'd still be my girl?"

Debbie nodded, but, before anything else was said, sleep overtook her.

That evening, she didn't cringe when he put the spoon to her lips. She forced herself to smile at him. After dinner, there was no pill, just the tape across her mouth.

He drove again, miles and miles over a smooth, fast road. When he pulled over, she heard cars speeding by.

He was going to let her go. He was going to let her out here at the side of the road, right where she could flag down a car. . . .

He climbed into the back of the van. Without speaking, he bent over her, removed the sleeping bag, and unwound the tape that held her ankles. She rotated her feet as he pulled the tape from her mouth. My hands next, she thought wildly. He's doing it. He's really doing it.

When he did take her wrists, though, and push her upright, he didn't unwind the tape. From the corner of her eye, she saw him reach one hand into the front of the van.

A knife! A huge knife under the front seat! She started to scream. "Please!"

"Deborah, be quiet," he said angrily. "I don't want him to come out and hurt you. I thought about what you said, but I can't let you go, because I don't think your mother would let you be my girl. We have to do something now. Do you promise you'll be quiet?"

She nodded, mute with fear. He dragged her between the seats to the front of the van. Headlights from a passing car flashed

159

briefly and disappeared. Opening the door on the passenger side, he shoved her from the van, keeping a hard grip on her wrists.

Weak-kneed, she staggered ahead of him across a roadside turnoff. There was a plaque mounted on a boulder. Where were they? Mountains. A view. A picnic table and a phone booth.

"What are you going to do?" she asked, almost crying with fear.

"You promised you'd be quiet." He steered her into the phone booth and pushed himself in behind her. His body crushed against hers as he tried to pull the door shut. She sobbed and struggled with him, unable to help herself. He put the knife to her throat, pressed it into her skin.

"Stop that! You've got to stop, Deborah. If you don't be good, you're going to make the Shark do something bad."

She stood with her face jammed into the corner of the booth, quaking with silent sobs. He lowered the knife and fumbled through his pocket for change.

"When you're quiet, Deborah, I'm going to dial your parents. You're going to tell them you're with your fiancé and they shouldn't try to break us up. Say this, Deborah. Say, 'He's the boy I love, more than anyone else in the world.' "

He told her all the things she should say to her parents. She stood as still as she could, but she couldn't make her body stop shaking.

"Quit moving! Say, 'He's the boy I love!' Say it out loud right now, to be sure you have it right."

"He's the boy I love, more than anyone else in the world," Deborah whispered.

"That was good, but you're going to have to say it louder." He held the tip of the knife close to her throat. "Do you promise to do that?"

She nodded. He lowered the knife and dialed.

Joyce shouted when she heard her daughter's voice on the phone.

"Debbie? Where are you? My God! We've been so worried. Frank! Debbie's . . ."

"I'm with the boy I love more than anyone else in the world," Joyce heard her older daughter say. "He's my fiancé. We're getting married. You shouldn't try to break us up. I know you'd like to, but we're in love and you better leave us alone."

"My God! Where are you? Please tell me. Debbie? Are you still there?"

Frank ran into the kitchen.

"It's Debbie?"

Crying now, Joyce handed him the phone.

"Debbie? Is that you?"

Frank held on to the receiver for a moment, and then winced. Looking at his wife, he shook his head. "She's hung up. She said . . ."

Frank's voice broke. He stumbled and Joyce reached to hold him.

"She said, 'Daddy, I really love him, more than you or Mommy or anyone else,' and then she hung up."

Later that night, when the initial shock of their daughter's call had left them and they sat dazed and hurt in their den, Joyce told her husband about the man.

"Frank, you may think I've really lost my mind, but I have an idea about who she's with. He's not a boy." As she told her husband about the dreams and the three different vans and the shark's tooth necklace, Joyce's voice dropped into bottomless despair.

Chapter 14

JOYCE felt the last of her composure slipping away like grains of sand slipping through her fingers. She had been all right a half hour earlier when Chief Debrito arrived. She'd shaken his hand and shown him into her kitchen and given him a cup of coffee like any normal woman would—any normal woman whose daughter had been missing for three days. Her words had followed the same line as her thoughts. Now, though, as Joyce described her daughter's phone call, her thoughts were being swamped by hysteria. Any moment now, she was going to start to say something and her words were going to be shrieks.

She'd told her story coherently—the first part of it, anyway. The policeman had listened patiently, his impassive expression slowly changing, showing interest. She described the brown car on the highway—an older Chevy, she thought. Then a familiar face. That same face in a grocery store, swinging a shark's tooth necklace in front of her daughter. And later, that necklace appearing in her daughter's pocket. But then Joyce's words had begun tumbling out as she described how that same familiar face had appeared in a white van, and a blue one, then finally in a black van with side windows that gleamed dark gold under a streetlight.

"Do you have that shark's tooth necklace?" DeBrito had asked, and she had to tell him that she hadn't been able to find it.

"But my husband saw it. He'll tell you. I didn't imagine it."

Joyce heard herself as he would hear her, paranoid, stumbling for direction. She talked about the man's face, vaguely familiar and somehow connected with something terrible, showing up at traffic lights, car washes, neighborhood meetings, haunting her sleep, jolting her into shocked wakefulness.

Talking about Debbie's phone call now, Joyce felt that the policeman was starting to doubt her. He had put his palms against the edge of the kitchen table and pushed himself back. That fed her nervousness and she stopped speaking and stared down at her hands resting on the table.

"Mrs. Neuhauser," he said, not unkindly, "your daughter told you the person she is with is a 'boy.' The person we're looking for is no boy. He's been described by several witnesses as being in his late twenties, or possibly early thirties."

The policeman paused. Joyce realized he was waiting for her to say something, but all she could manage was a weak sigh.

"Just a minute ago," he continued, "you yourself described the man you've seen in the vans as 'about thirty.'"

Joyce nodded without looking up.

"Your daughter just turned thirteen. I have kids of my own. To most kids your daughter's age, anybody beyond high school is geriatric."

It took an effort for Joyce to lift her head and meet his gaze. "But . . . I should have explained this. It's just so strange. When I've dreamed about this man, he *is* a boy. His face is younger. A teenager's face. I'm dreaming about someone out of my past."

It seemed forever before Chief Debrito said anything. Joyce saw him look at his watch, and she wondered whether he was thinking about the two-hour drive back to Provincetown. Four hours, round-trip, to listen to a crazy woman.

"Where are you from, Mrs. Neuhauser?" he asked.

"Lincoln, a few miles west of here. It's a small town. I mean, it *was* a small town. It's grown a lot."

Chief Debrito looked away from Joyce, back down at the kitchen table, where the two pictures lay. One, a glossy five-by-seven print, had been taken on a Cape Cod beach. It showed Debbie in her pink bathing suit, sitting cross-legged on a beach towel. The other picture on the kitchen table was the artist's rendering from the Provincetown newspaper.

Gus nodded toward the sketch. "And you suspect you might have known him when you were younger?"

"Yes," she said, trying to sound positive, though she couldn't be. "And I think there was some . . . trauma. Trouble." She shrugged helplessly. "Something that he did to me or someone I knew. Something happened that . . . ."

Her words trailed off.

"But you can't remember anything about him?" Debrito asked, sounding incredulous. "You can't remember what the trauma was? You're not that old, Mrs. Neuhauser. It couldn't have been *that* long ago that you were a teenager."

With each thing she said, he was becoming more skeptical. She had no choice. She had to explain why she couldn't remember.

"This past summer, I was in a psychiatric ward."

Now a tremor was noticeable in her voice. Did Chief Debrito's expression become more closed or did she imagine it? Joyce took a breath, gathering her courage. "I underwent a series of electroconvulsive treatments."

The policeman blinked, not comprehending.

"Shock treatments. For severe depression. They use electrical current to produce artificial seizures of the brain. Unfortunately, you can lose blocks of your memory. Temporarily, I mean. It usually comes back," she added hastily. "Mine has, mostly, but some of it is still like . . . Swiss cheese."

For a painful, prolonged moment, there was no sound in the kitchen but the hum of the electric clock on the wall.

"Oh," he said finally. "Well . . ."

164

"Chief Debrito, I know this all sounds crazy to you, but I don't think Debbie has run away with any 'boy.' Joyce jabbed a finger at the sketch. "I haven't seen this man driving around the neighborhood since the night Debbie disappeared. Between that and the shark's tooth necklace, it's too much of a coincidence. I think she's with him."

"That's possible," the policeman said. "It could be she was telling the truth when she called. Or thought she was. I'd like to have a dollar for every time my kids thought they were in love."

"She isn't 'in love,' " Joyce said emphatically. "Debbie hasn't reached the stage where she's that interested in boys, much less thirty-year-old men. I don't think she would have gone with this man willingly."

The policeman sat still as stone, staring down at the sketch. Joyce glanced at the clock. "My husband will be home soon. He knows I called you, but . . ." She tapped her fingers nervously against the tabletop. "Well, he's not sure what to make of this."

"Your husband thinks you may be wrong about this man?"

Joyce shrugged. "He doesn't know what to think."

Chief Debrito gave her a serious look. "Mrs. Neuhauser, I have to ask you this: If this man has been 'lurking' for a couple weeks, why didn't you tell the local police about it? Earlier today, I spoke to the officer handling your daughter's disappearance. He told me he didn't know anything about this man or the shark's tooth necklace until you called him this morning, about the same time you called me."

Staring down, Joyce shook her head. "My husband is worried that I'm going to slide . . ." She bit into her lower lip. "I didn't say anything because I was afraid people would think I was . . . crazy. And I've been afraid of the same thing."

The policeman didn't say a word.

Joyce's hysteria edged closer to the surface.

"You think I've wasted your time. . . ."

"Not at all," he responded as he stood. "You've corroborated Emma Stone's story. I just hope your daughter's okay. I'm going to stop by the local police station and talk to the officer in charge. I understand they've posted your daughter's picture around the neighborhood."

"Yes," Joyce said, then added, "I was thinking that I would put up this man's sketch, too."

"It can't hurt."

"I had better tell you this one other thing," Joyce said as Chief Debrito reached for the doorknob. "There's another reason why I didn't mention the strange man. Debbie has run away before. Twice. Once when she was ten, she spent the night in a friend's garage. Then, last year, she disappeared again. She turned up at my husband's parents' house in Connecticut."

"How long was she gone that time?"

"Two days. But this isn't the same situation. We've been doing better here. *All* of us. Debbie hasn't run away this time."

As Gus negotiated the labyrinth of wide, neat streets, his mind ran over what he had just heard. This was Emma's family. That, he was certain of. Teenage girl, a young girl, a boy about four, a baby. And a nervous, overweight mother, though not nearly as overweight as Emma had said. But how much of Joyce Neuhauser's story could he believe? Yes, she may have recognized the man in the artist's rendering as the man in Emma's store, but Gus had already heard the same thing from Emma weeks before and he hadn't had to drive two hours to hear it.

During his time on the Provincetown police force, Gus had investigated other killings, many of them involving people he knew. An unemployed laborer who had done some plumbing work for the Debritos had tried to hold up a bank. Things went wrong and a popular teller died. Temporary insanity. A commercial fisherman, exhausted after a week at sea, had arrived home unexpectedly and found his wife with another man. The fisherman, a man Gus had sailed with, picked up the ax he used to cut firewood and took care of both wife and lover. Temporary insanity. And then there had been two young men—friends since third grade and Gus's oldest child's schoolmates—and one of them had given the other one money to buy cocaine from someone else, and it turned there was no cocaine and somehow no money, either, because something went wrong, but everyone had a few drinks and—temporary insanity. There was a lot of that on the Cape, where seasonal unemployment and cold, damp wind could chill a man till nothing would warm him but the burn of whiskey in his throat. And almost always, after the insanity, there were witnesses—people in line at the bank, neighbors who saw the fisherman's wife and the friend, bartenders who heard the overheated, whiskey-slurred threats.

Who did he have for a witness now? A woman who had undergone shock treatment that had left her with a Swiss cheese mind. A woman who believed in her nightmares, and who believed she was being followed by a man in vans. Three *different* vans? Okay, so it was possible a man might drive a van on his job, and own a van, too. But where did that third van come from?

The one thin link connecting the Neuhauser girl's disappearance to Bobbie's killing, the thing that gave Gus hope, was the shark's tooth necklace. You could buy them in half the stores along Commercial Street and every other beach town on earth, but it was quite a coincidence that Debbie Neuhauser had ended up carrying one in her school uniform's pocket.

Sergeant Kennedy, the officer in charge of Debbie Neuhauser's disappearance, was rumpled and red-faced. He had a thick shock of white hair, and every time his phone rang he ran his hand through it in frustration.

It rang as he handed Gus the statement from the store detective at the Covered Bridge Mall. Before he picked up the receiver, he said to Gus, "The detective's a retired police clerk. Her name's Lorna Thompson. I looked at her personnel records. She's reliable, but some of these store security types can be a little overzealous."

Gus read Ms. Thompson's brief statement. At 9:20 the previous Friday night, the sixty-three-year-old detective had watched

167

the Neuhauser girl pocket three bottles of nail polish. When she confronted Debbie, the girl ran from the store into the parking lot. The detective did not see her again. At 9:30, while locking up the store's loading dock, the detective had heard what she first thought was a girl yelling "No, no." But there was a carload of kids horsing around the back of the mall, and the noise could have come from them.

Gus laid the statement back in the file, on top of the statement from the cosmetics clerk, a woman in her early seventies.

Sergeant Kennedy cradled the phone and nodded at the folder. "The stores at the mall hire a lot of these retired people because they're more reliable than kids. The problem is, sometimes you've got to take what they say with a grain of salt. Some of them don't have a lot of excitement in their lives. Kids grown, houses empty. They tend to make too much out of little things. You know what I mean?"

"Maybe so," Gus said, "but one of your men did find that broken bottle of nail polish. The same brand Debbie Neuhauser is supposed to have taken. Wasn't it found about where this detective thought the shouts were coming from?"

"Yes, we found a broken bottle of polish. Not necessarily *the* bottle. Look, Chief Debrito." Kennedy leaned across the desk. "The girl has already run away twice. What we figure is, after she stole the nail polish she hid out behind the mall until she was sure the store security people wouldn't come after her. For some reason, she dropped one of the bottles of polish. In any event, by that time her parents were due home. The kid knew she was going to get in trouble, so she split."

"Just like that? With enough money in her purse for a slice of pizza and a Coke? Wearing a blue-jean jacket? And no change of clothes? Wouldn't she have at least stopped by the pizza parlor to tell her friends?"

The sergeant shrugged. "Who knows what's going on with some of these kids?"

"What about last night's call to her parents?"

"You mean, 'I'm with the boy I love'?" A grin flickered over

Kennedy's face and then was gone. "Maybe there is a boy. Maybe there isn't. Maybe she made him up to stick the knife into her parents a little more. You know, she'd had a fight with her mother earlier in the week."

"Mrs. Neuhauser mentioned that when she told me about the shark's tooth," Gus said. "Did you happen to ask Debbie's friends about the necklace?"

Kennedy's phone rang. Reaching for it, he said, "I only heard about the damned thing this morning. I managed to reach the Moran girls at home before they left for school. Apparently, they found the thing on a path near their school." He picked up the receiver, then asked his caller to hold. "I'm going to have to take this one," he said to Gus.

"Sure." Gus stood up. "Just one more thing. What do you make of Mrs. Neuhauser's story about the man in the vans."

"Frankly, I don't know what to make of it. Considering Mrs. Neuhauser's background . . ." Kennedy shook his head, leaving Gus to draw his own conclusions about that.

"What I'd suggest you do is talk to Debbie Neuhauser's friends. The Moran girls. You can probably catch them at school until four. Those nuns don't mess around."

The afternoon sun that slanted through the window of the school principal's office fell directly onto a wooden crucifix mounted on the wall. The plaster Christ on the cross was at least eighteen inches tall, and its bloody wounds were vivid maroon against the alabaster skin. From time to time, as the girls answered his questions, Gus caught them glancing up at it. What the heck; he needed all the help he could get.

It was almost pointless, he had realized early in the interview, trying to get either of the Moran girls to acknowledge they had any part in the shoplifting episode. Of the two, the younger, Colleen, was more forthcoming, but neither of them was about to admit a thing. "We didn't know she was going to take something," the two agreed, sounding shocked by the very mention of it.

Getting the girls to talk about Debbie's disappearance was easier, though they were sharply divided on just what might have happened.

Lisa, the older girl, was at an age where boys entered into everything. Gus's question—Was it possible that Debbie had a boyfriend she'd met at the Cape?—was greeted with a burst of enthusiasm.

"I'll bet she did!"

The girl wore her curly hair long, and toyed with it continually as she talked to Gus. Winding a red ringlet around her finger, she said, "That's probably why Debbie didn't really want to go to Pop's Pizza with us. It wasn't because her parents were due home. It was because she was already planning to meet him!"

Gus liked to think of himself as having a rapport with teenagers. Certainly, he'd always been comfortable with his own children and their friends. But not more than two minutes into the interview, he had found himself developing a definite dislike for Lisa, along with a distrust of her judgment.

The younger girl, Colleen, disagreed with her sister, and Gus was inclined to go along with her. She didn't have Lisa's long curls or milk white skin. Freckles rioted across her face and her hair hung straight to her shoulders, but, as far as Gus was concerned, she was infinitely more attractive and credible than Lisa.

"If Debbie had a boyfriend, I would have known it," Colleen insisted. "Besides, she wouldn't have run away without telling me. We've been best friends since fourth grade."

"Maybe she didn't tell you everything," Lisa said.

"Did Debbie ever talk about her trip to the Cape with either of you?" Gus asked.

"Sure," Colleen responded.

"Did she say anything about meeting a man. Or boy?"

The girl shook her head. "No. All she said was that she hated going places with her parents. She said she was either bored or embarrassed the whole time."

"She got a nice tan, though," said Lisa.

Gus produced a folded sheet of paper from his jacket pocket. "I'm specifically interested in this man." He straightened it in front of the girls. "Have either of you seen anyone who resembled this sketch? Not necessarily with Debbie. He could have been anywhere around here. Maybe in a van."

The girls stared intently at the sketch, then shook their heads in unison.

"He's a little old for Debbie, don't you think?" Lisa said.

Gus ignored her. "What about any strange vans?"

"There are always vans around."

"Do you remember any of them following you when you were with Debbie?"

Again, the girls shook their heads.

"I'm also interested in anything either of you can tell me about a necklace Mrs. Neuhauser saw Debbie with—a shark's tooth on a chain."

Lisa gave a bored groan. "We already told Sergeant Kennedy about that."

"We found it in the woods," Colleen said. "It was on a gold chain."

"Plate," her sister added.

Gus looked at the older girl.

"Gold plate. Not real gold."

"You saw Debbie with this necklace?" Gus addressed his question to both girls, but his gaze came to rest on the younger one.

She nodded. "We were there when Debbie found it."

"She didn't find it," said Colleen. "I did. It was on the path. Debbie took it from me." Her eyes strayed to the crucifix. "I mean, I let her hold it. It was a piece of junk, anyway. I didn't know she kept it."

"Did the necklace seem to mean anything to her? What did she say when she took it from you?"

The girls exchanged surprised glances.

"She didn't treat it like it was anything special. She just said, 'Let me see that,' or something."

171

Gus looked at the younger sister.

"I don't remember exactly what Debbie said. But I remember she pretended to hypnotize us by swinging the chain."

"Tell me everything you can about finding the necklace," Gus said.

Now that they had something to tell, something real to talk about that had nothing to do with the mall and the nail polish, the girls were vivid, animated. Amazing, thought Gus. The two kids couldn't recall where the cosmetics counter was in the local department store, or remember what the store detective looked like, even though the episode had occurred just three nights earlier. But the story of the shark's tooth necklace found dangling from a branch a week earlier was detailed down to the exact branch on the exact bush.

"What did you talk about while you were on the path?" Gus asked. "Do you remember?"

"The necklace, of course. I thought those dorky boys from—"

Gus interrupted Lisa. "What were you talking about before you found the necklace?"

"I don't know."

"I remember," Colleen said. "Before we found the necklace, we were talking about what we were going to do Friday night."

"Go to the mall?"

"That's right!" she said, excited now. "You remember, Lisa? You asked Debbie if she was going to Pop's Pizza with us." The girl looked at Gus. "Do you think maybe that man in your picture was listening to us?"

"Oh, come on!" her older sister said. "How could a grown man be there without us seeing him? Anyway, Debbie never got to Pop's Pizza. We went straight there and she never showed up."

"Maybe he kidnapped her before she could get there. There *are* places on the path where a grown man could hide."

As Colleen described the path, the school's bell began ringing. Lisa immediately stood and started for the door.

172

"Before you go," Gus said, "I want you to promise me something. If you see anything suspicious—any more shark's tooth necklaces, any strange men hanging around here or driving around in vans, or in an old brown Chevy—you call Sergeant Kennedy. He'll get in touch with me. Okay?"

The girls nodded. "Sure."

"And," he added, "I want you to show me that path, and the exact spot where you found the shark's tooth."

"Now?" Lisa groaned. "I'm supposed to be at drama club. If I'm late . . ."

Her sister interrupted. "It will only take a minute to look at the path. It's right across the street. After all, Debbie is my best friend."

Gus followed the sisters from the bright office into a hall that now throbbed with young girls in plaid skirts and white blouses. He felt gigantic and clumsy as he pushed his way past them and through the main door.

Gus remained on the path after the Moran girls had gone. Sunlight through the canopy of trees covered the ground with a delicate lacelike pattern. The path was shorter than Gus had imagined, and wider, and much less menacing. From where he stood at the bend where the girls had found the necklace, the road that ran by the parochial school was just out of sight fifty feet away. He could hear girls calling out to one another. He could hear the hum of their parent's cars, the diesel engine of a school bus.

In the other direction, a row of backyards from Old Covered Bridge Estates was visible. In one yard—the only yard with a fence—a big scruffy dog ran back and forth barking. In the yard next to that, two women sat in lawn chairs watching a trio of children in a sandbox. One of the women was brushing a golden cocker spaniel.

Behind Gus, there was a slight rise. The trees there were more mature than those nearer the path, and the undergrowth denser. It was the only place around the path where a man possibly might hide. As Gus climbed the hill, brambles clung to his pants and a thick leafy tangle of vines thrust themselves into his face. Once at the top, he fought his way to the far side of the biggest oak.

The tree's trunk split several feet off the ground. The larger part of the split wasn't as wide as Gus's body, but there was a lot of leafy growth around the split. Would this disguise an adult man? Stooping, Gus peered back at the path. The leaves were losing their summer color. A patch of sunlight streaming through the trees lighted the orange leaves of the branch where the girls had found the necklace. A slight breeze stirred the air, and the branch moved almost imperceptibly.

Was it possible that, a week before, a man had crouched here in the thicket and watched three girls in parochial school uniforms, little girls maybe half his age, handle a shark's tooth he had placed over a branch?

Gus glanced at the ground around his feet. By now, rain would have washed away any footprints. As for any torn bits of clothing hanging on a bramble, the notion made him smile. Only in the movies. Slapping away a buzzing mosquito, he hurried out of the thicket.

Before Gus started back to the Cape, he called Joyce Neuhauser.

"I showed the Moran girls the sketch from the Provincetown paper. They didn't recognize the man, and they haven't noticed any suspicious vans. I also looked at the place where the girls found the necklace."

Joyce listened without interrupting as Gus told her about the conversation the girls had had that afternoon on the path.

"So this man knew Debbie might be at the mall on Friday night," she said when he'd finished.

"*If* he was on the path, he *could* have heard her say that. In any event, putting that sketch up around the neighborhood and at the mall isn't a bad idea."

"You believe me?" Joyce asked.

"I believe this man is a possibility, and we can't overlook any possibility. It can't hurt to spread that sketch around."

Gus helped Joyce work out the wording she would put on the man's sketch, then added, "Don't put your home phone number on it. Put Sergeant Kennedy's number at the station. Show the sketch to your neighbors, too. Especially the ones whose homes abut the path to the school."

"All right. And please let me know if you hear anything."

"Of course. Before you hang up, Mrs. Neuhauser, I have another question. Have you—or has anyone in your family or anybody you know—ever been involved with recreational scuba diving?"

Joyce answered without hesitation. "No. Nothing that I can recall."

"What about underwater research? On sharks," he asked. "Or wreck diving? Or Olympic swim competitions? Can you think of anything?"

"No. Nothing. I better go. I want to get dinner over with so I can get the sketch copied."

After he replaced the receiver, Gus remained in the phone booth for a moment, trying to fit what he had learned that afternoon in with Bobbie Yellowfeather's murder. The longer he thought about it, the more frail the connection seemed. Everything hinged on Joyce Neuhauser's spotty memory. It could well be that the face haunting Joyce Neuhauser was a figment of her own bedeviled imagination. It could well be that the shark's tooth the girls had found dangling over a branch was not the one purchased in Emma's store. And, he thought as he turned onto the turnpike and encountered a massive Boston rush-hour traffic jam, it could very well be that Debbie Neuhauser was at that moment standing on her grandparent's doorstep, apologetic, tearful, swearing she would never run away again.

Frankie missed his big sister terribly. When his mommy wasn't there, Debbie was the one he went to when he was frightened or when he fell down and hurt himself. Debbie knew how to put the white cream on his scraped knees and not sting him. And she was the one who would walk right into the dark closet in his bedroom and make sure there was no monster hiding there after Maryann had said there was a monster for sure.

His mom and dad had told him Debbie would be back soon, but he wasn't sure. They had so many secrets now, and they whispered all the time. Policemen had been there, too, talking to his mom and dad in the kitchen, with the door closed. There had been another one that afternoon, sitting at the kitchen table with his mom. He hadn't worn a policeman's clothes, but Frankie had heard his mother call the man "Officer." And a little while later, he'd seen the man again, on the path that ran between the backyard and Debbie's school.

Frankie stirred the sand in the Collinses' sandbox listlessly. The Collins children were younger—just babies—and after a while he didn't like playing with them. His daddy was in the house with Maryann and Andy. Right after dinner, his mommy had cut out a picture from a newspaper and pasted it on a clean piece of paper. She'd written words under the picture, but she wouldn't let him see them. Then she'd gone off alone in the station wagon.

It would be dark in a little while, but Frankie didn't feel like going in yet. Stepping out of the sandbox, he dusted the sand off his pants' legs.

Mrs. Collins was in a lawn chair, talking quietly with a neighbor.

"Can I take Goldie for a walk?" he asked.

Mrs. Collins glanced into the setting sun, and then looked at the little boy. "Do you promise you won't let go of her leash?"

"I promise."

"And you'll be back in five minutes, and you'll stay right in front of the house. I don't want her getting ticks again, so don't go near the woods."

Frankie nodded solemnly.

"All right. Her leash is on the doorknob."

176

"Come on, Goldie." Frankie hurried across the lawn, just in case Mrs. Collins changed her mind. The cocker trotted happily at his heels. She had been walking with Frankie many times. When he had attached the leash to her collar, he wrapped it tightly around his wrist and led the dog between the houses, walking with a child's sense of awesome responsibility.

Even before they reached the sidewalk, the little spaniel was tugging at her leash.

"I'm not going to let you go this time," Frankie said in a stern, childish voice. As they rounded the corner, Goldie strained harder against her red collar, pulling it taut.

Across the street from the last house, at the edge of the bare field that was full of weeds, Frankie stopped. From where he stood, he could see across the stretch of backyards. Mrs. Collins was still there, but she was looking the other way. The little boy stopped down. "Remember, Goldie," he said seriously, "if I let you go, you can't go in the woods. Okay?"

Goldie trembled with excitement as Frankie unclipped the leash. The moment she was free, the sturdy little dog raced across the field, a low yellow streak of energy in the waning sunlight, leaping after butterflies and birds. Frankie chased her, running first one way, then the other. She easily out-distanced him.

"Goldie! No!" he called when she ran to the path that led into the woods. The dog hesitated, glanced back at her pursuer, then bolted down the path, ears flapping.

Frankie paused where the shadows of the big trees fell onto the field. He could hear the dog thrashing through some low bushes, but he couldn't see her. Sometimes the woods were fun, but sometimes they were a scary place, a place where monsters and bad men crouched behind every tree, about to jump at him. Debbie always said there were no monsters in the woods, but Maryann had told him about one that hid in the thick bushes. It chased her, she said, and blood dripped from its huge long teeth. Now he had to decide. What if that wasn't Goldie making noise in the bushes? What if it was a monster?

177

He looked back across the yards. Mrs. Collins was standing up, looking his way. Her hands were on her hips. She knew he had let Goldie off the leash. Mustering his courage, Frankie took a few steps down the path.

It was dark in the trees, just like when the monster chased Maryann. "Goldie," he called softly. Ahead, around the bend in the path, something thrashed in the leaves. He held the leash hidden behind him; if Goldie saw it, she'd run again. "Come on, Goldie!" He stepped around the curve on tiptoes, ready to flee just in case it wasn't Goldie making all that noise.

"Aw, Goldie. Why did you do that?"

She was filthy, digging through a mulch of mud and fallen leaves. Keeping the leash out of sight, Frankie crept up to the cocker. To his relief, she didn't seem to notice his approach. He knelt and quickly snapped her leash onto her collar. She continued her frantic digging as he tugged at the leash.

"What is it, Goldie?"

Her head emerged from the leaves. In her teeth, she gripped a dirty little object. Frankie pried it out of her mouth. It was a tiny purse with colored beads on it. He pulled apart the thongs that kept the purse closed, and examined the page of the phone book he found folded inside.

Frankie knew some of his letters, but not all of them. This was a mystery. Maybe the monster had left this. Something disturbed the bushes behind him. There was a rustling of leaves, the crack of a branch. He looked around. The shadows were growing bigger, the light places on the path disappearing. Folding the page quickly, Frankie returned it to the bag, pulled the ties tight, and pocketed the little pouch.

"Come on, Goldie," he whispered, "let's go home."

Chapter 15

THE department store was almost empty, as it often was on Monday nights. Lorna Thompson, the store's detective, had time to talk.

"I raised five children of my own, three of them girls, and I've got a passel of grandkids," she told Joyce. "I know what a scared kid sounds like. When I first heard the girl screaming last Friday night, I thought she sounded scared." She looked at the sketch in her hand again. "But I never saw this man, either in the store when the girls were here or out back later."

"And no van out back?"

The other woman shook her head. "But I told the police that when that girl screamed 'No, no,'" the hairs on the back of my neck stood straight up. Half a minute later, though, a carload of kids comes roaring past—boys and girls both—shouting and raising hell like they do on Friday nights around here."

Joyce looked across the department store's bright, empty aisles, at the doors that lead to the parking lot. "That's the door she ran out?"

"That's right," the detective said. "I saw your daughter go as far as the first row of cars out there. Poor child looked so terrified, I figured she'd never try shoplifting again."

Mrs. Thompson started to hand the sketch back to Joyce.

"Is there anywhere you could post that?" Joyce asked. "Your manager wouldn't let me put it up in the window here."

Mrs. Thompson laid a sympathetic hand on Joyce's shoulder. "Sure. I'll get the guys in the mall's security office to put it up in there. The guards walk around all day and half the night looking at people. There's a chance one of them will recognize this character."

After two hours of walking store to store, Joyce was at the point of exhaustion and despair. Everyone was sympathetic, but no one had seen the man in the sketch. The record store's manager had allowed her to tape the sketch in a side window even while shaking his head. None of the clerks at the grocery store could remember seeing the man whose sketch now occupied a center spot on the bulletin board near the store's automatic doors.

When Joyce left the department store by the same door Debbie had run through the previous Friday night, fourteen of the twenty copies she'd made of the sketch were posted around the Covered Bridge Mall.

The last of summer's warmth had disappeared over the weekend. Joyce pulled her sweater closed as she walked into the parking lot's first row. This was where her frightened daughter had hidden from Lorna Thompson. "Oh, Debbie," Joyce said to herself. "If only that woman had caught you." Her eyes burned as she looked back at the store's bright windows. When she turned purposefully toward the back of the mall, Joyce could hardly see for her tears.

She walked beyond the lights that rimmed the parking lot, around the back corner of the department store, past the platform at the loading dock where Lorna Thompson had heard the girl screaming "No, no."

There was one of those huge semitrailers, like the one that had blocked Mrs. Thompson's view of the Dumpsters on Friday night. Bulbs shone over the back entrances to stores, but the light here was much dimmer than in the parking lot. Joyce picked her way carefully over the asphalt until she stood on the far side of the semi. The truck itself blocked the light from the department store's loading dock, and it was a moment before Joyce could even bring the dark green Dumpsters into focus. There were—how many? Six or eight of them standing in a jumbled line.

Stopping in front of the Dumpsters, she examined the ground. Here was where the nail polish had splattered on the asphalt, but the bright color was invisible to Joyce. Maybe it was already gone, worn down by tire treads and endless trips to the Dumpsters. Or maybe the stain was still there, hidden by the night.

Had Debbie really been in this dismal place? Was it her daughter Mrs. Thompson had heard, screaming in terror as a man pulled her into his van? Would he have threatened Debbie with a weapon? It wouldn't have been necessary: Debbie, with her reed-thin arms, couldn't fight off an adult male. Joyce stood shivering for a moment, then walked rapidly away from the Dumpsters.

The back of Pop's Pizza was at the other end of the alley. When Joyce passed the back of the store, a hot blast from the pizza oven's exhaust hit her. The smell of tomato sauce and sharp spices scarcely registered as she hurried around the corner to the restaurant's entrance. Debbie hadn't made it this far on Friday night, but maybe the man had.

Pushing through the door, she quickly took in the faces of the customers. It was a school night, and most of the weekend teenage crowd was missing. The rock music that blared on weekends played lowly in the background. Pop's few customers looked like tired shoppers, stopping to eat before hauling home their packages.

A short, muscular young man with a ponytail manned the counter. A second, older man stood to the side, near the ovens.

Before the young counterman in the white apron had a chance to ask what she wanted, Joyce had pushed one of the sketches across the counter.

"I want to find out if you've ever seen this man in here," she said rapidly. "Especially last Friday night?"

He lifted his shoulders and let them drop listlessly. "A lot of people come in here. Most of the faces don't stick in my mind." He held the picture toward the other man. "You remember seeing this guy around here?"

The other man wore wire-rimmed glasses. He pushed them up his nose, squinted at the sketch, and shook his head.

"My daughter Debbie disappeared Friday night. She was last seen at the other end of the mall."

"Oh, yeah!" the young man said, his indifference gone. "She was supposed to meet some friends here, but she never showed up. Right?"

"That's right."

"The police were in Saturday afternoon about her. I talked to them myself. I'm the owner's nephew," he added, as if establishing his credibility. Tilting his head, he gave the sketch a long look. "The cops didn't show me that."

"Yesterday, the police weren't aware of this man," Joyce explained wearily. "I wonder if you would put this up in here somewhere where people will see it."

"Sure. Happy to do it," the young man said. "Wish I could help you more, but I was here Friday and I don't remember anyone like this. Of course, Friday nights are wild in this place. You don't have time to breathe. Even my uncle—he's Pop—works the counter Friday nights. Most of the time, all he does is count the money."

"Is your uncle here now?" Joyce asked. "Maybe he saw someone. . . ."

"No. He's not around."

"Hey, you know something?" The other man approached the counter. Taking the sketch from his coworker, he examined it carefully. "I remember Pop saying something Friday night about throwing some guy out of here." He looked up at Joyce and shrugged. "I never saw the guy, but could be worth checking. . . ."

The younger man interrupted. Whether he was in charge in his uncle's absence wasn't clear, but he seemed to have acquired the mannerisms of a boss. He told Joyce that his uncle had been out of town since Saturday but would be back the following day before noon.

Joyce's attention was still riveted on the second man. "What was the man doing that made Pop throw him out?"

"Don't know anything about it," the older worker said, shaking his head. "When I work this counter Friday night, I don't see or hear anything but pizza. All I know is, Pop wanted him out of here."

"Do you know about what time this happened?"

"No. Pop didn't even mention it until later, when I was sweeping up."

"I'll show this to Pop as soon as he gets in," said the younger man." He read the few lines Joyce had printed neatly under the actual sketch. "Says here he should call the police."

"I'll call your uncle myself," Joyce said. "About eleven?"

"Yeah. Sometimes he doesn't make it in until a little later."

"I'll call at eleven."

Sometime after midnight, when the rest of the family slept, Joyce remained slumped in the recliner in their den. Across the room, the big color television flickered. She'd turned the sound down until only the delirious screams of a talk-show audience could be heard.

Exhausted, and too upset to sleep, she played over her two conversations with Chief Debrito. Some of the recollections were painful, and none more so than the way he'd pulled back when she'd mentioned the shock therapy. But, skeptical or not, he'd gone to the local police. He'd questioned the Moran girls. He'd examined the path where Debbie had found the necklace.

But where, Joyce wondered, had his curious questions come from—the questions about Olympic swimmers and deep-sea divers? What did she know about that? Only what she glimpsed on television. Sleek bodies poised on the edge of diving boards during the summer Olympics. National Geographic specials. Jacques Cousteau. Shipwrecks. The world beneath the sea was as foreign to Joyce as the world of Arctic explorers or great white hunters.

The wild screams from the television turned into the steady hum of a test pattern. Joyce used the remote switch to turn off the set. Rising from the recliner, she turned out the remaining lights and walked up the stairs.

Before she fell into an uneasy sleep, something flicked through her mind. It was the same image that had been there before—the water, rippling, clear turquoise—and the same face was there, just as before. This time, though, it wasn't part of a dream. It was a clear waking memory that clutched her. She was in the Lincoln Township swimming pool. She was trapped underwater, unable to surface and get air into her lungs. She was dying.

Joyce's night was long, her brief stretches of light sleep broken again and again by startled awakenings. Frank woke once, and Joyce watched him sit hunched on the edge of the bed, his head in his hands. Finally, she moved to his side of the bed and touched him. It seemed to Joyce that at first Frank couldn't even feel her hand on his back, then he turned and put his arms around her. His hands explored her body. She started to pull away, thinking, Not now, but suddenly she wanted to make love as desperately as he did. Afterward, when they lay awake, he spoke softly to her.

"Whatever happens, Joyce, we've got to think of ourselves," he said. "You may or may not be right about Debbie, but I have a feeling that if she is with this man, or any man or boy, she's there willingly."

"I don't think so," Joyce whispered.

He continued as if she hadn't spoken. "Debbie grew up an awful lot while you were away. We both know she's got a mind of her own. I don't want the whole family to fall apart over something that might be hopeless."

Joyce lay silent, telling herself, It's not hopeless.

"Life has to go on," Frank said before he fell asleep.

In the morning as soon as Frank and Maryann had gone, Joyce systematically, diligently searched her older daughter's bedroom. As she forced her hands under Debbie's mattress, she saw the morning light play across the flowered quilt Debbie had chosen from a catalog. She searched each of the five drawers in Debbie's white chest of drawers and looked through all the pockets in the girl's crowded closet. She searched for nothing in particular. She searched for a hint, any single clue that Debbie had matured to the extent that boys, men, and sex occupied a major part of her thoughts.

She disturbed the stuffed animals atop Debbie's bookshelf and turned the pages of the young-adult mysteries Debbie sometimes read. At the end of her search, Joyce had found nothing. The only possible hint of an interest in boys was a poster of a popular male rock star Debbie had taped on her closet door. Before Joyce closed her daughter's door, she took a parting look at the young man's face. He looked about twelve.

A little later that morning, Joyce dressed Frankie and the baby and took them to the basement.

"Do you want to see what Goldie and I found yesterday when I took her for a walk?" Frankie asked as he followed his mother into the storage room.

"Not right now. There are some toys Daddy used to play with in this box. You might like them."

Minutes later, Frankie was engrossed in the Lincoln Logs, a miniature fort rising around him. Joyce propped Andy in his walker and went to work.

Dead tired, she moved on nervous energy. This was no longer a casual excursion into her past. Unless she was willing to concede to Frank that her search for Debbie might be hopeless, she had to find the stranger in the van. He fit somewhere, at some moment in the past. She was going to find that moment, recreate it piece by piece. When she found it, she would find the stranger's identity. And when she found that, Joyce prayed that she would find her daughter.

She lifted the hinged top on the cedar chest, the one she had brought from her teenage bedroom. Frankie got to his feet.

"What's in there, Mommy?"

"Old clothes and things, honey. This used to be mommy's hope chest."

"Hope?" He peered into the chest. Disappointed by the stacks of old clothes, Frankie wandered back to the Lincoln Logs.

"Hope," Joyce repeated softly. Even fifteen years earlier, the hope chest, given to Joyce by an unmarried aunt whose hopes had soured, had seemed to her embarrassingly old-fashioned. Were there still girls who hoped, now, and pinned their hopes on embroidered tablecloths and lace-trimmed pillowcases? Or perhaps on the promises offered by white lace negligees, carefully folded between layers of tissue paper. Probably not.

She pulled out the ankle-length dress she had worn to the senior prom. Blue chiffon, masses of it, crushed and faded beyond any hope now, but what a dress it had been! She pressed the dress to her bosom. Over her breasts, the chiffon was sewn in a series of tiny pleats. Frank had brought her an orchid corsage, and she could remember how his hand had slid boldly beneath the pleats as he'd pinned it on her dress. They'd been dating for what? About six months, and on that prom night she finally lost her virginity, in the backseat of Frank's father's four-door Buick, buried in yards of blue chiffon.

Laying aside the blue dress, Joyce quickly searched through the chest. Long-forgotten wool sweaters released the wafting pungent scent of camphor and cedar. For a moment, she thought the yearbook wasn't there. Then her fingers brushed across the rough burlap cover.

Frightened by what she might find but more frightened that she might find nothing, Joyce settled onto a cushion near Frankie's log fort and began flipping the yearbook's pages.

At the front were candid photos of teachers and staff. Some were strangers to her; most were not. There was poor Mr. Finney, who taught biology and cried. And Miss Sanders, who wore miniskirts and smoked marijuana during lunch hour. Joyce quickly passed over these, onto the middle of the book where the senior class, 1978, stared up from the pages with two-by-three-inch studio-portrait smiles.

Turning the pages slowly, Joyce examined each face in its turn, dozens, scores of them. Those she recognized, she locked onto, spending a moment securing them in her past. With each new page, she prayed the stranger would reveal himself, but none of the portraits offered even a slight resemblance.

The students had signed one another's books, and she read over their cryptic comments. "I gave it up for Lent," a smiling boy had written above his photo. Another had written merely, "Nasty!" The words' meanings were mostly lost, but still Joyce began daydreaming, slipping fifteen years back.

Under each portrait was a list of activities. She skimmed past her own photo, unaccountably embarrassed, but her gaze was drawn back to it. It showed a round-faced girl, with the long, straight hair common to many of the girls in the book. Chorus, art club. She had been pretty, in a soft way.

There was Pete Robbins, beaming out from the center of the page almost as if the photographer had put a special spotlight on him. She read the words he had scrawled hastily around his picture.

"Joyce, I'll always remember that red bathing suit and the summer of '77. Pete 'the Shark' Robbins."

The Shark. Joyce's hands were suddenly cold.

A frightening stranger buys a shark's tooth necklace in a beach-town store. Her own drowning becomes a recurring nightmare. A policeman asks about water sports.

Joyce whispered Pete's nickname—"the Shark"—and the present disappeared as a wave of remembered past washed over her. Her eyes were on the glossy pages of the yearbook, focused on the scrawling letters Pete Robbins had left fifteen years before, but the basement storage room had ceased to exist.

Summer 1977

The public pool. The sun glitters over the surface of the water. Pete Robbins is in his lifeguard chair, stretching lazily. Joyce looks at him from the deep end, where she's treading water. He lifts his hand and waves, but the wave could be for any of them. Everyone likes Pete.

And that boy is there—the one she laughed at earlier in the girls' dressing room. It's spooky, the way he's always so quiet.

Joyce drifts onto her back and feels the sun beating down on her face. She floats, moving her arms lazily.

Suddenly, that spooky boy is right beside her. His hands reach to her shoulders. She thinks he's fooling around, but then he's pushing down hard, so that her face slips beneath the surface before she can get a breath. He's strong. One hand is on her shoulder, the other on her head. He's holding her under. She fights his arms with her nails, struggling to free herself.

It goes on and on until she's sure she'll die there in the public pool. Where's Pete? Doesn't anyone see what's happening?

And then the boy's hands are gone. Joyce shoots to the surface, gasping, hearing the last piercing scream of a whistle.

"Joyce and Ronnie! Cut out the horseplay," Pete Robbins calls across the pool.

The incident is over. Pete is already looking the other way at some kids playing on the slide at the shallow end. Joyce stares into the young man's face as he floats away. His pale gray-green eyes show no emotion. "Moron," she sputters after him.

Shaking her head, Joyce brought herself back to the present. Though confusion and surprise jangled through her mind, and the fear for her daughter remained, she experienced a profound sense of relief. The thing that had terrified her for so many nights was real. Half a minute with her head held underwater by a boy she had laughed at in the girls' locker room. And the boy had a name—Ronnie.

Frankie was still happily engrossed with his fort. Andy

bounced contentedly in his walker. Leaning against the cedar chest, Joyce closed her eyes and pieced together the missing earlier portion of that summer day.

It had begun as nothing more than horseplay. There had been five or six girls in the locker room, starting to change into their bathing suits. Before they'd changed, though, there had been something they'd had to do. How had the girls discovered the small peepholes in the wooden partition? Joyce couldn't remember. She hadn't been in on the discovery. She had been enlisted into the prank for no reason other than that she had been there.

She remembered how she and another girl had stayed behind as decoys, undressing slowly, and even now, sitting in her basement, Joyce could recall the heightened emotions she'd felt— the nervous, giggling sensuality.

The other girls had crept into the boys' locker room. They'd stolen up behind the boys who had been standing on the bench peering through the peepholes.

There had been sudden shouts of surprise, insults hurled, and laughter, too. "It's safe," a girl had called from the boys' side of the partition.

Joyce had immediately stripped off her remaining street clothes. She'd had a new bathing suit—a red one-piece with a low back. She had just pulled it over her hips when bare feet raced across the wet floor. That boy—the one with the pale eyes—had raced into the locker, pursued by a trio of teenage girls. His face had been white with panic.

He'd stopped, face-to-face with Joyce. His gaze had dropped to her bare breasts. She had never seen a look of such repulsion.

The girls had chased him from the dressing room, screaming after him. "Creep. Moron. Pervert." Joyce had been as eager as any of them, her shrieks joining the chorus of laughter and taunts. She had never been an extrovert, but for that moment she had been. She'd felt popular. She'd fit in.

Joyce flipped quickly through the rest of the yearbook. The stranger's face was not among any of the lower classmen, nor did she see him in any of the candid photos at the back of the book. There was the swim team, the Lincoln Sharks, posed around the diving board at the high school pool.

She examined the faces in the photo. The stranger wasn't there. Pete Robbins was, as always, in the center of the group. A white towel was draped around his neck. He smiled broadly and held a trophy. Had Pete dreamed of diving for sunken treasure, or maybe of Olympic competitions? Joyce didn't know; she'd never really been a part of Pete's crowd. If he had dreamed those dreams, they hadn't materialized. He'd gone to law school. Joyce knew that much. She had heard he worked for a firm in Boston.

She glanced at her watch. Closing the book, she picked up the baby. Her summer infatuation for Pete Robbins had passed with the ending of the season and the closing of the public pool. He was important for only one thing now: He'd known the stranger. Pete Robbins had called the boy's name across the pool. Ronnie.

"I have to make a phone call, Frankie. Do you want to come upstairs?"

"No. Who are you going to call now?"

"A man at Pop's Pizza, and then a man I used to know a long time ago."

Joyce reached Pop with no difficulty. The difficulty came only as they spoke. She learned that the man thrown out of Pop's Pizza on Friday night had been making the customers nervous, that he had stared at the girls, touched one of them.

Joyce shuddered as she listened to this. "Do you recognize him from the sketch?" she asked Pop.

Pop seemed to consider his words carefully. "I can't be sure," he finally said. "Not positive. The guy I threw out had a short haircut and he was clean-shaven. Looked kind of weird. You know the type? Like a grown-up Boy Scout. The character in this sketch has longer hair and it looks like he's got a beard. Don't get me wrong," Pop added. "There's a real resemblance,

190

and the height and weight seem about right. I just can't swear to it."

"Did you get a look at the man's car?" Joyce asked.

"No. Wish I had. I watched him until he walked into the parking lot. If I see him again, though, I'll call you. And the cops, too. And I'll be sure to find out what he's driving. I feel real bad for you, Mrs. Neuhauser. If one of my daughters was missing, I'd be out of my mind."

Joyce was close to tears. Pop's sympathy, added to his ambivalence about the man in the sketch, made it hard for her to thank him and say good-bye without weeping into the phone. She stood quietly for a few moments. When she felt composed again, she dug the Boston Yellow Pages from a kitchen shelf and turned to the listings for lawyers.

Chapter 16

THE sign on the highway was small, and almost overgrown with vines. Ronnie slowed as he approached it. It read, TUCKER'S COVE RECREATIONAL VEHICLE HOOKUPS. The Indian woman had mentioned this place when she talked about Dromedary Point. Pulling onto the dirt road just beyond the sign, Ronnie followed it through the woods until it ended at Tucker's Cove, on the Atlantic. He parked the van at the far side of a big sand and gravel lot, away from the shabby white trailer with OFFICE printed over the door.

Deborah lay on top of the sleeping bag, hands and feet bound, mouth taped. She looked terrible, her hair hanging in dirty clumps and her face greasy and puffy. He couldn't stand seeing her like this. She smelled badly, too, and whenever he got close to her he felt like turning his face away.

"Deborah?"

Her eyelids were so swollen that she looked back at him through ugly slits.

"I'm going to get us a place to park for the night, with a hot shower."

As Ronnie crossed the lot, a thin, bent old man with a gloomy face stepped from the trailer. The old man took a hard look at the van, and Ronnie saw his mouth move as if he was cursing under his breath.

As Ephraim Tucker saw it, there were two kinds of people in this world: the smart ones—a select group comprised of him, sole owner and proprietor of Tucker's Cove Campsites and Recreational Vehicle Hookups, and whomever he happened to be talking to—and all the others. A bunch of damned fools, that's what the others were. Oh, they were a mixed bag, he'd give you that much. There were the big damned fools in Washington and up in the capital building in Boston, good for nothing but hot air and wasting Ephraim's hard-earned money. There were the fools who populated big cities. There were damned fool foreigners. There were women, blacks, liberals, and anyone who had anything to do with any of them. Look at his friend, Little Ned up in Provincetown. There was a fool for you. Errand boy for that old battle-ax Emma. Lucky to have two dollars to his name on a Saturday night.

And, of course, there were the biggest damned fools of all— the customers of Tucker's Cove.

They came every summer, "Like a swarm of flies zeroing in on a fresh pile of cow flop," he like to say to his friends at the Fo'c'sle Tavern. "With their screaming brats and their overfed wives lying around in curlers and pants they should be ashamed of wearing. And what do you suppose they talk about?" Ephraim would ask any of the local people he could still corner. "Nothing but their gas mileage and their shower stalls and their damned fool compact toilets. Make me laugh, the whole bunch of 'em." No one could remember ever seeing Ephraim Tucker laugh.

Now, here it was mid-October. The tourists had finally left, just before the fierce wind from the Atlantic peeled off their useless hides, and here was some joker in a black van. Ephraim took a good long look at the Hawaiian scene decals blocking out the side windows. "Damned fool things," the old man muttered.

He stared, unblinking, as the driver approached the trailer that served as Ephraim's office and home. Short hair—a plus. Could use a shave—a minus. Youngish—a minus; but too old to be driving around in a old clinker like the Dodge—a real minus. As the other man got closer, Ephraim saw that his eyes were red-rimmed and watery.

Ephraim had his number, by God! A vagrant, no doubt about it. Probably lost his job, home, and family to the bottle. Bad news.

Ephraim's nasal twang was honed to a fine pitch by years of complaining. "Season's about over," he replied when asked about a hookup site.

"I only want somewhere to park for the night, with a hot shower."

There was an tired, begging quality to the man's voice that didn't get past Ephraim. "Looks like your van's seen a lot of miles," he said. "What's your name, anyhow?"

"Ronnie."

"Smith or Jones?" the old man asked, tickled by his own wit. He didn't wait for an answer.

"How many of you are there? Just you?"

"Huh?"

What a fool this one was! Ephraim glared at Ronnie. The furrows lining his forehead deepened. He gave a sigh that seemed to come from a glut of petty annoyances. " 'Cause," he explained in a long-suffering voice, "if there's more than one of you, you pay two fifty extra for the shower. You think fresh water comes cheap out here on the Cape, you try to get yourself a glass of it in one of those high-priced restaurants over in Orleans or Hyannis. You'll see. You'll be down on your knees, begging some waiter. . . ."

Ronnie shook his head. "There's just me."

Ephraim nodded. "All right. That'll be ten dollars for one night. Let you stay two for sixteen."

One of the few traits Ephraim admired was thrift. When his offer was ignored, he was pretty sure he had a fool on his hands. He watched Ronnie—if that was his real name—maneuver the black van down to the last site at the far edge of the lot, the one back in the dwarf pines where the sand blew so hard it could pit a beer can overnight. Another damned fool. Probably harmless, but maybe not. A little funny, Ephraim said to himself. Him hiding off by himself like that. Better keep my eyes open. Not that he wouldn't have anyway, but just in case this was one of those sneaky lowlifes, trying to hide a freeloader in the back of that van, trying to put one over on Ephraim. And in that case, Ronnie was as big a damned fool as you'd ever run across.

That afternoon, Ephraim watched carefully. He saw Ronnie lift the hood to check his oil. He watched him study the road maps they were all so interested in. By early evening, the only really suspicious thing Ephraim could put his finger on was how Ronnie didn't seem to want company, how when Ephraim crossed the sandy lot and headed toward the dwarf pines, this Ronnie character met him partway.

"Wanted to tell you to get your shower by nine. Lights out after that."

"All right. Is that all?"

Ephraim nodded. " 'Cept you should know, there's hurricane warnings out. Two storms. One off the Carolinas, second one—a big one—down in the Caribbean. Tide's already high here. By tomorrow morning, wind's going to be real rough. Maybe you want to move that van of yours closer."

"I'm fine back where I am."

"What have you got in that thing, Ronnie?"

Ronnie had started walking away. He stopped midstride. Ephraim, fine-tuned to what he considered suspicious behavior, saw the other man's shoulders tense.

"What do you mean?" Ronnie asked.

"Just curious. You know, the tourists pull in here, they're always showing each other how they got their vans fixed up. Sinks. Toilets. Some of them even have little showers. Damnest thing I ever saw. Close the toilet seat, pull a curtain around it, and push a button. There you are, showering right along with your toilet. And this last August, I had a couple from Toronto even had a hot tub fixed up in their Winnebago.''

"I've just got what I need. Nothing special.''

It had been Ephraim's experience that the van and RV people were, by nature, exhibitionists, that there wasn't one of them wasn't ready to show his vehicle's innards to the world. There was something here needed watching.

"Just curious,'' Ephraim said. He turned, then looked over his shoulder. Ronnie hadn't moved. "You're only paid through one P.M. tomorrow. You know that.''

"That's all right.''

Ephraim felt the other man's gaze following him as he walked to the trailer. Throughout the afternoon, he nursed his temporary defeat, coddling it, worrying it until, by evening, the possibility he might catch this Ronnie character at something, anything, had become as tantalizing as the possibility of a new love affair or a winning lottery ticket would be to another man. His frustration grew when, just before the sun disappeared, he saw Ronnie leave the men's shower room, a duffel bag in one hand, a towel in the other.

A heavy fog had drifted down from Canada that night, mixing with the winds coming up from the south. When Ephraim threw the switch that turned on the floodlights, the lot was shrouded in a swirling mist so dense, it looked as if a light snow was falling.

Ephraim cleared his dinner dishes and turned out the kitchen light. Then, as he had planned, he dragged his three-legged stool over next to the kitchen door and pulled aside the curtain just a bit. Through the haze, the light from inside the van was barely visible. Ephraim waited. He felt the crick in his knee that told him his rheumatism was laying in for its yearly siege. His eyelids grew heavy and his head began to drop. Then something startled him: a flash of light, out at the edge of the lot. He jerked up and squinted, straining to see. By the time he realized that the interior lights in the black van had brightened, they had darkened again. He was cursing his bad luck when, suddenly, he caught a glimpse of a figure moving through the thick pine shadows. And then—and if Ephraim had been given to howling with glee, he would have done it then—there was another figure, right behind the first one. Without looking away, the old man reached for his glasses on the edge of the sink.

They were hugging the edge of the lot, sometimes blending together as one hulking shadow, sometimes separating. They disappeared, and he wondered whether the fog or his own eyes were playing tricks on him, whether one wasn't the shadow of the other, or whether maybe there was nothing at all but wind shifting through the sand and trees. Only when the couple reached the cinder-block building that housed the showers was Ephraim sure. The floodlight caught them—two figures in silhouette against the gray stone. A satisfied cackle escaped the old man. He leaned so far forward, his glasses scraped the windowpane.

A girl, just like he'd suspected.

Right away, Ephraim noticed the strange way the pair moved. Odd how the girl hesitated and stumbled, how her feet dragged through the sand, how the man's hand on her arm pulled more than guided. He saw her hands reach out to feel the doorway to the ladies' shower like a blind person would. She disappeared into the shower, leaving Ronnie at the door.

Ephraim's opinion of this odd behavior was quick and definite. Drugs. No doubt about it. Damned fool junkies in his campground doing God knows what. He waited for the lights he was sure would brighten the women's shower. Nothing. Just like a sneak thief, showering in the dark, he thought. He let the curtain fall into place. "Damned fools, thinking they're going to put one over on me, do me out of my two fifty," he muttered as he carried the three-legged stool back to its corner. Before he went to bed, Ephraim took his car keys off the hook by the trailer door. "Wouldn't trust them not to break in here tonight

197

and steal them," he said to himself. He tucked the keys under his mattress, and fell into a sound sleep.

The shower was Debbie's second—no, her third—freedom that day. He was starting to trust her. That morning, there had been no pill after breakfast. She had eaten two candy bars from his hand and drunk a carton of orange juice through the straw he held for her. Then he'd driven again, but not so far. As the groggy fear that had enveloped her for days lifted, she had experienced her situation with a clarity that was almost worse than being drugged. Wasn't anybody looking for her? Did they think it was like the times when she'd run away? Had her mother and father really believed that horrible phone call?

Earlier that evening, he'd taken the black tape off her mouth, as he did regularly three times every day, and spoon-fed her a carton of yogurt and an orange he'd peeled and sectioned. She hated the way he knelt so close when he fed her, the way he stared so hard at her mouth closing around the white plastic spoon, but she ate eagerly. After he wiped her mouth with a paper towel, he tore a fresh strip of black tape from the roll.

She hated the tape as much as she hated the meals. The thought of saying his name actually made her stomach feel sick, but she did it, knowing he would like it. "Please, Ronnie," she had said sweetly. "If you leave the tape off, I won't make any noise."

The tape was taut between his two hands, the sticky side poised over her mouth. He had looked at her thoughtfully and asked, "You won't scream, will you?" Debbie shook her head. When he lowered the tape, her lips turned up in a small smile. "Thank you, Ronnie," she said, and in the dimly lighted van she had seen his blush.

Now she shivered in the dank shower stall, letting cold water run over her and wash the filth from her body and the last of the haze from her mind. She thought this was her sixth night in the van, but she couldn't be sure. The only thing she felt certain about was that he was close to where he wanted to take her.

More and more, he talked about the special place they were going. Whenever he talked about that place, his voice got all whispery. "The most romantic place in the world," he kept saying. She hated him when he talked that way almost as much as she hated him when he swore at her.

There was a faucet for hot water in the shower, but by the time the water began to run warm he was already calling her.

"Deborah? Are you okay?"

His voice was too close. He had said he would wait outside, but she was sure he had stepped into the ladies' shower room. "I'm coming," she answered, quickly drying herself. As she peered around the edge of the shower stall, he disappeared through the door.

Taking the bundle of clothes he'd brought for her, she slipped a flannel nightgown over her head and buttoned it down the front. This was one of his mother's things. It was ugly and faded, but at least it was clean.

This was a public place he'd brought her to, she was sure. A public place somewhere at the shore. She'd heard the boom of the waves as soon as he'd turned off the engine that afternoon; and when she'd stepped out of the musty van, she'd smelled salt water.

As she put on clean socks and her sneakers, she shined the flashlight he'd let her use around the shower room. There was no way out of the place other than the exit, where he stood guard. The fog-blanketed night sky showed through some high windows, throwing cold blue light over the concrete-block walls. There were three shower stalls with moldy pink plastic curtains. Debbie towel-dried her wet hair with paper towels from a rusty dispenser, then combed it. She strained to see her reflection in an aluminum mirror that hung over a dirty sink. There were five sinks in a row, and five aluminum mirrors over them. Hooks were mounted on the wall for hanging clothes.

An open door led into a smaller room where five grimy toilet cubicles lined the wall. If she could only put him off for a few more minutes. . . .

"I'll be through in a minute," she called. When he didn't respond, she added, "Okay, Ronnie?"

"That's all right, Deborah."

Her denim jacket was draped over one of the hooks. On the way into the room with the toilets, she reached into a pocket and took one of the bottles of nail polish.

The paper towels were cheap, with a hard finish. Tearing one free, she carried it into one of the cubicles and fastened the door behind her. She opened the bottle of polish and spread the paper towel across a closed toilet seat.

Help. I'm kidnapped. D. Neuhauser. Black van.

Her heart sped as she hurried to print the words. The polish seeped into the paper, blurring the letters, but she could read them well enough. She was taking a big chance. He might search her when she was finished. The nail polish smell was noticeable, too, but she couldn't do anything about that. She blew across the towel until the polish felt dry. On her way out of the ladies' room, she shoved the towel into her jacket pocket.

He met her at the door.

"You didn't leave anything in there, did you?"

Glancing at the bundle of clothes she held in her arms, she shook her head. "I don't think so, but if you want to check, go ahead."

He stared at her for what seemed an age. Finally, he smiled. "Your hair looks nice," he said, steering her toward the van.

"Thank you."

As they walked, she tried to take in everything around her. They were in a big empty lot where poles stuck from the ground like at a drive-in movie. The lot was surrounded by trees and bushes on three sides. On the fourth side, surf broke against a shore. There was a short pier, with a shack near it. They were at some kind of campground. She didn't think it was deserted. Floodlights focused on the shower room and a couple of other

200

buildings. Someone had to turn them on. She noticed a small white trailer near the trees.

Once they were in the van, he taped her hands behind her, but he didn't pull the tape as tightly as he usually did. "You'll be more comfortable this way. Now your feet."

She stuck out her feet. It was becoming routine. As he wound the tape around her ankles, his hand wandered across her calf. She cringed and pulled away. "It's okay, Deborah," he said quickly. "It's okay. We won't do anything until you're ready." Drawing the sleeping bag around her, he zipped it to her neck.

"Let's not forget your milk."

Almost every night, there had been the pill along with her milk. She shook her head. "I'm really tired. I can sleep all right without it."

"No," he said. "Pretty soon you won't have to take them, but not yet. Now—" He held the pill to her lips.

She wanted to scream, to spit at him again or to bite him. But that would make him mad, and every time he got mad it was worse. She opened her mouth. He put the pill on her tongue, then held a paper cup of milk to her lips. When she had drained it, she laid her head on the pillow.

He climbed to the front of the van. She could make out his outline against the front window. His back was against the passenger door and his legs stretched over the seat, over the place where he kept his knife. He shifted slightly. She knew he was looking at her.

"Deborah? Are you still awake?"

She was silent.

"You were real good today. You're starting to like me, aren't you?"

She didn't answer.

"If the tide is down in the morning, we'll make it out to Dromedary Point. When you see this place we're going to, you'll love it. You can fix up the house any way you want."

Dromedary Point. They were back at the Cape. Deborah felt herself drifting into that awful drugged sleep. As her eyes closed,

201

he pulled the curtain that separated the cab from the back of the van.

Ephraim was up with the sun, watching. It was a little before ten when he saw Ronnie open the van's back door and start shaking out some sleeping bags.

Time is money. That was one of Ephraim's favorite sayings, and he had wasted about enough time on this joker. He set out across his lot, full of purpose.

Ronnie tossed the sleeping bag into the van and slammed the door shut the moment he saw Ephraim coming. Ephraim did a neat side step when Ronnie walked out to intercept him. The old man didn't stop until he stood with one arm resting comfortably against the side of the van. They were on his property, by God, and he wasn't going to let this loser put anything over on him.

"Sleep all right?"

"Fine. I'm leaving now," he said, stepping toward the van's passenger door.

Ephraim nodded, then moved nearer the rear of the van. "You enjoy your shower last night?"

Ronnie moved nearer the old man, his expression blank.

"I was wondering, because . . ." Ephraim, fast for a man his age, darted around the van. He had his hand on the back latch before Ronnie could reach him. ". . . because I'm hoping your girlfriend had enough hot water." With that, and a self-satisfied nod, he twisted the handle and pulled the door open.

She was young, just a child. She stared out from the murky dark at him. Her awful puffy eyes blinked and watered in the unfamiliar daylight. Her thin legs stuck out from under her flannel night-gown. Wide black tape wound around her ankles and wrists. She opened her mouth and whispered to him, but there was something wrong with her. She couldn't seem to get her words out.

Ephraim bent over the girl just as Ronnie drove the knife into his lower back. Gasping, the old man took a few staggering steps. Before he collapsed into the sand, he heard the girl moaning. "Don't kill him," she was saying.

Chapter 17

JOYCE was surprised at the size of Pete Robbins's office. After calling the attorney the day before and speaking first to a receptionist, and then to an English-accented secretary, Joyce had imagined Robbins in a baronial corner suite with fifteen-foot ceilings and Oriental rugs. Robbins office was, in reality, smaller than the bedroom Maryann had to herself. Robbins had a wood-veneer desk, two bookcases, a couple of chairs, a couple of plants, and stacks of files. The spires of taller structures showed through the window behind his desk. A slice of gray afternoon sky peeked through a narrow gap in the other buildings. Robbins's office, Joyce thought as she sat in a chair facing his desk, looked a lot like Frank's, except it wasn't as large.

No, the office was not grand, and neither was Pete Robbins. The years since their graduation had left their mark. Nothing devastating. He was still an attractive man, but the blond of his hair was duller, and his skin had a pallor to it that suggested too much time indoors. Joyce, particularly attuned to weight increases, was surprised to see that a slight paunch strained the front of his gray pinstripe suit.

"Of course I remember you, Joyce," he said as he walked to

the other side of his desk. "You haven't changed a bit. So what's this all about, anyway? Planning for our fifteenth-year reunion already? Amazing how fast time passes. I've got to tell you, I had a blast at the tenth."

Robbins had the start of a double chin. He wedged a forefinger under his collar and tugged at the cloth as if it was too tight. "I don't recall seeing you there."

He hadn't remembered her at all. Joyce had felt that from the moment he extended his hand in the firm's reception area. As he'd lead her past the posh offices of senior partners, past secretaries tapping on word processors, she sensed that he was trying to place her.

He had taken a checkbook from a desk drawer. "My time's pretty limited. I won't be able to do any committee work, but I can help out."

Before she could say anything, he was writing a check. "Reunion Committee. Right, Joyce?"

Joyce began apologetically. "I'm afraid I'm not here about the reunion, Pete."

"I go by Peter these days." He looked up at her. "Then what can I do for you? Is this a legal matter?"

"Our thirteen-year-old daughter has been missing for almost a week. Since last Friday, to be exact," Joyce said, all in one breath.

Two tiny creases appeared between Robbins's eyebrows. "I'm sorry to hear that," he said after a moment had passed, "but isn't that a matter for the police?"

"We've been to the police. They think Debbie may have run away."

The tiny creases deepened. "Well, Joyce, I'm not sure what to say. I'm certainly sympathetic. I'm a parent myself. I have terrific kids—a girl nine and a boy five. . . ." He nodded at a series of photos on one of the bookcases—two smiling children and a pretty woman Joyce didn't recognize. "But I don't know how we can help you. I deal in real estate law. The firm doesn't even handle divorces, much less get involved with runaways."

204

He lifted his shoulders and let them fall, a gesture of helplessness. "I might be able get you the name of a private investigator. One of my colleagues used someone."

Robbins was clearly accustomed to working fast. He was reaching for his phone when Joyce interrupted.

"Peter, I'm not here to ask for that kind of help. I don't think Debbie ran away. I think she's been kidnapped." Joyce slid the Provincetown newspaper across Robbins's desk. The paper was open to the article about Bobbie Yellowfeather's murder and the sketch of the suspect.

"I think you know this man," Joyce said.

Confused, Robbins replaced his receiver and looked down at the paper.

The office's quiet was broken only by the hum of traffic from the street far below. Joyce sat quietly, watching the lawyer. When Robbins had finished reading, his gaze moved to the sketch. For an instant, Joyce thought there was a reaction— nothing large—a mere tightening of the muscles in his jaw. When Robbins looked back at her, though, his expression gave away nothing.

"You do remember him, don't you?" she asked. "From the public pool that summer before our senior year. His name is Ronnie."

Robbins folded the newspaper and handed it back to her. "I'm sorry, Joyce, but you're mistaken. I can't imagine why you think I know this man."

"He was a friend of yours. Maybe not a friend, but at least an acquaintance," she added, remembering that everyone had been a friend of Pete's. "He spent time at the pool that summer. I remember you speaking to him."

Robbins swiveled his chair to the side and looked out the window. "I'm sorry this has happened to you and your family, Joyce, but there is absolutely nothing I can do."

Joyce could think no further than Peter Robbins. If he couldn't, or wouldn't, help her, she didn't know where she would turn. "Please try to remember," she pleaded. "I think my daughter is with this man. He's a suspect in a murder. You have a daughter. Think about how you would feel if she was with someone like this."

Robbins faced Joyce, then pushed himself away from his desk and rose. "All I can say is, I'm sorry, but I don't recognize the man in the sketch." Stepping around her, he opened his office door. "I don't mean to rush you, but I'm expecting a client shortly."

Joyce rose, her entire body shaking. How could this happen? She'd been so sure, and now Robbins was telling her she was wrong. Fury and frustration roiled in her. She wouldn't cry, not in front of this complacent man with the pretty wife and cute kids, but at the same time she knew that the moment she was away from Pete Robbins she would break down and give in to her doubts. As she started through the open door, she swayed as if she might faint. Robbins reached to take her arm, but she lurched away from him and stumbled into the hall. Joyce pressed her hands against her temples for a moment. Taking a deep breath then, she hurried past the secretaries and toward the reception area.

She was almost at the end of the long hall when something—not a vague feeling but a knowledge that was real and terrible—hit hard. Stopping abruptly, Joyce retraced her steps.

Peter Robbins was still in his office door. Annoyance showed across his features when he saw Joyce coming back. He opened his mouth to speak, but she didn't give him a chance.

"By the way," she said, her voice flat but strong. "How is your little sister? What's her name? Angela, isn't it?"

Robbins paled. He slumped against his door frame, as if Joyce's words had taken away some vital thing that held him together.

"I guess she's not so little anymore," Joyce continued. "She must be . . . what? In her early twenties by now?"

After a moment, Robbins straightened. "Angela's fine. She's a college senior these days. I'll tell her you asked about her."

"Better yet, give me her phone number," Joyce said. "I'd like to get in touch with her."

Robbins stepped back into his office. Before he closed the door, he made a quick movement with his head that indicated that he didn't want the secretaries to overhear them. Joyce stepped into his doorway. "I'll talk to Angela and see if she wants to call you," he said quietly.

That evening while his wife spoke to Chief Debrito on the phone, Frank listened from the den, bewildered and a little angry. He had never been able to tolerate uncertainty, and suddenly his whole world was uncertain. He was being pulled along in the avalanche of his wife's ideas. And some of those ideas!

If Joyce was wrong—and Frank could easily believe that she was—what on earth had Pete Robbins thought of her that afternoon? The company Frank worked for occasionally dealt with Robbins's law firm, and the idea of Robbins's reaction to Joyce's visit made Frank feel almost sick with embarrassment. Still, there was a part of Frank that admired, and perhaps even envied, Joyce. Misguided as she might be, she had a courage he lacked. The fear of making a fool of herself was not a part of Joyce's nature.

When Joyce had finished her conversation and joined him in the den, Frank pushed the button that switched off the sound of the evening news.

"You went to see Pete Robbins today, Joyce? The big jock from your high school?"

Joyce nodded, and glanced at Frankie and Maryann. The two children were sitting on the sofa looking at books. Sliding between them, Joyce hugged them both. "Why don't you two go upstairs and get ready for bed. I'll come up in a few minutes."

"Will you read us stories?" Maryann asked.

"Of course."

As soon as the children left the room, Joyce said to her

husband, "Yes, I went to see Pete Robbins." She hesitated, waiting for Frank's reaction. He sat quietly, staring at her.

"Do you remember something happening with Pete's little sister, at the beginning of my senior year?" she asked.

Frank shrugged. "At the start of your senior year in high school, I was starting my senior year in college."

Joyce leaned back into the sofa cushions. "But you knew Pete Robbins, didn't you?"

"I knew of him. Everybody in town knew of him. I was a little old for his crowd, though."

"I wasn't part of his crowd, either," Joyce said, "but I do remember this kid from the pool . . . the one I've been dreaming about. He was there a lot that summer. I had a incident with him. It came back to me yesterday." Noticing Frank's startled look, Joyce quickly added. "It was nothing. I mean, almost nothing." She told Frank about the scene in the girl's locker room, and her later scare in the pool.

"Actually, I shouldn't say it was nothing. For a few seconds, I was terrified. But you know how careless kids can be about danger. Once my initial fright was gone, I sort of dismissed him. He was pretty forgettable. Then senior year started; I met you. . . .

"And then, suddenly there were all these wild rumors. First I heard that some kid had taken Pete's little sister out in the woods behind the Robbins's house and raped her. Then I heard that it was this kid from the pool. . . ." Joyce's voice trailed off. "I never really knew much about what happened, but . . ." She paused again.

"But what?"

"But I think it's possible that same kid who molested Pete Robbins's sister is the man I saw driving the van."

Vans, Frank said to himself. Three different vans. Jesus! "What did Robbins say?" he asked.

"I showed him the sketch. He said he didn't recognize the man, but I think he did."

"What about the police chief. What does he think?"

"I'm not sure. He's interested in what I'm saying, but he says there is nothing concrete to place the man in the sketch anywhere in this area."

"There is also nothing concrete to connect the kid you think you remember from the pool with the man in the vans," Frank said with an edge to his voice. "And please tell me why Pete Robbins would lie about recognizing the man. We do business with them," he added. "I hope this doesn't cause problems there."

Joyce was jolted by anger. "Debbie's missing, and you're worried about that?"

"You'd be worried about that, too, if you were paying the bills around here," he snapped back.

The couple sat without speaking for a few seconds, both of them nursing anger and hurt. Joyce noticed the lines of fatigue etched around Frank's eyes. He rubbed at them as if they could be erased by his clenched fists.

"Fighting with each other isn't going to help," she finally said.

He nodded in mute agreement.

A few minutes later, as Joyce was on her way upstairs to put Maryann and Frankie to bed, she heard the phone ring. She felt a now-familiar quickening of her pulse as Frank answered.

"For you again, Joyce," he called from the kitchen.

She glanced up the stairs, where the children were waiting. "Who is it?"

"I think you better take it. I'll put the kids to bed." He had walked to the bottom of the stairs.

"It's Angela Robbins," he said. "Pete Robbins's sister."

Angela Robbins gripped the paper cup firmly and blew three quick, sharp breaths across her hot coffee, sending ripples over the surface. She took a quick sip, then set the cup back on her tray.

"As I told you over the phone, Mrs. Neuhauser, nothing really happened."

Joyce, sitting across the table in the crowded student cafeteria, almost felt herself withering under the younger woman's forthright stare.

Angela was crisp, infused with self-confidence. She had none of her brother's gloss or charm, and, in fact, looked nothing like him. She was short, with a stocky frame. Her dark brows were thick and straight, almost meeting over her nose. Her wiry brown hair had been twisted into a makeshift knot at the back of her head. Loose strands fell over her forehead. On another girl, the look might have been a conscious attempt at a wistful charm. On Angela Robbins, it was messy, and strangely severe. She might have been announcing to the world that she didn't have time for vanity.

"Poly sci and urban studies," she had said, letting a pile of books drop onto the Formica table with a thud. "Groundwork for law school."

"Oh. Like your brother."

The girl looked at Joyce as if Joyce were mad. "Not *exactly* like my brother. I want to defend corporate America's victims, not corporate America."

As Joyce talked about Debbie, and about the stranger in the van, a new anxiety gnawed at her, for surely this self-possessed young woman was nobody's victim. The day before, in Pete Robbins's office, she had unfolded the Provincetown newspaper with little trepidation. Her hands shook, though, as she took the newspaper sketch and handed it to Angela.

"If you would simply take a look at this and tell me if it could be the same person."

Lifting the sketch, Angela stared straight at it, unblinking, unfazed. After a moment, she shook her head. "I really can't say. It's sort of ridiculous, don't you think? You're asking me to identify someone I haven't seen for fifteen years. I was a child the last time I saw the boy you're thinking of," she added indignantly. "If I ever knew his last name, I don't remember it."

Angela swallowed the rest of her coffee in a long gulp. "I have to get to the library, and I'm sure you have a lot to do." The younger woman's tone softened. "I'm sorry about your daughter, but I'm sure she's all right. Girls can be pretty mature at thirteen. I volunteer at legal aid. I've seen thirteen-year-old girls with children of their own."

She pushed back her chair, as if to leave.

A spasm of anger gripped Joyce. She knew her daughter. This brusque young woman did not. Reaching across the table, she took the younger woman's wrist. "Debbie just turned thirteen this summer. I know my daughter, Angela. She is not mature, and she is not ready to have children of her own."

The younger woman was flustered by this show of temper. She took a deep breath. "Look—" she began.

Joyce didn't let her finish. "How old were you, Angela, when you were molested? Or was it okay because you were a mature little girl?"

"I was eight, for Christ's sake," Angela snapped. "I was only eight." She let the books fall onto the table and slipped back into the chair.

"Oh. I didn't realize there was a cutoff age. Like driving a car, is it? Or drinking beer? Little girls can be picked off the street and molested once they pass puberty? Is that right?"

Joyce's voice had grown shrill. Conversations at adjoining tables quieted. Angela looked around, then said to Joyce, "What do you want from me? I told you I don't recognize man in the picture." She glanced at the sketch again, then back at Joyce. "You don't want me to point the finger at somebody who I truthfully do not recognize, when you have absolutely no proof it is the same man. If that's what you want, you can forget it."

"I want to find my daughter," Joyce countered, "and I think this man has her." She paused for a second to collect her thoughts. "Look, I believe you don't recognize the man in this sketch, but would you please tell me what happened when you were eight. I know a little about it because there were rumors all over school. All over town."

"My reputation precedes me," the girl said. "Pete Robbins's little sister was raped at the creek. That's what you heard.

211

Right?" Angela drummed her fingers on the table. "It didn't happen. And even if it had, it's history."

"Not to me," Joyce said. "I want to try to understand why this man . . . if it is the same man . . . has taken my daughter."

Angela slowly released her hold on the edge of the table. She looked down at the sketch again. "I need another cup of coffee."

"It was late summer. This kid—I knew him slightly. He was someone my brother knew. Of course, Pete knew everyone. My big brother had a million friends. He was the center of everything, like the sun with the planets rotating around it, absorbing a little of its light. He and this boy—Ronnie—weren't close at all. Ronnie was—you know—" Angela frowned with the effort of trying to find the right word. "—An outsider. I think that even before the incident at the creek, the other kids thought he was kind of strange. The only thing he and Pete had in common was the swim team—the Sharks. Apparently Ronnie hadn't made the team, but he planned to try out for it again."

"Our house was kind of a meeting place for my brother and his friends. They'd work on their cars—my brother had this Mustang convertible—or else go up to Pete's room and play records. Sometimes I'd sit there, out of their sight, or maybe just beneath their notice. I'd listen to them while they talked about girls and sports and music. When they caught me eavesdropping, I made fun of them, but I thought they were pretty great." A slight smile played at the corners of Angela's mouth. "It's nice, you know, when the most popular kid in town is your big brother.

"This Ronnie—anything I say is going to sound pretty damning—but even I noticed that he was . . . odd. He was a little younger than my brother, but it was more than that. I hate to say *weird*, but he was childish, and kind of fawning. I remember one day my brother and some of his friends were upstairs playing records. Ronnie knocked on the door and my brother had me

212

tell him they weren't there. When he was gone, I heard them laughing about him."

The young woman tilted her head toward Joyce. "Have you ever heard how a group of animals will pick on the one sick animal? I think that's how it was with Ronnie, even before he took me to the creek.

"The first time I met Ronnie was one evening when Pete gave me a ride somewhere. For some reason, Ronnie was already in the car. I got in the backseat with him. He was friendlier to me than my brothers friends were usually, but I still didn't like him as much as I liked Pete's closer friends. Probably because I knew Ronnie was only tolerated by the other boys. Or maybe I sensed that something about him was not right."

Angela spoke slowly, in a monotone, seldom lifting her gaze from the pattern of rings from old coffee cups covering the table. When she did look up at Joyce, her eyes were dark and troubled.

"Please understand, Mrs. Neuhauser. I'm not suggesting he was foaming at the mouth or anything like that. This Ronnie kid made almost no impression on me. That is, until . . ."

"Until he molested you?" Joyce asked when the girl hesitated.

Angela's gaze shifted back to the table. "He didn't. Not the way you're thinking. I'm not sure he would have. If I'd been calmer, if I'd tried to explain to him that he was frightening me, I think he would have stopped what he was doing."

"Angela," Joyce said kindly, "Don't you think you're expecting an awful lot from a eight-year-old?"

The younger woman appeared not to have heard. "One afternoon, Ronnie came to the front door late, about four. My mom was in the basement doing laundry. He asked for Pete, but Pete was out somewhere.

"Ronnie seemed to want to hang around—with me, I mean. It was the same kind of thing I'd noticed when we were in Pete's car. My brother's other friends, they would give me about ten seconds of their time: 'Hey, Angela. Tell Pete I came by.' Ronnie, though . . . he stood in the front door for a few minutes. How was I? he wanted to know. Had I been upstairs playing? What with? Where was my mom?

"I had this . . . this thing . . . an obsession, for frogs." She shook her head, loosening a few of the pins holding the precarious mass of hair. "There was muppet character on TV. Kermit the frog. That afternoon, I was wearing shorts and a T-shirt with the Kermit logo. They were new, and I was so proud of them. My mother had sent away for the set . . . six box tops and a ten-dollar bill or something like that. Ronnie commented on my outfit, and then he asked me if I wanted to go see some real frogs.

"There was a creek near our house. Ronnie said he'd seen frogs sitting on a log. He told me he'd help me catch one. I wasn't supposed to go to the creek unless my parents or Pete were with me, but, well—" Angela shrugged, and smiled again. "I was really into frogs."

"I went with Ronnie across the street and down to the stream," she continued. "It ran through one of those abandoned apple orchards. Lincoln Township hadn't been built up like it is now. There was a lot of undeveloped land.

"When we started climbing down the bank to the stream, he reached out for my hand. I told him, "I can do it myself," but he still kept reaching his hand out toward me. I'm not sure, but maybe that's why I fell. Maybe he was making me nervous and I was trying to avoid touching him. I had climbed down there by myself before, but this time I didn't make it. I slid on some loose rocks and ended up at the bottom, covered with mud.

"He climbed down after me and helped me up. I'd gotten my shorts dirty. I twisted and looked at the back of my leg. I'd scraped myself and my calf was bleeding. It didn't hurt much, but I got upset and started crying.

" 'Don't cry. Don't cry,' " he kept saying. 'I'll take care of you.' "

"He got the shorts off me." Angela looked up at Joyce. "Remember, I was around teenage boys all the time," she said defensively. "Maybe I was naïve, even for an eight-year-old. I certainly wasn't trying to be provocative."

"You don't have to explain that to me."

"He took off his shoes and socks and waded into the creek. He rinsed my shorts. And then . . . then he said, 'You're awfully dirty, too, Angela. Maybe we should wash you off before you go home.'

"I was wearing the T-shirt and my pink nylon day-of-the-week pants. I stepped into the creek and he splashed water over my legs. I think that's when he started touching me. I knew he shouldn't be doing that, but I don't think I was scared of him yet. I mean, not really frightened. I just wanted to go home. I was still crying a little and I said something like, 'Give me back my shorts.'

"He got out of the creek with my shorts in his hand but then . . . I told you he was kind of childish. He hid my shorts behind his back, like he thought this was a game I'd enjoy."

Angela seemed to hunch more deeply into the oversized sweater she wore. "I started crying harder, and then he said this awful thing. He said, 'I don't want to do anything dirty, Angela. I know you're a good girl. I just want to look at you.' "

The young woman's voice had dropped to almost a whisper. "Then . . . then he said he loved me." She glanced at Joyce again, then let her gaze drop to the tabletop.

"I got really scared and made a grab for my shorts, but he got hold of my hand. That's when I got hysterical. I mean, wild, screaming and crying. He seemed surprised by the way I was acting. He pulled me close to him and kept saying, 'We won't do anything dirty. I promise we won't do anything dirty.' And he kept patting me on the head and back, like he was stroking a frantic animal. I struggled and broke away from him, finally, and climbed up the bank. I ran all the way home, shrieking at the top of my lungs.

Tears sprang to the young woman's eyes. "My brother had just driven up when I got home. My mother came running out of the house, and some of the neighbors heard me, too. Somebody noticed that the elastic had been torn off the leg of my pink panties. After that . . . well . . . everybody was hysterical. And, I'll tell you the truth, at that point I don't know if I was more frightened by what had happened with this boy, or the way everyone was acting, or because I'd disobeyed and gone to the creek. But everybody was overwrought and I was so upset that I kept sobbing and screaming.

"One neighbor—she was a nurse—she was kneeling beside me, asking me all these questions. 'Did he touch you here? Did he take down your pants?' And . . . and I don't know." The young woman blinked, trying not to cry. "I just kept nodding and saying, 'Yes.' By then I was so upset, all I could do was agree. And then she—this nurse—said, 'But he didn't pull down his pants?'

"I remember agreeing, he didn't pull down his pants. The truth is, if she had put it another way, if she had said, 'So he pulled down his pants and touched you there with his thing,' I might have agreed to that, too.

"I rode to my doctor's office in my brother's car, sitting in the front seat on my mother's lap. Nothing showed up in the examination." She shrugged. "There was nothing to show up. My parents never brought formal charges; I suppose they wanted to shield me.

"Anyway, that evening my brother and a group of his close friends went out and found Ronnie. They took him to the locker room at the pool after it was closed for the night. My brother had a key. They beat him bloody. My brother—he's a solid citizen these days, but he used to be a little wild. I think I liked him better then," she added.

"Of course, everybody in Lincoln heard about it," Angela said, louder now. "And what they heard! Half of it wasn't true, but the boy was totally hated. If his family had stayed here, he would have been a leper."

Joyce wanted to ask where the family had moved, but she was afraid to interrupt the young woman's story, afraid that if Angela stopped, she wouldn't start again.

216

"About a week after the incident at the creek, the house that Ronnie and his mother lived in caught fire in the middle of the night. It burned to the ground. The fire was suspicious, but nothing was ever proved. Unfortunately, the mother was badly burned. Her hand. I've always felt guilty about that, in some odd way."

Joyce put her hand over the younger woman's. "It doesn't sound like you did anything to feel guilty about. You acted like a little girl."

Angela frowned, not placated. "Later on, when I was older, I found that out that I carried this weird stigma. I mean, everyone was almost too nice to me. Like, even in high school, I went out with some boy and when I wouldn't have sex with him, he got this stupid, condescending look on his face. 'Because of what happened at the creek?' he asked me, as if that five-minute episode was what kept me from flinging myself at him. In Lincoln," she added bitterly, "I'll always be the little girl who was raped at the creek."

"Do you know where Ronnie and his mother went?" Joyce asked.

"They just disappeared," the young woman said.

"You know the boy's last name, don't you?"

The girl blinked, seemingly surprised that Joyce had repeated her earlier question. There was a sudden surge in conversation around them. Angela spoke sharply, making her words heard above it. "I told you I didn't."

And I didn't believe you, Joyce said to herself. "I don't think the incident is as buried as you pretend," she told Angela. "It's very close to the surface. Right under the skin." Without waiting for Angela's response, Joyce began fumbling through her handbag.

Once again, Angela gathered her books. "I really have to go."

"Before you do, let me show you another picture. This is Debbie. It was taken six weeks ago at the Cape. Does she look *mature* to you? She doesn't, does she? She probably doesn't look much older than you did when you were eight."

Angela took the photo in her hand. As she stared at it, her eyes clouded. "Maybe you're right. Every time I've seen something in the paper about a local child being molested, I ask myself, Could it be the same boy? But it never has been. I follow child-molesting cases the way some people follow plane crashes. I can't help it. But, for all I know, Ronnie is leading a perfectly normal life. People change, Mrs. Neuhauser."

"Some do," Joyce said. "And some sink deeper and deeper into their own secret torments until they are overwhelmed by them."

Angela examined Debbie's picture once more. "The boy's last name was Haddon," she said finally. "Ronnie Haddon. The last I heard, he was living with his mother in Rockville, but that was years ago."

Ronnie Haddon. Finally there was a name to go with the face. It meant everything, and, at the same time, Joyce knew it meant nothing definite. Yes, she had a name, but that was all she had. A name to go with a face she saw in her nightmares. What could she say to the police to get them to investigate a man who, more than a decade before, had taken a little girl to a creek to look at frogs. As she drove home, Joyce wondered how she could convince Chief Debrito that the man she had seen at the Cape was the boy who, years before, had caused her a moment of fear at a public swimming pool.

When she pulled into their driveway, she saw Frankie sitting on the rim of the sandbox next door, staring down and looking utterly dejected.

"Frankie," she called. "Want some lunch?"

He didn't look up right away. When he did, his lower lip was pushed forward in a pout. She forced herself to smile as she crossed the lawn to the sandbox.

"Let's pick up Andy and go home. I have to make a phone call, but after that we can have lunch together."

"You always talk on the phone. You promised you'd tuck me in last night, and then you didn't. And I'm tired of staying with

Gloria all the time." His lower lip quivered. "And you never even looked at the doll's purse I told you about."

Joyce sat next to the little boy and took him in her arms. "Oh, sweetheart, I'm so sorry I've neglected you. Do you want to show me the doll's purse now?"

Frankie pulled away from his mother and bent over the sandbox. Dangling his hand, he ran a finger through the sand. Joyce thought he was tracing a picture, but then he withdrew his finger. Hooked over it was a leather string from which hung a small beaded leather bag.

"We found it by the path in the woods." He held the bag toward her. "Goldie and me."

"You know you and Goldie aren't supposed to go in the woods."

"But our name is in the purse," Frankie said.

"Our name? What do you mean?" Joyce asked.

Frankie spelled out the letters. "N-E-U-H-A-U-S-E-R, like I'm supposed to say if I get lost. I'll show you." He pried the strings of the bag loose and reached his small fingers into it. "Here." He handed his mother the piece of paper. "Here's our name."

Joyce opened the folded sheet and stared at it. A page from the local phone directory. After a moment, she asked, "Did you check the phone book for our name and draw the circle around it with a pencil, Frankie?"

He shook his head, happy now to have his mother's attention. "No. It was that way, in the bag."

"You didn't tear this page out of our phone book? Or Gloria's?" she asked excitedly as she took the leather beaded bag from her son.

"No," he said, annoyed. "It was in there already, like I told you."

Joyce felt as if everything in her field of vision had gone except for the few words etched into the leather on the back of the bag: Great Plains Leather. She stood abruptly after a moment and hurried home, pulling her little boy with her.

"The man who left the bar with Bobbie Yellowfeather was on the path the girls took," she told Gus Debrito as soon as she reached him. "I can prove it. And I know his name."

She sounded defensive, but that was the way she felt. The police chief's response surprised her.

"I've been trying to reach you, Mrs. Neuhauser. Earlier today, I got a call from Sergeant Kennedy at your precinct. A sixteen-year-old girl spotted one of the sketches you put up at the shopping center. She claims a man in a brown Chevy picked her up when she was hitchhiking in your area one night last week. Apparently, he frightened her so badly she jumped out of his car while it was moving. She hadn't told anyone about this because she's not supposed to hitchhike, but after she saw one of those posters she had second thoughts. She swears it's the same guy, only now he's got a short haircut and a close shave. The girl told Kennedy that this guy was having fantasies about an Indian woman."

Chapter 18

AFTER speaking to Joyce that evening and learning that Bobbie's medicine bag had been found on the path behind her house, Gus Debrito got the Department of Motor Vehicles to run a computer check on all the Haddons in the Boston area. Within hours, the search narrowed down to a Ronald Haddon in Rockville, who had recently registered a used Dodge van and recently sold a 1980 brown Chevrolet. Gus's remaining doubts about Joyce Neuhauser's story vanished. The man who had been with Bobbie Yellowfeather in the Fo'c'sle Tavern was the same man who had cruised Joyce's neighborhood, the man who had hung a shark's tooth necklace over a branch for a young girl to find, and frightened a young hitchhiker.

The next morning, Gus and Perry sat in their unmarked car outside the Haddon residence. The two men talked softly, taking in the Rockville street. It was a gray day, with pale clouds hanging low in the sky. The morning air was especially still, the way it sometimes is before a storm.

The street seemed like a safe one, without the barred windows and vandalized automobiles seen in some Boston suburbs. There was little traffic, and the few pedestrians they spotted seemed to be on their way to work. At one corner, a yellow school bus stopped for a few children, then pulled away.

The small frame house they were parked in front of varied little from the other houses on the street: one story, with steps leading to a front porch wide enough for a couple of chairs. Some of the homes were better kept than others, but only the house they were in front of actually looked neglected. The browning grass was overgrown, and weeds sprouted freely among the shrubs banking the house. A plastic grocery bag had wrapped itself around a dying azalea plant.

"Too darned quiet for a Friday morning," Perry said. "Seems almost unnatural. That joker's probably sitting in his window right now with a rifle sight trained on us."

Gus smiled. "Sure glad I brought you along, Perry. You have a way of looking on the bright side of a situation." The chief twisted in his seat and nodded to the two uniformed patrolmen in the city police car that was parked across the street. If anything went wrong, he wanted them. Needed them. And it *was* their jurisdiction. But it was his case. His and Joyce Neuhauser's.

Gus unlocked the glove compartment and took out the holstered gun he had put in there earlier that morning. Shifting his body, he strapped the holster around his waist.

"I'm going in. You wait here."

"Got you, Chief. If I hear shots, I'll come running."

Gus glanced at his deputy. "You won't be hearing shots."

"You're probably right. This guy uses a knife."

"You're a comfort, Perry."

As Gus walked up the path to the little house, he adjusted his sports jacket to hide his gun. He fervently hoped he wouldn't be needing it. He was out of shape by ten or fifteen pounds, and out of his prime by as many years.

The concrete steps that led to the house's narrow porch were chipped. There was no bell at the front door, so Gus knocked on the screen door, tentatively at first, then hard enough to make the screen rattle against the frame. While waiting for an answer, he lifted the lid on the mailbox that was mounted next to the door. It was jammed with unretrieved mail. He resisted his urge to shift through the contents. He knocked again, then stepped to a window.

Gus was staring through a crack in the curtains, peering at a small, neat living room when a woman said, "Ronnie hasn't been around in a while."

She was standing on the porch of the neighboring house, holding herself erect with the aid of a cane. She was tiny and stooped, with thin gray hair and glasses as thick as the bottom of an old soda bottle. Already self-conscious about the pistol's weight on his hip, Gus fastened his jacket's bottom button.

"Is this Ronald Haddon's residence?" he asked, walking back down the steps.

The woman nodded. "I haven't seen Ronnie all week, though."

Her eyes, already magnified by the glasses, grew enormous when Gus held up his identification.

"Police? Why are you asking after Ronnie?"

"Do you live here?"

The woman wore a print dress with a prim white lace collar. When she nodded again, more nervously, her head bobbed like a bird's bobbing out of its ruff. She introduced herself to Gus as Mrs. Adele Pierson, and told him that she owned the house Ronnie lived in, adding, "He's never been gone this long before."

"I'd like to ask you some questions, if you don't mind," Gus said.

"Well . . ." Adele Pierson glanced at Gus's identification again. "I suppose it would be all right. Would you like to come in? I could fix some tea."

Gus walked up the three steps onto Mrs. Pierson's porch and stood at her open door. One lamp burned in an otherwise-dim room. Heat billowed through the door, enveloping him. He quickly moved back onto the porch.

"No, thank you, Mrs. Pierson. This will only take a minute.

Why don't you sit down?" He indicated the single white metal porch chair.

"No. I'm fine," she said.

While Mrs. Pierson leaned heavily on her cane, Gus asked her whether she had any idea where Haddon had gone.

The old woman shook her head. "The truth is, Ronnie's not a very outgoing boy. He's been living next door for fifteen years, and I could count the times we've said more than 'Good afternoon,' on my fingers. I always dealt with his mother," she added.

"Is his mother around?"

Mrs. Pierson blinked, shocked by the thought. "Goodness no. She's dead. It must be almost six months now. She had a stroke and died within a few weeks of it. These days, Ronnie slips the rent under my door. I hardly ever see him. I suppose if something needs repair, he does it. The only way I know when Ronnie's around is by his car or the van in the driveway."

"What kind of car does Haddon drive, Mrs. Pierson?"

"A couple weeks ago, he got a big black van. Up until then, he drove his mother's Chevrolet. But last Thursday afternoon—I know it was Thursday because I do my grocery shopping on Thursdays and I was putting things away in the kitchen—I glanced out the window and saw a young man talking to Ronnie in the driveway. A minute later, the young man left in the Chevrolet." She wrinkled her brow uncertainly. "I wondered then if Ronnie sold—"

"The Chevrolet—is it brown?"

"Why, yes." Mrs. Pierson shifted her weight on the cane to peer at the police car parked across the street.

"Has something happened to Ronnie? He hasn't been in an accident, has he?"

"Not as far as I know." Gus pulled a copy of the police artist's original sketch from his pocket. "I'd like you to look at this. Does it resemble Ronnie Haddon?"

Mrs. Pierson moved away from the dark doorway into the gray morning light and squinted at the picture. A disapproving frown crossed her face. "Lately, he does look that way sometimes. Until his mother died, I never saw Ronnie when he didn't have a clean shave and haircut, but the last few months he's been letting himself go. A shame. Ronnie's a nice, clean-cut boy. He has such pretty eyes." She handed the picture back to Gus. "I've always wondered why . . ."

She hesitated, reconsidering what she'd been about to say.

"What have you wondered, Mrs. Pierson?"

The woman's gaze shifted away from Gus, as if the conversation was taking an embarrassing turn. "Well, it seems to me that a clean-cut young man like Ronnie would have young women interested in him, but, as far as I could see, he never has. He was devoted to his mother, though," Mrs. Pierson said with another birdlike nod. "No one would fault Ronnie on that."

"You never see Haddon with women," Gus said. "What about other men? Have you ever met any of Haddon's friends?"

Mrs. Pierson thought about that for a moment. "Ronnie doesn't seem to be much for going out or having people over. Not that I mind. He never makes a bit of noise. No loud parties or music. When you have renters, you have to be careful. Occasionally, I've seen Ronnie drive off at night, but he's always alone." She paused, then said timidly, "I don't like to gossip, but don't you think it seems a little . . . abnormal? Especially now."

Gus tugged at his earlobe. "Could you explain what do you mean by abnormal?"

"Well, it's a fine thing to care for your mother, but now that she's gone, wouldn't you think Ronnie would want to make a new life for himself. And . . ."

"And?"

Mrs. Pierson leaned toward Gus and said in a low voice, "To tell you the truth, I always felt kind of sorry for Ronnie. I know I shouldn't speak ill about the dead, but Mrs. Haddon used to berate that poor boy something awful." She glanced around the quiet street as if afraid someone might catch her gossiping. "It seems to me Mrs. Haddon's passing would have been a relief for Ronnie."

225

"You could hear the Haddons fighting?"

"I couldn't help it," she said defensively. "I wasn't trying to, but we've got no yards at all. There aren't ten feet between my kitchen and theirs. I wouldn't say they were fighting, though. Ronnie would never have raised his voice to his mother. She was the one who made all the noise."

A man of Haddon's age, who didn't date, who didn't go out with friends. How did Ronnie Haddon spend his time? Gus asked Mrs. Pierson about that.

"Well, while his mother was alive, Ronnie kept the house immaculate. He washed the windows every couple weeks and kept up the lawn. Once I dropped by and saw him polishing the furniture. The old-fashioned way," she added, "with real polish. None of that spray junk." A small frown creased Mrs. Pierson's forehead. "His mother could have done more to help, you know. Her hand had been burned in a fire, but that was before they moved here. But I must admit, sometimes a woman's presence does encourage a man to keep things in order." She looked past Gus, at the Haddon's house. "Since his mother died, Ronnie has let the place run down. I've never seen the lawn look so untidy. I suppose I'll have to speak to him about that."

"Does Haddon have a full-time job?"

"Yes! Indeed he does! Ronnie works for Vittucchi's. The cleaning plant out next to the main highway. He's been there for years. You know you have a responsible tenant when he can hold a job, but . . ." She hesitated, averting her eyes from Gus. It struck him that there was something else on her mind. After a moment, she went on. "I hope nothing's wrong. It might be hard finding another tenant. Ronnie always pays his rent on time. My husband didn't leave much. I depend on that rental."

Gus wrote down the name and location of the cleaning plant. "I'd like to get my deputy and take a quick look at Haddon's house, if that's okay. We won't touch anything."

The suggestion obviously made the woman unhappy. "Why, I don't know if I should do that," she said nervously. "After all, Ronnie's rent is paid through the month."

"Or if you'd prefer," Gus said, feeling guilty as hell, "I'll get a search warrant."

Mrs. Pierson swayed on her cane as if she might topple over. Gus quickly took her elbow.

"A search warrant? Goodness! What's Ronnie done? Oh, no. Don't tell me. I don't want to know. Just let me get my sweater and I'll open the door for you."

Gus returned to the car and talked with Perry for a few seconds. The two men then followed Mrs. Pierson, making slow progress up the steps to Haddon's front door. They stood to one side as the old woman fumbled with the lock. When the door opened, Mrs. Pierson peered through it, then smiled back at the policemen.

"He's a good tenant, just like I told you. Clean as a whistle. Ronnie's bedroom is the one on the right, off the hall," she added. "His mother had the best room—the one at the back. It catches the morning light. I don't think Ronnie's moved into it. I still see him cleaning in there. He usually lifts the shades, but they've been drawn all week."

"Keeps a neat house, that's for sure," Perry said.

"Why don't you wait out here," Gus said to Mrs. Pierson.

Mrs. Pierson stepped aside. Gus was following Perry through the door when she laid a frail hand on his arm.

"You know, I heard those rumors years ago," she said softly. "I never knew whether to believe them or not. Ronnie seemed like such a good boy to me."

"What were the rumors, Mrs. Pierson?" Gus asked.

What little color the woman had seemed to drain from her. Gus thought that perhaps something in his expression or voice had frightened her. When she finally spoke, he realized that it was what Mrs. Pierson had to say that reduced her words to an embarrassed whisper.

"I heard that when Ronnie and his mother lived in Lincoln, he did something to a little girl that he shouldn't have done. I heard they had to leave town. One of my neighbors down the street even suggested I shouldn't rent to them."

227

The admission seemed to draw the last of Mrs. Pierson's strength. She turned the lock in the door. "I'm going back to my place. Please pull the door behind you when you leave."

Gus watched her move slowly away before he joined Perry in the house.

"Don't touch anything you don't have to," he said to his deputy.

"Guy's obviously a psycho," Perry said.

"How can you tell?" Gus asked, taking in the small living room.

"No normal man's this clean."

The furniture was inexpensive modern, covered in a light fabric that would have shown stains had there been any. Vacuum tracks were visible across the spotless beige pile rug. Tabletops were bare but for lamps. The only disorder was an accumulation of unopened mail tumbling across a table near the door. Using the tip of his finger, Gus shuffled through that. Mostly advertising circulars. A recent phone bill. There were no personal letters.

The room smelled of the kind of furniture polish Gus's own grandmother had used, but as he stood there he detected another odor lurking behind that clean, old-fashioned one.

Oh, God! he thought. I hope we don't find that little Neuhauser girl's body here.

Perry had wandered into the kitchen. "You could eat off the floor in here," he called.

A fluorescent bulb shone above the kitchen sink, illuminating the shiny white porcelain. A few dishes were stacked in a dish drainer. The towel folded neatly over the rod looked fresh. The trash can had been emptied. A clean paper bag, turned down neatly at its edges, lined it.

"Clean as a whistle, but . . ." Perry lifted his chin and sniffed, delicate as a hound sniffing for game. "Do you smell something funny?"

"I sure do."

"Hell! You don't think that poor kid's . . ."

Gus drew a sharp breath. "I wondered about that myself for a second, but I don't think that's a body we're smelling."

"You're right," Perry said. "Smells more like a sewer."

The two men moved quickly out of the kitchen and down the short hall to the back of the house. The first door at the end of the hall opened into a small bathroom. Expecting that the smell originated here, Gus took a deep breath outside the half-open door. Stepping inside, he glanced into the clean toilet, then shifted the shower curtain and stared down at the gleaming bathtub. The grainy remains of powdered cleanser lay across its bottom.

"The smell's not coming from here," he said to Perry.

"Maybe it's just old plumbing acting up."

"I've got old plumbing that acts up and my house never smells like this."

The first bedroom on the hall was small and dim. Gus moved cautiously around it, using a handkerchief on the tip of his finger to open the dresser drawers.

"See anything?" Perry asked.

"Nope. If this is Haddon's room, he's taken his underclothes with him."

Perry opened the closet door. "Couple uniforms in here. A hat on the shelf. That's all." He read the label from a uniform pocket: VITTUCCHI'S.

Gus was standing near the neatly made bed. He peered down into the space between the mattress and the wall, then carefully pushed his hand into the opening. Something fell to the floor. Perry got onto his knees. "I know what kind of books I hide behind my mattress," he said, sliding a magazine from under the bed. He flipped a page, and another, and suddenly lifted his hand from the pages. Gus looked down at the magazine. The unclothed girls posing seductively were children.

"This guy really *is* a pervert," Perry finally said.

Gus stood stock-still. "Sure looks that way. We've got enough to call in the forensic team. After we take a look at the other bedroom, I'm going to leave one of the local cops here to be sure nobody else touches anything."

"There's one thing I'm wondering about," Perry said as they left the room. "Why would a guy who likes little girls end up out on Dromedary Point with Bobby Yellowfeather?"

"Don't know," said Gus. "Maybe we never will. We've got something else to wonder about, too: Would a normal girl like Debbie Neuhauser go off willingly with a man like this?"

"You think the girl's been kidnapped?"

"I'd bet my pension on it."

The two men stood outside the door to the last room on the hall.

"The smell's coming from in here."

Using his handkerchief to shield his nose, Gus opened the door.

"Shit!" said Perry, his voice muffled by his hand over his face.

"You've got that right!"

Streaks of excrement stained the white bedspread and the wall beside the bed. Dried yellow and brown stains spread across the even cylinders of the pillows. The mirror over the dresser was smeared brown. Its three drawers hung open, and the smell of urine wafted from them. Through the filthy mirror, Gus glimpsed his deputy peering wide-eyed over his hand.

"Looks like Haddon had a few unresolved problems with his mother," Gus said through his handkerchief. "The forensics guys are sure going to enjoy lifting prints out of that," he added, hurrying after Perry through the door.

Sal Vittucchi's normally pink face was blotched crimson in the heat of the cleaning plant. Dark half-moons of perspiration stained the underarms of his bright pink polo shirt. The tiny office was airless and smelled of chemicals and stale cigar smoke. Gus sat sweltering in the worn plastic chair on the other side of Vittucchi's cluttered desk.

"I never had any major complaints about Ronnie," Vittucchi said. "Showed up, did his job. Drove the van." He chewed on the tip of a cigar, then struck a match to it. "I teased Ronnie when he bought it, about maybe wanting to get laid in back. What I really think is after twelve years Ronnie got so used to driving the van, he couldn't stand losing it when the new one came in."

"He was in the same position here, all that time?" Gus asked.

The police chief hadn't intended to be critical. Vittucchi, however, turned defensive.

"So? You're telling me I should have made him manager?" He flipped his hands toward Gus, palms up. "Ronnie—he's like a kid. Mind wanders. He forgets things. I couldn't promote him, have him overseeing things in the plant, forgetting to turn off the mangle or a pressing machine. Fuckin' burn the place down. Carlos, now, he's got a good head on his shoulders. Careful with the equipment. Likes the ladies a little too much, but what am I supposed to do about that?"

Gus nodded, agreeing that there wasn't much Vittucchi could do about that. He then asked whether Vittucchi knew where Ronnie spent his vacations.

Vittucchi shook his head. "He got his holidays and his two weeks vacation, same as everybody else. I don't know what he did with them."

"What were Haddon's hours?"

"Eight A.M. to five P.M. Or whenever he got through with his deliveries. I never made a big deal about that. Sometimes he took the van home with him."

"You have a record of when he took his vacation?"

The fat man's wooden chair creaked as he shifted his weight. "Do I have records? I got records up the kazoo, Chief. I got Equal Employment records; I got OSHA records."

"Just vacation records. I'm interested particularly in the Friday before Labor Day," Gus added, knowing that if Haddon had, in fact, been at work, he couldn't have been in a traffic jam near the Bourne Bridge.

Vittucchi shook his head. "It's not likely Ronnie was on

vacation then. Holidays are busy for me. I do a lot of work with restaurants and motels."

Vittucchi kept his records in a three-drawer steel file cabinet. He thumbed through one manila folder, then another. "Son of a gun," he said after a few seconds of this. "Ronnie called in sick that Friday." He eased himself back into his chair. "Unusual. Ronnie was almost never sick. But, you know"—the big man shrugged—"last few months Ronnie was acting sort of different. Got downright sloppy-looking for a while. Let his hair get too long, wasn't shaving every day. I had to speak to him about that. Gave him a pep talk about being my front man."

Gus went through some of the same questions he'd asked Mrs. Pierson. How did Haddon pass his spare time? A shrug from Vittucchi. Male friends? Another shrug.

Girlfriends?

"Girlfriends? Ronnie?" The fat man snorted, then settled down and regarded Gus seriously. "I got a feeling you're not asking me about girls his own age. You asking me about little girls? Like in children? Right?"

"I'm asking for anything you know about Haddon's relationships with females."

Vittucchi leaned across the desk. "I heard a story about Ronnie. A long time back—high school—he's supposed to have messed with some little girl. Like maybe he's a pervert."

"Did you ever see any evidence of that?"

"You kidding? Far as I could tell, Ronnie wasn't much for *any* girls." He nodded toward the back of the plant. "I got some foxy girls working here. You think Ronnie ever looked at any of them? Never. I used to tease him if he came in a few minutes late. 'Hey, Ronnie! Out getting yourself a little ass last night?' The kid, he'd turn red, couldn't look me in the eye. I sure never figured on Ronnie having a fiancée. What's he done? Married some jailbait?"

"Haddon has a fiancée?" Gus asked skeptically.

"That's what he says. Last Friday evening, Ronnie tells me he's quitting. No notice, no nothing." Vittucchi picked the

232

cigar from an ashtray and took a drag. Smoke billowed around him. "Got this shit-eatin' grin on his face. Told me he's going off with his fiancée. No reason for a guy to lie about that."

It was midafternoon when Gus finally got to the Neuhauser home. Leaving Perry in the car, he went in to talk to Joyce, something he had been dreading for hours.

Joyce sat quietly with her hands clutched as Gus told her what he knew. He pulled a few punches, but not many. She looked even more exhausted than she had the previous Monday, but Gus was beginning to think that Joyce Neuhauser was stronger than either of them had realized.

"We've called in the forensic team now," he said as he watched the Neuhauser's youngest child scoot across the kitchen floor on his stomach. "I should be hearing from them by tomorrow morning. Even late today."

Joyce slapped the tabletop with the flat of her hand. Gus looked up, startled.

"That's not going to do Debbie any good, Chief Debrito. Forensics won't tell you where Ronnie Haddon has taken her. A known child molester has my daughter," Joyce said, her voice rising angrily. "Think about that!"

"I do think about it, Mrs. Neuhauser. We're doing everything possible to find them. Every cop in this state can identify that van and has its license number. We've called the FBI, as well. Haddon could have crossed a dozen state lines by now."

"I don't mean to snap at you," Joyce said. "I'm just so damned upset."

"Anybody in your position would be," Gus said. "We'll have Haddon's picture on the news tonight. Debbie's, too, unless you object."

"Object?" She stared at him, not understanding.

"Remember—Haddon has probably killed one woman. We don't know what set him off that time, but, if he starts feeling that having Debbie around is a problem, who can say what he might do. From everything we've heard, it seems like Haddon's infatuated with your daughter. He wants to keep her with him, but . . .''

He paused, letting Joyce absorb exactly what he meant.

She bent down to pick the baby off the floor. "It's so easy when they're this age. You mentioned you have children.''

"Three. The youngest one's twenty.''

"If one of your children was in Debbie's predicament, what would you do?''

Gus shook his head. "I honestly don't know.''

Joyce lifted Andy onto her lap. Looking at Gus again, she said, "I'd like to talk to Frank about releasing Debbie's picture, but I expect that we won't object.''

Chapter 19

AS soon as Ronnie had dragged the tarp halfway off the old man, the stench hit him. He glanced quickly at Deborah, but she didn't seem to notice the smell. She kept her face turned away.

The old man was heavier than he looked. Ronnie strained as he pulled the body across the sand to the hole he'd dug at the back of the cinder-block locker rooms. He rolled it into the hole and used a broad-edged shovel to push sand into the shallow grave. As he worked, the harsh wind coming off the Atlantic stirred the sand, uncovering the scuffed tip of a shoe and a bit of the old man's yellow windbreaker, stained brown with blood. The blood seemed to upset Deborah; she hadn't spoken a word since the Shark had stabbed the old man the day before and the old man's bloody spittle sprayed on her. All she had done was scream, until Ronnie had feared her horrible hoarse wailing would never end. It had taken a slap across her face before Deborah was quiet. More than one slap, he remembered, and the memory shamed him. Sometimes the Shark was right about those things, though. Sometimes the Shark knew how you had to handle women.

Ronnie worked quickly to cover the body and hide its ugliness. When the last traces of the old man were covered by sand, he looked at Deborah. She was sitting in the sand a few feet away from the grave. Her hands were tied behind her, but her feet weren't bound. She could have run, he knew. Could have tried to get away, but she hadn't. He'd told her to stay there and she'd stayed. Quiet, too.

Ronnie leaned the shovel against the cinder-block building and smiled at his girl. He thought she was liking him more and more, but it was hard to tell. The Shark was there so much now, whispering, telling him Deborah was bad. Ronnie knew he couldn't always trust the Shark. Once the Shark even told him to hit his mother. Slap the nagging old bag right across the face, the Shark had whispered, and Ronnie had clasped his hands behind his back to keep from doing that. Now the Shark kept whispering to Ronnie, talking about filthy things he could do to Deborah.

"I told you I'd take care of everything," Ronnie said to her.

She stared, blank-eyed. Ronnie looked past her across the stretch of water that lay between them and Dromedary Point. The water was rough, whitecaps rising.

"Want to go down and look at the beach?"

Deborah got to her feet without having to be told. Taking her arm, Ronnie led her past the cinder-block building, past the pier, and down the beach.

The beach at Tucker's Cove was strewn with sea grass and broken shells. Waves crashed into the shore, and the cold wind blew needles of sand into Ronnie's eyes. At the water's edge, they stopped. Ronnie pointed into the distance.

"You see that piece of land out there? That's where we're going, as soon as the water is calm. If we can't get the van through," he added, "we'll take the old man's boat."

He hoped for a reaction, but she gazed glassy-eyed into the distance, saying nothing. Her hair whipped around her face, blown by the wind. He could feel her arm trembling through her blue-jean jacket. He made a mental note to get her a warmer coat. He didn't like her jacket, anyway. The shiny patches on it made her look cheap.

"You're cold. You want to go back now?"

She nodded almost imperceptibly. He turned to lead her back across the dune, and her hair brushed across his face. He couldn't help what he did. He pulled Deborah close so that she pressed into him. Opening his windbreaker, he wrapped it around her back. She stiffened but didn't fight, and he savored the feel of her body.

"Is that better, Deborah? You're so cold, aren't you? Poor Deborah. I'm going to take care of you. It's too rough for us to try crossing today. You know, instead of staying in the van tonight, we're going to stay in that old man's trailer. I looked through it yesterday. He has a refrigerator and stove. I'll make us a real meal. You'd like that, wouldn't you?" Ronnie bent his head until his face nestled in her hair.

He moved them into the trailer that morning. He loosened Deborah's hands, and she helped him carry a few things from their small stock of food and clothing. After a while, Ronnie was glad to see that she'd warmed up enough to take off her trashy denim jacket and drop it in the van.

While Deborah sat rigid on Ephraim Tucker's tweed sofa, staring vacantly at a movie on the old black and white television, Ronnie looked through the trailer's little refrigerator.

"Look at this, Deborah. Hamburger meat."

He crossed the floor and held the package in front of her. "It's still fresh. There are noodles on the shelf, and a can of tomatoes. I'll make spaghetti. Mother taught me how. You'll like Mother's recipe."

Deborah looked at the cellophane-wrapped package of raw meat, then turned her head into the sofa cushion. She shuddered, and her body convulsed with muffled sobs.

"What is it, Deborah? What's the matter?"

"You killed that old man," she said. "You just stabbed him and killed him."

Ronnie frowned and shook his head. "No. I didn't. Don't

237

you understand? The Shark killed him. He had to. The old man was trying to break us up."

He moved quietly around the trailer's tiny bedroom for a few minutes, checking windows, making ready for the night. He wouldn't use the electric lights, and he had brought in the kerosene lantern from the van. When he damped the wick and only a thin light shone through the windows, Debbie opened her eyes.

She watched, her face half-covered by a blanket, as he propped open the bedroom door with one of the kitchen chairs. She saw him lean toward the television, adjusting the sound, then sink onto the old sofa. Light from the television flickered against the bedroom wall.

She had been disoriented and dazed for an entire day after he'd killed the old man. After he'd hit her, she'd stumbled through the hours, doing whatever he asked. Shock. She knew the symptoms from her personal-health class. It was the hamburger that brought her out of it: the blood oozing from the plastic wrap just like the blood had oozed out of the old man's mouth when he'd tried to talk to her. That had jolted her awake.

When she thought Ronnie wasn't watching, she started working the tape around her wrists. It wasn't tight, and she found the tape's edge easily. The pill wasn't working yet, and she prayed she could fight it. If she could get her hands free and make herself stay awake until he was asleep, maybe she could get past him. *I'm wide awake. I'm wide awake,* she kept saying to herself. As she struggled with the tape, though, the familiar fatigue began, even stronger and quicker than usual. She tried to force herself awake. *I'm wide . . .* The fog closed quickly over her.

Ronnie kept the kerosene lantern dim. He set it on the floor beside him, next to her bed. There had been enough time for the pills to work, but he didn't want to risk waking her, not tonight, with what he was going to do.

He'd been thinking about it since he'd pressed against her on the beach. The urge had embarrassed him at first. He'd tried to make it go away, but it had strengthened through the afternoon and evening until he could hardly look at her without feeling the sweat and the tightening in his groin. He couldn't take a chance on her waking, though. When he poured Deborah's milk that night, he had dissolved a second pill in the liquid.

He pulled the blanket until it lay below her waist, and then the sheet, stripping back the layers gently. How pretty she looked in his mother's yellow flannel nightgown. She'd buttoned it all the way to her neck. He took a deep breath. This was no time to get nervous.

He'd planned it all evening, picturing how he would touch her. Putting his hand to Deborah's throat, he loosened the first button. She didn't stir. His fingers fumbled with the next button, and the next. His breaths quickened. By the time he eased the button near her waist from its hole, his fingers shook violently.

He lifted his hands. Stop it. Stop shaking. Don't do anything to ruin this. When the trembling eased, he lowered his hands again. Taking both sides of the nightgown's collar in his fingers, he slowly, gently folded them back until the bare V of Deborah's skin lay visible beneath the open nightgown. Lifting the lantern, he held it so that light shimmered over her.

She was as beautiful as he had thought she would be, as beautiful as an angel. Even more beautiful than Angela. His breath quickened. He lowered his free hand slowly until it lay over one of Deborah's breasts, barely touching her.

She felt like satin. Smoother, even. His skin was suddenly hot and sweat-soaked. Breaths came out of him in quick gasps. He'd never gone this far with a real girl before. Never.

There were other things he wanted to do, other places to explore. He fought the desire. His breathing slowed until he trusted himself to fasten her nightgown hurriedly. When he had pulled the blanket over her, Ronnie hurried out of the bedroom. Stripping, he lay on the sofa.

It was the best sex ever. Much better than with the girl on the phone. He came quickly and felt drained of everything, as if every bit of confusion and tension had gone from him. Deborah was his angel. His new Angela.

Could it have been this sweet with Angela, if he hadn't moved too fast? His thoughts wandered back over the years, back to Angela, back to where it had started.

It had began on an afternoon in mid-August, a Saturday when the temperature soared. The Shark offered Ronnie a ride home from the pool in his Mustang. Another boy, one of the Shark's friends, already occupied the front passenger seat, so Ronnie climbed into the rear, grateful, hardly believing this was happening. It was the first time it had ever happened, and the last. Why had it happened at all? Why had the most popular boy in town offered a strange, quiet boy with no friends a spot in his back seat? The reasons were lost in time and in the aftermath of what came later.

The Shark had pulled over at his house and blown the Mustang's horn. A eight-year-old girl in shorts and sandals climbed into the backseat next to Ronnie.

"This squirt is Angela, my sister," the Shark had said with a fake gruffness that masked his real affection. "I've got to drop her somewhere."

The little girl had smiled, making Ronnie catch his breath. She was the most beautiful girl he had ever seen. So innocent, so cute. The way her legs were too short to reach the floor and her feet swung over the custom floormat the Shark had installed made Ronnie feel dizzy with pleasure. Angela had gotten out of the car on Ronnie's side, climbing over him, brushing against him with her bare knee, and finally he'd known what the others meant when they talked about girls.

He'd always gone along with the things they said, pretending he understood, pretending he enjoyed peeking into the girls' locker room at the pool, but he'd never really understood until he met Angela.

A few weeks later, the bad time had started.

Ronnie shuddered and rubbed his hands over his eyes to erase the ugly image that had suddenly clouded his memories. The sudden plunge into the dark at the back of his mind disoriented him. Shouldn't think about it, he said to himself. Think about the nice things. Angela is in the past. Now there's Deborah.

He strained to bring himself into the present. It was hard. The past—the bad time—it didn't want to let go. He was hardly aware of the images flickering over the television, of the Boston newscaster's muted voice. They only registered when the man had said his name for the second time.

"Haddon is believed to be driving a black 1979 Dodge van. . . ."

He sat up, half-dazed, and focused his eyes on the screen. His picture—the one from his driver's license—showed on the television.

". . . considered extremely dangerous," the commentator was saying.

Ronnie came alive. Leaping to his feet, he turned up the volume. His fists tightened as his van's license number was read over the air. And then came a picture of Deborah. It looked like a yearbook picture. Her white collar was buttoned high at her throat, and her hair hung straight over her shoulders.

". . . may be traveling with Haddon. It is believed that the girl may have been kidnapped and is being held against her will."

Kidnapped? The word hammered into him. How could they think she'd been kidnapped? Deborah had told her mother they were getting married. Ronnie's mind dwelt briefly on what this meant. It had to be her mother doing this, trying to break them up. That Indian woman, or else her cat-faced friend, had talked to Deborah's mother.

Lying bitches! His confusion subsided, replaced by a rage that shook him.

Hateful, stupid woman. It was the dirty Indian woman who had done this. The cat-faced girl had never seen the van, but the Indian woman had. Ronnie paced the trailer's little living room in a fury. When the Indian woman went to his house at night

241

and took back her leather bag, she'd seen his black van parked in the driveway. Now they were looking for it. He had to get rid of the van. Hide it somewhere. Grabbing his jacket, Ronnie hurried from the trailer.

It was long after daybreak when Debbie woke. She felt awful, groggy and sweaty. Dragging herself from the bed, she stumbled into the living room.

He was at the stove, frying eggs.

"I have to go to the bathroom. Would you undo my hands please?"

Her tongue felt mushy in her mouth, and her early-morning voice slurred more than ever. He didn't seem to notice her. Something was different with him this morning. There was no stupid smile, no 'Hope you slept well, Deborah.' When he looked at her, his eyes looked dead. He laid down a spatula he'd been using. Taking a paring knife in his hand, he sawed through the tape that held her wrists. When she was free, he turned back to the stove.

She rubbed her wrists, hardly believing he wasn't going to go with her, wasn't going to wait outside the half-open door. She walked back into the bedroom to get her clothing, expecting every moment to hear his footsteps right behind her or feel his hand on her arm. Nothing. On the way to the bathroom, she passed within inches of the trailer's door. He didn't make a move toward her.

The bathroom was horrible—a tiny room with a plastic folding door. Debbie pulled the door shut. There was no point in locking it. His knife would go right through the plastic. But he wasn't hovering. That was the main thing. She hadn't had tape on her mouth or legs the day before. Maybe now he was going to leave her hands free, too. And if that happened, she was going to get away, even if she had to stick a kitchen knife in him.

She turned the water on hard and immediately went through the cabinet over the sink. Soap, toothpaste, aspirin. A safety razor, the kind with dual single-edged blades. And a plastic case with a supply of blades. She pried one of the blades from the case and examined it, but she couldn't think of how she could use it.

Under the sink, next to the pipes, there was a round cardboard container. She read the label. Lye. Could she use that? She read the warnings on the label.

As she washed her face, she made plans for the day. She'd be nice to him again. Smile and say, "Thank you, Ronnie." She'd eat everything so she would have lots of energy. And if she saw a chance, she would run for it.

She began unbuttoning her nightgown, starting at the neck. The top button had been put in the hole for the second, but she gave it little thought. Her fingers, still stiff with sleep, fumbled with the tiny buttons. The fourth one—it was in the wrong hole, too. And one down near her stomach . . .

Her legs started shaking. She opened her mouth to cry out, then shut it again. She kept her lips clamped tight, whimpering quietly so he wouldn't hear. Tears rolled down her face. He was doing things to her at night while she was asleep.

Debbie knew the things boys and girls did. She'd read about it in school and heard about it a million times from Lisa. Her parents did it—Debbie had heard them—and that had to be weird. This was the worst, though. Horrible.

She dressed herself when she was able. Before she opened the bathroom door, she slid the container of lye behind the toilet where he couldn't see it.

The table was set, juice poured. He was waiting for her at the table. She pulled out a chair and sat across from him. He scooped scrambled eggs and a couple pieces of sausage onto her plate without looking at her.

"This looks so good, Ronnie. I'm starved." She took a sip of juice, then a forkful of sausage, watching him all the while, ready to flash a smile the second he looked at her.

"Your mother's such a bitch, passing on those lies!"

He spat the words at her. She dropped her fork.

"She told the police you were kidnapped. I know she talks to that Indian woman. Why didn't you tell me? Maybe she's an

Indian, too. Is that why you didn't tell me, Deborah? You didn't want me to know your mother was an Indian?"

Crazy, crazy. He was getting worse and worse. She couldn't make sense out of what he was saying. His face was so white and angry. More angry than when he'd hit her. More angry even than when he'd killed the old man. She tried to smile at him, but hot tears burned her eyes.

"My mother's not an Indian."

He looked away. "She told them about the van," he finally said, his voice calmer. "I had to hide it. It took me almost all night to walk back."

She picked up her fork and took a bite of the eggs. She couldn't taste them, but she chewed and swallowed. "That's too bad. What are we going to do without it?"

An age seemed to pass before he answered her. "I couldn't find the keys to the old man's car. We'll have to take his boat. We can't go today, though. The water's rougher than it was yesterday. That old jerk doesn't have anything but a rowboat. There's not even an outboard motor. I found a shotgun in the shed," he added. "And some shells."

"What do you want that for?"

He shrugged.

They finished breakfast in silence.

"You must be tired," Debbie said. "You could take a nap while I do the dishes."

He shook his head. "You didn't tell me the truth about your mother, Deborah. How can I trust you?"

"How was I supposed to know my mother was friends with the Indian woman," she blurted. "She never told me."

He stared thoughtfully at her, then slid his chair back. "You can do the dishes, but I'm going to watch you."

He never slept all day, and he never stopped watching her. He wouldn't let her turn on the television, and time passed slowly. She spent her time studying the trailer, any part of it she could get to without making him suspicious. The knives were in the drawer beside the sink. A couple of them were pretty sharp, but she couldn't take one, not with him watching. He had leaned the shotgun against the bedroom wall, but she didn't know whether it was loaded or not. Alongside the door that led outside was a row of light switches. One of them was larger than the other, and surrounded by a metal plate. Maybe an alarm? Or maybe it operated the outside floodlights. The lye was still behind the toilet, but he didn't let her close the bathroom door again that day. He stood in the door while she used the toilet, his back turned. He could hear everything she did.

When dusk fell, he took the black tape from the counter and bound her to one of the kitchen chairs. He didn't tape her mouth, but her hands were fastened to the arms and her feet to the legs. When he finished that, he took more tape and wrapped it around her chest and then around the back of the chair, so tightly that she could hardly breath.

"I'm going to sleep in the bed tonight. You keep quiet." At the bedroom door, he hesitated. "I wanted to do it with you, but I'm not sure anymore. I thought you were a good girl. Now I don't know. Maybe the Shark is right about you." He doused the lantern. A moment later, he was snoring.

He was getting worse and worse. He hadn't given her lunch or dinner, and she'd been too scared to ask. One good thing, though: He hadn't given her a pill.

While she struggled with the tape, the phone suddenly rang, startling her. She sat still. The phone was in the bedroom, where he slept, but if he heard it, he ignored it. It rang half a dozen times before it stopped.

Debbie fought with the tape until her arms ached. It didn't give an inch. There was no way she could use a knife, or the lye, not bound the way she was. She started scooting the chair across the floor. Finally, she was directly under the light switches. It took all the strength in her legs to get herself up as high as the switches. When she had, she grasped the big one in her teeth and pushed it up. A powerful light beamed through the curtained windows from outside the trailer.

★　★　★

On the other side of the Cape, Little Ned Mayo was perplexed. First Saturday night in years his friend Ephraim Tucker hadn't made it into town for a few beers. Ned left the Fo'c'sle Tavern and walked down Commercial Street toward Emma's, wondering whether she would let him use her car. Old man like Ephraim, living out there alone. Ned had tried calling Ephraim's number earlier that evening. There hadn't been any response. You never could tell what might have happened. Heart attack, maybe. Or a stroke. And there's old Ephraim, lying there and nobody gives a damn! Hell of a world!

Ned stumbled over the curb in front of Emma's and grabbed at a windowbox to keep from falling. Should have stuck to beer. Shouldn't've had those two whiskeys. Old man can't afford a bad fall. Could be that's what had happened to Ephraim. Poor Ephraim, sprawled on the floor of his trailer, broken hip. Somebody should check on him.

Ned looked up at Emma's window. The lights were out. Wouldn't she get riled up if he woke her and asked for her car keys. Emma had a nose like a bloodhound. One whiff of the liquor on his breath and she'd throw him out in the street so fast . . .

There was another way.

He slipped around the side of the building and made his way along the narrow walkway, past the garbage cans, to the plank walkway under the store's pilings where Emma kept her big old motorboat. His fingers scraped across the boat's bottom. Nice and dry. That woman sure took care of her stuff. The winch was there, too, greased and waiting. He stretched his arms into the wooden lattice of the store's subflooring and pulled down a pair of oars. Wasn't about to fire up that motor until he was out of Emma's hearing.

One of the oars rapped against a pipe, sending an echo shivering up the metal. Ned waited, his heart pounding. That old firecracker might have woken up. She'd start screaming thief and shooting out the window with that antique revolver she kept under her bed.

He reached into his jacket pocket for the half-pint bottle of whiskey he'd lifted from behind the bar at the Fo'c'sle, and took a long swallow to soothe his nerves.

The rattling stilled and there was only the sound of water lapping against the pilings. Ned lowered the boat into the water. Locking the oars into place, he pushed away from the pilings.

A bad night for this, he realized immediately—rough water and a cold wind. The razor-edged sliver of the new moon was blanketed by a smoky mist. Boats moved through the night cautiously, with lights straining to force a path through the heavy air and foghorns calling across the water. Ned took another pull on the bottle. He'd have to stick real close to the land.

His fear diminished with the level of the liquor in the bottle. By the time he was far enough away from Emma's to start the powerful inboard motor, he was enjoying it. A sure-fire adventure, like in the old days. Ned could just picture old Ephraim's expression when he pulled up at the Tucker's Cove pier. Letting the throttle all the way out, Ned left the secluded waters of the bay and roared into open water.

About twenty minutes later, Ned had rounded Race Point and was heading south. That was when the engine began to cough. He lowered the throttle, but the thing kept sputtering. He was about an eighth mile offshore and a good mile north of Tucker's Cove when it died.

He cursed out loud. Out of gas. A half-full can banged around in the bottom of the boat, but that wouldn't get him far. Spooky out here, too. Water real turbulent. Guy could easily be swamped. The little boat lurched violently in the waves, slamming Ned against the hull.

He was going to die out there for sure. He gripped both sides of the boat and held on. When the boat quit rocking, Ned poured the rest of the gas into the tank and started toward Ephraim's.

Might not make it, he thought after about ten minutes of this. Waves getting rougher and rougher, and around the bend of Dromedary Point, over toward Ephraim's that was a real bad spot. Nightmare Point, they'd called it in the old days. He took another long pull on the bottle and stared across the water.

Son of a gun! Danged if Ephraim didn't have his floodlights on. Nothing else over there. Had to be Tucker's Cove. Why would a tight son of a gun like Ephraim have the lights on in the middle of the night out of season? Cheaper even than Emma, and running electric lights that way? As Ned watched, the lights went off. Then they went on again. Then off. Ned squinted, peering through the night. What the devil was Ephraim doing?

Taking up the oars to save gas, he started rowing toward Tucker's Cove. The waves turned him back. Too rough for a boat like Emma's. Needed a big boat to get past Dromedary Point. Maybe he'd get Emma's car in the morning and drive out. If Emma wouldn't give him her keys, he'd go to the police. Somebody had to check on Ephraim. Turning the boat, Ned began the trip back to Provincetown.

Chapter 20

AT about 8:00 A.M., a bird-watcher named Milton Snyder trained his binoculars on the poplar trees at the southern end of the Herring Marsh near Wellfleet. Wind whipped the tall trees, sending leaves showering onto the water. The bird-watcher was certain he had spotted something special in the lower branches of one tree. He held the glasses steady, and after a few minutes his patience was rewarded. An immature bald eagle flew from the tree and circled the marsh.

Snyder followed the movement, carefully noting the whitish feathers on the underside of the young bird's wings. Where had the eagle come from? If there had been an eagle's nest around the marsh, he would have spotted it. The eagle disappeared back into the poplar tree. Snyder lowered his binoculars and jotted some notes in the spiral notebook he always carried. When he had finished, he raised the binoculars again, hoping for one more glimpse of the bird. He kept the glasses trained on the poplars for a moment, then moved them until the far edge of the marsh was in his view.

Wasn't that odd? It looked as if someone had driven a black van partly into the mud. There were patches of quicksand over there, and the front of the van was sunken, so the driver's window was completely submerged. Snyder stepped a few feet to his right, trying to get a look at the van's side. There was no business logo, but someone had put orange shades in the side windows.

Snyder considered circling and getting as close to the van as possible, but even in the short time he'd been there the wind had picked up. It looked like the Cape was going to get the tail end of the hurricane that had lashed the Carolinas the day before.

He covered the mile between the marsh and his home quickly on his three-speed bike. Snyder's wife, Bea, had been sleeping when he'd left, but she'd be up now. Bea always made pancakes on Sunday morning.

When Snyder walked into the kitchen, Bea was mixing the batter in a bowl.

"I saw that eagle again at the marsh," he told her. "Somewhere around here there's a big nest. Don't know how I've missed it."

Bea was never too talkative in the morning. She nodded absently as she poured the batter into the frying pan.

"I saw something peculiar while I was at the marsh. Someone's tried to dump an old van. It's half-buried in the quicksand. The county's going to have some job getting it out."

"A van? It's not black, is it?" Bea hadn't been to the marsh in weeks, but she had seen the news the night before. When Milton nodded, surprised, she asked with real alarm in her voice, "Did it have orange shades in the windows?"

"How did you know that?"

"Did you look inside?"

"Couldn't." Milton's surprise grew when Bea left the pancakes sizzling and hurried to the phone. "What are you doing? Breakfast is going to burn."

"You dozed off during the news last night," Bea responded. "There could be a kidnapped little girl in that van. I need the number of the police in Provincetown," she said to the operator who answered her call.

Joyce hadn't believed that she could get any more anxious than she already was, but when the call came from Gus she was seized by the most profound and debilitating fear imaginable. A black van had been spotted on the Cape.

"Mrs. Neuhauser? Are you all right?"

It was a moment before Joyce forced out a weak yes.

"Okay. I'm heading down to the marsh in a couple minutes. It's about a twenty-minute drive from here. We've already called a tow truck to meet us. If the weather doesn't get any worse, we should have the vehicle out of the quicksand by noon."

Joyce was almost surprised to hear herself speak. "I'm leaving for the Cape right now, as soon as we hang up."

"Why don't you hold off until you hear from me," Debrito said. "It will just be an hour or two. I'll call you as soon as we have the van out."

She couldn't hold off. Her anxiety would only increase until it became unbearable. "I can't," she told him. "I can't sit here waiting for your call. I'll be in Wellfleet in two hours. I have a map that will show me how to get to the marsh. If you're not there. . . ."

Joyce's mind had begun racing. Get Gloria to watch the kids; reach Frank at his office. . . .

"Okay, okay," Gus said. "Please drive carefully. I'll be there. But you have to realize we may find nothing. It may not be the same van. And if it is . . . ."

If it was the same van, would they find her daughter in it? Was it possible that Ronnie Haddon had tried to sink the van with Debbie in it, alive?

"Damn," Patrolman Perry muttered as he steered the squad car down the bumpy road toward Tucker's Cove Recreational Vehicle Hookups. He'd been in on everything, right from the start. Right from the point when they'd found Bobby Yellowfeather's body in the dunes. Hadn't he crawled through the scrub pine

251

right behind the chief, and smelled the same awful smell of that decayed flesh? Hadn't he gone through that weird sucker's house, too, and stood right in the middle of that stinking bedroom? And what did that get him? Nothing. Things were finally heating up and there could be some real action, but what does Gus do? Sends him on an errand to check out Little Ned Mayo's wild story about blinking lights.

Little Ned. There's a reliable witness for you. Taking out Emma's boat in the middle of the night in rough weather. Probably drunk as a skunk when he saw those blinking lights. Surprised the old coot didn't report UFOs.

The patrol car's front tire hit a pothole and the vehicle shimmied. Piece of junk cruiser he'd been assigned, too. Worst one in the Provincetown PD. No suspension, no pickup, transmission shot and the police radio worked only half the time. Perry swore again. "Damn!"

When the cruiser bounced over that deep pothole, the car's frame rattled. The sound broke through the sound of the wind whistling through the trailer. Debbie shifted the chair until she could peek under the curtain that covered the window in the door.

A police car! Her heart started beating fast. They're coming to get me. But—Oh, God! There's only one policeman. How could they just send one? Don't they know how crazy he is?

No, no. They didn't know. Someone had seen her signal with the lights. That's why the policeman was there. He didn't know she was in here tied up, or that the old man was dead. She could tell that from the way the policeman acted when he got out of the car. He just stood there for a minute in the deserted lot. He didn't look worried at all. The wind lifted his hat off his head. He ran a few steps and retrieved it. He wore a gun around his waist, but he hadn't taken it out of the holster. In her mind, she shouted to the policeman: Take out your gun.

At the back of the trailer, the bedsprings creaked. Debbie

looked over her shoulder. Ronnie had shifted in the bed, but she could still see his legs sprawled across it.

The *wham* of the slamming car door seemed to thunder through the trailer. Debbie held her breath as Ronnie moved again. When he kept on breathing like a person who was asleep, she peeked back through the curtain. The policeman had been looking in the old man's car. She held her breath as he took a few steps toward the trailer and called out loud.

"Ephraim?"

He was about twenty feet away from her now.

Oh, please, she prayed, don't make any noise. Don't wake him up. Just get me out of here.

"Ephraim? You around?"

The policeman started toward the trailer. The noise of the wind muffled the sound of his feet crunching over the gravel. "Where you hiding, Ephraim?" he shouted.

The policeman looked young, almost like a high school kid. As he got closer, Debbie could see less of him until, when he stood at the trailer's door, only his waist was visible. He still hadn't reached for his gun. Even worse. He was holding his hat in the hand he should have used to draw his gun.

Desperate, Debbie whispered into the crack at the edge of the door, "He's crazy. Please get me out of here."

The policeman didn't hear. He knocked hard. When there was no response, he tried the doorknob. The lock held.

Debbie heard the bedsprings creak again. She was almost too frightened to look, but she did, and she couldn't see Ronnie's legs anymore. When she turned back, the policeman had already walked across the lot to the wood pier. He checked the old man's boat and the padlock on the shed, then walked back to his police car. Debbie took in a deep breath. If she had to, she would scream to stop him from leaving. He wasn't leaving yet, though. He reached through the window and talked to someone on his police radio. When he'd finished, he stepped around the car and started toward the trailer again.

253

"You in there, Ephraim? You going to make me break a window?"

The sound of feet crossing the trailer floor made her stomach flip. Ronnie was behind her. He had the shotgun in his hands. Had it pointed straight at the window. She shook her head wildly, but he wasn't looking at her. He was going to kill the policeman. She could tell by his expression.

Terrified, Debbie screamed, "He's got a gun." Ronnie's hand was over her mouth in a second. Debbie crashed her body into the door, trying to make as much noise as she could. Ronnie pushed her hard. The chair fell onto its side, with her tied to it. She watched in horror as Ronnie raised the shotgun and pressed the trigger. There was a loud click instead of the roar she had steeled herself for. Maybe the old man's gun didn't work. She looked up through the window. From her place on the floor, she couldn't see whether the policeman was there or not.

Ronnie cracked the gun's barrel open, and clicked it shut. He peered under the shade, then moved slightly so that the gun was at an angle.

When he pulled the trigger the second time, there was a earsplitting roar. Glass from the broken window splattered around her. By the time the glass stopped falling, Ronnie had opened the door and run from the trailer. In a panic, Debbie pushed herself along the floor until she lay in the open door.

The policeman was down on his stomach in the sand and gravel between the trailer and his car. Sand blew over his pants legs and across his back. His holster was empty now, but Debbie didn't see his gun. He was so still that she was sure he was dead. When she saw his legs move, the tension she'd been holding in let go and she started screaming.

"Shut your mouth!" Ronnie shouted at her. He placed the shotgun barrel on the back of the policeman's head.

"If you kill him, I won't love you anymore," Debbie yelled, desperate to stop him.

There was a second when she heard nothing but the wind.

254

Then there was another click as Ronnie squeezed the trigger and the gun misfired.

"I mean it, Ronnie!" she screamed. "Didn't you hear what I said? Don't you want us to get to our special place today? Please, Ronnie. Don't hurt the policeman any more."

Ronnie moved the gun barrel away from the policeman's head. "I'm not sure about you anymore, Deborah. You're not the good girl I thought you were when I brought you here."

"Yes, I am. I swear to you I am a good girl."

"If you love me, how come you wanted this cop to find you?"

"I didn't. I only yelled when you brought the gun. I don't like killing. Your mother doesn't like killing, either," she cried, trying everything she could think of to stop him. "And I do love you. All I want is to be with you."

The fury began fading from Ronnie's face. "It wasn't me who shot him," he said finally as he lowered the gun. "It was the Shark."

"I know that. If you'll untie me, I'll help get us packed."

Ronnie took another look at the fallen policeman. Then, with the shotgun in his hand, he walked back to the trailer door.

Debbie's face was swollen and streaked with tears. Sand clung to the wet trails down her cheeks. Ronnie slid the shotgun behind the sofa. Crouching near her, he untied the tape that held her to the chair. As he lifted her up, he whispered into her ear, "I knew you'd start to love me."

Debbie was quiet while he held her and talked about their special place. The feel of his breath on her skin made her cringe. She was still shaking, but even through her fear she realized that her chances were better than they had been. She was untied, and if she could be alone for just five seconds maybe she could find the policeman's gun. His car was right there, too. She hadn't seen what he'd done with the keys, but they had to be either in his pocket or in the ignition.

After a few seconds, she rubbed her ankles. As she did, she

leaned forward, trying to spot the policeman's gun. Ronnie reached over and flicked at the sand on her face.

"Poor little Deborah. Your skin is so red and puffy. Wouldn't you like to get cleaned up?"

It disgusted her so much when he touched her that she jumped up out of his grasp.

"We've got lots to do if we're moving today. What should I do first? We could even take the police car. Want me to look for his keys? Maybe he left them inside it."

She started moving toward the cruiser. Ronnie got to his feet and took her hand. "You're all dirty, Deborah. Your hair smells bad. I like it when you smell sweet, like right after your shower. You never did get your shower yesterday."

Her terror rose again as he led her back into the trailer. At the bathroom door, she forced herself to smile at him. "Well," she said, "I'll take my shower right now. You wait right here. Okay?"

She could only mean one thing. Why else would she smile like that? Sure, he had suggested the shower, but he hadn't made her smile at him. Not that way. Deborah wanted him to watch her. Ronnie was sure of it.

The background sound of running water thrilled him. Maybe she even wanted . . . No! No! He wouldn't try that. He didn't want to scare her. That had been his mistake with Angela. He'd moved too fast and scared her. This time, he was going to do it right. When Deborah got used to letting him watch her take her shower, then she'd let him touch her while she was awake.

He pushed the folding door wide.

This wasn't right. It wasn't like he expected.

Deborah was standing in front of the sink, dressed in the same dirty clothes she'd been wearing. She had a hard, mean expression on her face. He started to say something, but her hand lashed out toward him.

He put up his hands and wrenched his face sideways. A hot, fiery liquid splashed across his face, hands, and neck. Writhing with the sudden pain, Ronnie stumbled back from the bathroom. He felt her brush past, but the pain made him powerless to stop her. Rushing into the bathroom, he stumbled desperately into the shower stall. The running water was hot. He screamed as it hit the open wounds on his skin.

The policeman had crawled until he was hidden behind a trash can at the side of the trailer. He had his gun in his hand. Dots of blood were seeping through his shirt, and there was blood on his neck. He was alive, though. As Debbie crouched next to him, his eyelids opened.

"Why is he screaming?" he asked weakly.

"I threw lye on him."

The policeman winced, then looked away. Debbie followed his gaze and realized that he was looking at his car.

"It's an automatic," he whispered. "Can you drive?"

"I think so."

"Then go get help."

The screaming stopped as suddenly as it had started. The only sound was the wind whistling around them.

"The keys are in the ignition. If he comes outside, I'll try to shoot him."

The shotgun roared again before Debbie reached the police cruiser. Spraying gravel stung her legs. Changing direction, she circled back past the policeman and around the trailer. She dashed to the far side of the cruiser, her breaths coming in shallow gasps.

The key wasn't in the ignition; it was on the seat. As Debbie fumbled for it, she heard the sharp *pop* of a pistol. She saw Ronnie running across the parking lot. The policeman's shot had missed him. She quickly locked the doors and pushed the key into the ignition. As soon as the engine fired, she pressed her foot on the accelerator. The engine raced, but the car didn't move.

Gears, she thought wildly. She shifted the lever on the floor into drive and tried the accelerator again. The car jerked forward. It felt as if something huge was holding it, keeping it from moving.

He was there now, right at the back of the car. Turning the steering wheel, Debbie gunned the engine hard. The car lugged forward. What was wrong with it?

He ran beside the car, staring through the window at her, calling her names. He was soaking wet. Raw, bleeding sores streaked his face and made mottled patterns on the front of his shirt. One of his eyes was half-closed, and through the slit the white looked bloodred.

The brake. Debbie remembered about the emergency brake. She felt for it, but she wasn't fast enough. The shotgun came up. She steeled herself for another roar, but he swung the gun like a club, breaking the cruiser's window.

Joyce switched off the ignition and stared across the marsh. The van sat on solid ground now, anchored by wire lines reeling from a tow truck. She searched the group of people milling around the van, desperately looking for a thin young girl. She saw no one even remotely like Debbie. The van's back door was open, and Joyce saw a man step into the vehicle. Gus Debrito stood outside, his back against the wind.

Joyce found it hard to get out of the station wagon, afraid that when she learned what the police had found in that mud-covered black van, she would learn the worst thing a mother could.

It was a few minutes before she realized that Gus was waving to her, indicating that she should join him. Would he do that if Debbie's body was in there? No, he wouldn't, and she groaned with relief.

She fought the wind around the water's edge, walking on shaking legs. Chief Debrito met her before she reached the van. He had something bundled in his arm. "It's Haddon's van, Mrs. Neuhauser," he told her. "There's no one in there now, but we have evidence your daughter was there."

Taking Joyce's arm, he led her to a police cruiser. When she was sitting on the edge of the front seat, he showed her the thing he had bundled under his arm.

"This is Debbie's, isn't it?"

It was the blue-jean jacket with the sequined patches she'd bought for her daughter in the shop on Commercial Street. Joyce fought back tears when he showed her the note her daughter had scrawled with bright pink nail polish on a cheap paper towel.

Joyce waited in the cruiser while Gus made arrangements for the marsh to be dragged. Before he got into the cruiser, he asked for Joyce's car keys. "I don't want you driving. I'll have someone take your station wagon back to Provincetown. We'll meet them there." He glanced at the dark clouds hovering overhead. "It's going to start pouring any minute now. I have to make one stop on the way back. It should take only a few minutes, but I'm having another car with two officers follow us in case there's a problem."

Joyce nodded, hardly listening as Gus said something about his deputy and the police radio that didn't answer. "Last we heard from Perry," the chief said as they drove away from the marsh, "he was at Tucker's Cove. He reported in that everything looked fine, but we can't reach him now. Radio's probably gone out again."

It started sprinkling during the fifteen-minute drive back up Route 6. Gus turned off at the sign for Tucker's Cove and took the bumpy dirt road slowly. While he maneuvered the cruiser around potholes, Joyce sat still, scarcely noticing where they were going.

"Looks quiet," Gus was saying as he reached the end of the tree-covered drive and looked over the windswept open area that led to the Atlantic. Suddenly, then, he twisted the steering wheel to the right and jammed on his brakes. Along the left side of the lot, the land sloped down about twelve feet. Cranberry bushes were thick in this gully, but the top of the police cruiser showed clearly.

"You lock the doors and stay here," Debrito ordered Joyce.

In the next instant, Joyce heard him telling one of the men in the other cruiser to radio for help. When he and the third policeman descended into the gully, they had drawn their guns.

Joyce sat in silence and watched until their heads had disappeared. There was a knock on her window. Startled, she looked through the rain-streaked glass. The third policeman had thrown a plastic raincoat over his head. He was gesturing toward a trailer on the far side of the lot. "Going to look in there," he shouted over the strengthening wind.

Heavier drops of rain were splattering the car's windshield now. Joyce followed the third policeman with her eyes until she heard a sharp cracking sound from somewhere near the water. She shifted her eyes.

Something had moved across the lot. A humanlike form, running almost doubled over. Leaning nearer the windshield, Joyce strained to see the pier and the shack next to it. There was nothing there now, but there had been something an instant before—or someone. She twisted in her seat, frantic to catch the policeman's attention. He had disappeared into the trailer. She looked back at the pier. Someone *was* there. The small boat that seconds before had hung suspended on ropes next to the pier was slipping slowly into the water. Joyce opened her door and began running through the rain toward the Atlantic.

Rain and wind lashed at her face, and above the sound of the storm she heard another crack as the boat slammed into the pier's wood pilings. Racing onto the pier, Joyce looked over the edge. The boat lurched three feet below where she stood, its stern floating free, its bow still fastened.

She spotted him first, but she didn't know him. He was a blur in the storm, struggling to get the boat's front clear from the lines that still held it. Glancing back to the land, Joyce saw Chief Debrito and the other officer climbing out of the gully. She shouted to them, but they didn't hear her. He heard, though, and he looked up at her from the pitching boat.

Joyce saw the familiar pale eyes, surrounded by red welted flesh. Then she looked beyond him. Her daughter was huddled into the boat's bow. She screamed for the police once again. Then, without another second's thought, she jumped off the pier. Her daughter cried out as Joyce crashed into the bottom of the boat. "Mommy! Help me, Mommy."

Fighting off his hands, Joyce crawled to the front of the lurching boat. She cradled Debbie with one arm as her free hand tore at the tape that bound the girl's hands. The wind ripped at Joyce and its howl blocked out all other sound. His hands were pulling at her shoulders when the boat rocked so violently that she was thrown on top of her daughter.

Chief Debrito was in the boat then, struggling with Ronnie. The boat tipped. Water churned around them. For a sickening second, Joyce lost her hold on Debbie. She felt herself falling, sinking, but then Debbie's bound hands clutched desperately toward her mother and Joyce had the girl again. She pulled herself and her daughter back into the boat as Chief Debrito and Ronnie disappeared under the waves.

The second officer had dropped into the water, a life preserver in one hand. Seconds later, Chief Debrito surfaced. He gripped the ring, gasping in the churning gray Atlantic. Sirens screamed through the gale as the second policeman's head emerged from the water.

Debrito was pointing out to sea. Footsteps pounded across the wood pier. Ronnie's head poked above the whitecaps about twenty feet out. A massive breaking wave rushed into him and Joyce saw his body tumbling through the Atlantic. Men wearing yellow slickers were running on the pier now. They threw lines into the water toward the place where Ronnie had surfaced. The lines skidded over the waves and came back to them.

Joyce clung to her sobbing daughter as two of the men in yellow slickers secured the boat's stern to the dock.

The Shark stayed under until his lungs felt as if they would explode. Salt water burned into his raw skin. He heard the sound from somewhere above. It was a howl crying out above the wailing of the wind. He didn't intend to surface, but the ocean

261

threw him up and he saw the flashing lights over the dock. He sank beneath the surface and the wailing melted into the surging salt water. He held his breath and swam until his body screamed out for oxygen. When the pain in his lungs grew too great, he surfaced again. Before he could draw a breath, the Atlantic had tossed him up, then dragged him back beneath its surface as if he were a child's toy. The Shark went under head first. His body—that machine of nerve and muscle—was suddenly an alien, useless thing and he was afraid. He had to have air. He struggled toward the surface, but it was too far away. When he opened his mouth to scream, water rushed into his lungs. The violent storm carried his body out to sea.

Joyce and Debbie Neuhauser spent that night in a small hospital on the Cape, Debbie in a bed, Joyce dozing in a chair next to her daughter. As the hurricane blew across the Cape, the hospital's steel girders groaned and creaked like a ship's rigging in rough water. The buffeting wind made the floors and walls tremble. Rain smashed against the room's window. At some point in the night, there was a loud crack, followed by a fearful crash. Joyce woke with a start, her heart thumping. She looked out the window and saw that a huge elm tree had fallen across the hospital's lawn, landing a few feet away from Debbie's room. Debbie slept soundly, but the fears Joyce had been living with remained. It would take time for them to disappear.

The doctor who examined the girl had said she would be fine physically. She was bruised, dehydrated, and had lost weight, but she was sound. As for the emotional bruises Debbie had suffered, no one could say, but Joyce was certain of one thing: Whatever happened, she would be there for her daughter.

There were footsteps in the hospital corridor. Going to the door, Joyce saw the night-duty nurse coming from the room next to Debbie's. Earlier that evening, she had seen Deputy Perry wheeled into that room on a hospital gurney.

"How is he?" she asked.

The nurse was young and pretty, with a blond ponytail. "The

doctor says he'll recover." She smiled over her shoulder as she made her way down the hall. "I think he's already feeling better," she added, but she didn't elaborate.

As Joyce stepped back into Debbie's room, the corridor lights flickered. Debbie stirred and moaned in her sleep. Her eyes fluttered open. Hurrying to her daughter's side, Joyce took one of Debbie's hands.

"I was so scared I'd never see you again," Debbie whispered. She blinked and stared at her mother. "I love you, Mommy," she said before she drifted into another deep sleep.

The following morning, when the wind from the hurricane ebbed and the roads onto the Cape cleared, Frank Neuhauser arrived at the hospital. He knew Debbie was all right. That was the most important thing. The night before, when he'd talked to the doctor who had examined her, the doctor had said Debbie was a strong kid, pretty resilient. Frank had wept with relief when he learned that his daughter hadn't been sexually molested.

He walked toward the hospital, stepping over the rivulets of water draining from the soaking lawn. A huge elm, once regal and green, lay like a dead elephant on the grass. In the main corridor of the hospital, near the reception desk, a group of reporters and newspaper photographers waited. Chief Debrito had already made a statement for the press, but the reporters still hoped to interview Joyce, and maybe even Debbie. Frank made his way past them, trying to remain inconspicuous.

He wasn't to blame for what had happened to Debbie, but he couldn't absolve himself of one thing: If Joyce had listened to him, if she had given in when he thought Debbie's situation was out of their control, Debbie would probably be dead. For that, Frank had to shoulder blame.

As he hurried up the hall, Joyce stepped into the door of Debbie's room. She looked drawn and pale. He had dreaded this moment. He felt awkward and ashamed, felt like hanging back and begging his wife to forgive him.

Joyce nodded toward the room.

"Debbie's waiting for you. She's eager to go home."

"I hope you are, too." He searched her face for a clue about how she felt.

Joyce smiled affectionately. "Of course I am. What did you think?" Stepping forward, she took Frank's hand and led him into Debbie's room.

Four days after the Neuhausers left the Cape, Forest Service employees discovered a bloated body that washed up on the beach at Dromedary Point. The corpse, that of a white male, was identified as Ronald Haddon's. One of Haddon's legs had been severed at the thigh. A scientist at the Wood's Hole Oceanographic Institute, speaking off the record, suggested that the wounds on Haddon's stump were consistent with those of a shark attack.